GREEDY INTENTIONS

Derrick "BJ" Williams
&
Dionte Matthews

TABLE OF CONTENTS

CHAPTER 1

T.Z. exhaled the weed smoke out his nostrils trying to relax his nerves as his main man Derrick drove the stolen 1987 Caprice Classic down the street in the pouring rain. T.Z. Looked in the backseat at the two faces which had the same look of nervousness and determination on it as he did.

"Yall good?" T.Z. asked.

"We Gucci!" Roxy answered.

"Just Checking," T.Z. said with his reassuring smile show casing 12 golds across the top and bottom.

Roxy and CiCi sat in the backseat quiet trying ease the butterflies that invaded their stomach and seems as if they spoke one might fly out and expose their nervousness. Derrick made a right on Lamar still bobbing his head to 2Pac's "Ambitionz as a Ridah", getting his mind prepared for one of the biggest moments of his life cause Derrick knew just as anybody else in that car knew if something goes wrong it could cost them their life. T.Z. Put the doobie out in the ashtray as Derrick pulled in the parking lot of what you would think was an abandon building if all the different cars wasn't park round at the back.

"Everybody remember their instruction?" T.Z. asked in his taking lead tone.

"Yeah!" they all said at once like soldiers heading to the battlefield.

T.Z. loaded a bullet into the chamber of his baby .40cal, grabbed his umbrella from the floor and step out into the raining night with his three soldiers next to him.

Redmack walked over and viewed all the patrons having a good time even the ones who were losing their money was seeming to be having fun. Redmack didn't own the illegal gambling spot he felt proud of it as his own because he ran it. He had say-so over everything and everybody who enter the illegal establishment from bartender to card-dealers to security only person he couldn't order around at will was Jax, the owner, the boss man that gave him the position that he got now, but Redmack didn't sweat that cause he knew that Jax very seldom ever showed up doing business hours unless his present was a must everything else was left up to Redmack. Besides a couple fights nothing major really occurred since no weapons were allowed inside beside for Redmack 9mm and security's pistols and Redmack was well respected especially since nigga's knew he worked for Jax.

"I'm taking all bets!" the dude yelled standing at the crap table.

Redmack smiled as he watched the men place several hundred-dollar bills all around the tables knowing the house get a cut on 6 & 8's.

"Point eight!" Redmack heard the crap house man say.

Redmack knowing the house man switch the dice to make sure they get a share of the cash. Redmack caught eyes with the house man and gave a slight head nod giving him a good job signal. Redmack noticed the 5'7 dark skinned woman who skin looked as if it was Hershey covered heading his way. The silver one-piece dress hugged her ass and hips so tight. Guys stared at her perfectly round ass as she walked pass them heading toward Redmack.

"What's up baby girl?" Redmack asked as they both embraced each other.

"Happy to see you!" she said looking up into Redmack's hazel eyes as he stood 6'2 215 pounds. Women always have had a thing for Redmack since he was a mix breed nigga, half black the other half Mexican the other part Indian. Long hair if you didn't know the nigga you would swear he was a pimp or something like it, and if you didn't know him he damn sure would try to act as one too, that always seem to be his downfall with the woman as well.

T.Z. sat in front of the slot machine deposited quarters inside pulling down on the handle as if he was concerned about winning. He was actually paying more attention to his people making sure everybody was where they supposed to be. When he seen CiCi walking to the back with Redmack it was time. T.Z. Made eye contact with his people placed in different area. He took a deep breath "All or nothing!" he mumbled to himself as he followed CiCi and Redmack to the back office room.

T.Z. Knocked on the office door.

"What?" Redmack yelled from inside the office.

"It's a problem sir" T.Z. said changing his voice removing the twin .40cal from under his shirt. "What da fu-" Redmack's sentence was cut short when he seen the twin barrels looking at him when he swung the office door open. Redmack instantly froze with his hands in the air in fear.

"Get in there and don't say shit!" T.Z. ordered with murder in his eyes. T.Z look over at CiCi as she straightened her dress out. "Good work!" T.Z. told her as he kicked the office door closed.

Redmack looked at her wishing he could cut her head off right now knowing she set him up. "Where's the safe?" T.Z. Asked coldly. "Ain't no sa-" T.Z. Smacked Redmack in the face with the gun. "I'm ask yo bitch ass one mo time nigga, where's the mafucking safe at", T.Z. Demanded placing the barrel of one of the guns at his dick. "Behind the full length mirror on the wall", Redmack said dropping his head in defeat. CiCi went and pulled the mirror out exposing a large wall safe with digital numbers. "I guess I got to ask for the code as well", T.Z. Said being sarcastic. "4276". CiCi entered the code and turned the handle when she seen the green light flash. "Jackpot!". CiCi smiled at T.Z. T.Z. Took the neatly folded black trash bag out his rear pocket for CiCi so she could put the money inside it and tossed it to her. Redmack grew with more anger by the second as he watched CiCi empty the safe of its contents. Redmack thought about reaching for the 9mm that was tucked in his waistband from the back but knowing the trigger-happy youngster wouldn't hesitate to kill him where he stood but was the few hundred

4

thousand worth it to Redmack. It wasn't. The disrespect of robbing him was worth more. Right when T.Z. looked over at CiCi, Redmack made his move. T.Z. Caught the sudden movement out his peripheral view "bloc, bloc, bloc," T.Z. Fired the twin 40's as Redmack made a lifesaving dive behind the large oakwood desk. "Bloc, bloc", the twin 40's sounded like cannon's going off inside the office as bullets slammed into the desk. CiCi hurried and emptied the rest of the money inside the trash bag and headed for the door. "Tat, tat, tat, bloc, bloc, T.Z. Returned fire at Redmack as he crouched shielding CiCi making sure neither one of them got hit by Redmack's wild firing heading out the office. T.Z. And CiCi emerged out the office unharmed. T.Z. Hoped that phase 2 of his plan was being executed precisely if not they would be in for it. T.Z. Nerves settled when he seen all the patrons who were just gambling having a good time laid all across the dirty floor only in boxer shorts for the guys and panties & bras for the woman, while Derrick, Roxy, Ape, Marcus, Flex and Black held them at gun point with all their cash and valuables inside trash bags. T.Z. was impressed. He and CiCi stepped over various people heading for the exit, "I see things went pretty smoothly out here" said T.Z. to Derrick, "Better then back there I heard", said Derrick hearing the shootout between T.Z. And Redmack. "That hoe still alive so let's burn asap!" T.Z. Said still heading for the exit. His crew followed behind but keeping their weapons aimed at the people as they exited one by one.

The crew trotted threw the rain headed for the getaway cars. Roxy got in the driver seat of the stolen caprice with CiCi, Flex, and Black while Derrick got in the driver seat of another car, a delta 88 which was also stolen and previously parked. T.Z., Ape, and Marcus got in with Derrick,

5

speeding into the raining night as Roxy drove the opposite direction into the night as well. Derrick drove the speed limit when he felt he was at a good distant from the gambling spot. They were almost home free and didn't want to risk getting pulled over for speeding in a stolen car while armed with guns. Since the gambling spot was an illegal operation, they weren't concern about anybody calling the police. They knew the beef would get settled in the streets. Derrick drove down a dark empty street parking behind a white 2010 Camaro on "22in Forgiato's. "This is it!" said Derrick looking next to him at Ape "you right!" said T.Z. From the backseat "boom, boom, tat, tat, tat '. Blood and brain matter flew on the car windows as T.Z. Put two holes in Marcus's and Ape head and Derrick popped the trunk to get the bottle of lighter fluid out. They poured lighter fluid over the body and inside the Delta 88 to destroy any evidence. T.Z. put a match to each body. T.Z. could see the flames consuming the inside of the Delta as he looked back in his rear-view mirror before turning off the street.

Redmack paced around his office furious about the situation that just occurred, how could he let his operation be infiltrated that easy. All the customers were gone and the only people who remain were the workers and none of them were allowed to leave because they all were under investigation especially since it was his own team who help rob him. The even worse part bout this is he had to call Jax at 4:40 in the morning and tell him about losing Jax's money. Redmack looked at his iPhone 4 hating to make the dreaded call found Jax name then pressed talk on his touch screen. Redmack grew more nervous with every ring hoping Jax wouldn't answer "What is it?" Redmack heard the unpleasant greeting on the other end of the line. "Umm, umm, Jax we got a problem."

6

Redmack stuttered speaking. "What's the problem?" Jax asked fully woke now. "The spot got hit!" Redmack told Jax like a burden was lifted. "Hello? Hello?", Redmack looked at the phone noticing the line was dead. Redmack knew Jax heard him and was on his way. Jax was from the old school he didn't believe in talking business over any line beside two pay phones even then the conversation was limited. Redmack had all his workers under investigation until answer came out and he knew Jax would probably do the same thing with Redmack as a prime suspect. Redmack understood thats how this type of business went, that meant he had to come up with an answer quick.

T.Z. parked his Camaro in front of the building of his apartment that him and Derrick shared waiting on Roxy to arrive. When he seen the H.I.D. Lights parking behind him he knew that was her. The rain had eased up to a light shower so T.Z. Got out the car with his 5'10 frame weighing 190 pounds solid still in great shape from his 4-year bid he just finish doing 4 months ago. The sound of Roxy's stilettos' echo off the ground as she approached him with Flex on her side with the black trash bags in hand. Roxy kissed T.Z. Light brown cheek as rain fell on him making his skin sparkle in the moon light. "Y'all handle everything?" T.Z. Asked already knowing the answer. "Done Dolla!" Flex said handing T.Z. Two of the four bags he carried. Flex and Roxy was the other two members of T.Z.'s crew. Roxy and T.Z. Grew up down the street from each other most people would assume that they had something going on with each other but their love for each other was platonic. That was only by their choice cause Roxy was a dime, standing only 5'2 135 pounds high yellow skin tone with an ass that could get her an Apple Bottom modeling deal. A nigga would kill over her that's only if she didn't kill him first cause the pretty face is only an illusion when it comes to Roxy. Flex and T.Z. were celly for 2 years while T.Z. was in prison. Flex got out 9 months before T.Z. And kept it real so when T.Z. Got out it was a must they fucked with each other. Flex still held his size as well at 6'2 weighting 220 pounds brown skin complexion covered in prison tattoo's. T.Z. Only had one tattoo that said RIP Travis on his chest. Derrick Got out the car joining the circle in the drizzle. Derrick, T.Z., and Roxy all went to Jr. high school together. T.Z. Found out that Derrick liked smoking weed right before their 7th grade football games, they been friends ever since. They both accepted Roxy as a sister. Derrick was only 5'8 150 pounds with smooth dark skin and long braids. "I see y'all took care of business". Derrick stated "Have it ever been a time a bitch didn't?" Roxy said with arrogance "Whatever"! said Derrick "T. T Hello? Roxy said snapping her fingers in T.Z. Face breaking the trance he was in looking at the crescent moon "What's up?" he said coming back to reality. "Damn what's up there that got your attention?" Roxy said looking up while rain drops fell in her eyes. "Just thinking that's all" he answered. "Well let's think inside before I'm soaked!" she complained. "Aight, aight!" T.Z. Said taking one last look as the crew headed inside. "Damn psych pills fucked my bro head up in the joint" Roxy joked as they went in the apartment. "Fuck you Roxy!" T.Z. Said hearing the comment.

CHAPTER 2

Jax's gators echoed through the empty building as his 6'1 frame 200 pounds walked across the tile floor. To be 58 Jax was in great shape he had a few wrinkles in the corners of his eyes on his light brown skin and his salt and pepper goatee was the only give away about his age. Only sign of tiredness Jax presented was the street life he was so ready to cut all illegal activities he sponsored from gambling spot to the drug trade. Jax had money invested in many legal resources from tax companies to real estate to cattle and horse breeding he even help sponsor the mayor campaign. He just can't seem to pull away from the lucrative illegal tax-free life style that built his empire Even though it's been over 20 years since Jax lived in the slums of the Dallas, TX streets. Jax has and always will be a street nigga at heart that's the main reason why he got to get to the bottom of this shit.

The 300 grand that was stolen was punk money to Jax. He wants to find out what mafucker had the balls to rob his spot cause whoever did it he hope the cash was worth there life cause didn't to many big moves take place without Jax knowing the little details of it. The chatter instantly stop when Jax stepped into the same office where Redmack almost lost his life bout 2 hours ago. Jax looked the people in the room in their eyes trying read any sign of betrayal in them. All the people did the same thing by dropping their heads not wanting the old man looking them in their eyes as if he could see into their souls and expose there deepest darkest secrets. Jax viewed the bullet holes in the walls and inside the large oak wood desk as he approached the desk that Redmack sat behind. "How you doing Jax?" Redmack broke the silence jumping up from his seat offering it to Jax. Jax took the seat in the large Italian leather chair crossing his right leg over the left and his hands together in a pyramid shape as he always sat when discuss business matters. "Blessed!" Jax said in his deep baritone voice. Jax was a man of self-control so to see him get loud and upset was seldom to none even when he was truly upset. "Let me explain Jax bout what happen" Redmack pleaded. "First let me see the tape" Jax said to him. Redmack remove the remote control from his pocket and pointed it towards the '50-inch flat screen on the wall. Everybody's eyes turned towards the screen watching the video as if they hadn't already watched it 10 times already. Jax watched how the entire scene unfolded from start to finish, actually amused at the little circus show. When the tape ended Jax had the answers to some of his questions. First, he knew by the scared shitless look from Redmack on the screen he had no parts. Second, he had the face of the little nigga he was damn sure that master minded the lick. He could tell the lil nigga was no older than 24, 25. Jax daughter was only 23. He thought back to when he was that age he remembered being hungry the same way but he also knew the code of the streets at that age. "Live by the sword, die by the sword!," Redmack? "Yeah Mr. Jax," Redmack answered. "First of all relax, breath, I don't think you or none of them sitting here played a part in this mess!" Jax said easing the tension in the room. "Tell me this, how do you allow you own security to help rob you?" Jax asked. "I…I…I…" "Save it!" Jax said cutting Redmack off. "Redmack if you ever want to be a productive business man and Boss, you need to learn not to mix business with pleasure", Jax stated how Redmack let CiCi allow him to put his guards down and get caught slipping. "You right!" said Redmack. "Well its yo turn to do something right, find them three fake ass security men and find out that nigga's name who almost killed you and them two bitches that was with him and the other niggas as well. Names, address, everything you can find out bout these little mafucker's," Jax explain expecting it to be done. Redmack was already on top of it, he had niggas on the hunt at the crack of dawn trying to find something. One thing for sure, Redmack wasn't an amateur in street wars at 39 years old he seen his fair share of bloodshed. At times being the one causing the blood shed with his own hands. "I'll be expecting to hear from you by tonight", Jax said rising from the Italian leather chair leaving out the room.

T.Z. And his crew had just finished counting all the earning's from last night's lick. The money out the safe including the loose cash all the patrons had plus the money the dealer's held, they ended up coming up on $345,540.00. T.Z looked at the stacks of cash on the table in front of him and his crew thinking about the plans he had with his share of the money. "T what you gone do with yo money?" asked Roxy. "Probably try and take over the world", Derrick said jokingly. Everybody was laughing at his joke but T.Z, "I might!" T.Z said looking serious, "Aight Gotti!" Roxy cracked.

"Reporter: "Breaking news, police have just discovered 2 bodies inside a burning vehicle when police were called out to a car fire. No, I'm sorry, it has been 2 different cars found burning with bodies inside". The crew instantly turned to pay attention to the morning news. "Reporter: "Police are still investigating to see are the crimes related to each other, no identities have been discovered at this time. Police ask that you contact the Dallas Police if you have any information. You can remain anonymous, stay tuned to Fox 4 Good Day for more updates". T.Z watched the screen looking at his work. Feeling more self-assured bout Flex seeing he followed plans effectively by killing CiCi and Black. T.Z knew he could trust Roxy and Derrick with his life but he was still getting to that level with Flex. T.Z knew that Flex carried his-self as a real nigga. Never showed any signs of being liable to the crew or T.Z, that's the main reason T.Z had CiCi, Black, Ape, and Marcus knocked off because he was sure if the pressure was on them from different directions. Especially from Jax's direction, they would crack. T.Z has been plotting this take down since he was still in prison. Roxy and her home girl CiCi got the security guards to cross over after a few good head jobs and some pussy and a fairy tale dream about how they could become kingpin status.

At first when T.Z presented the idea to Roxy and Derrick it sounded unrealistic but every time one of them come to visit that's all he would talk about so they finally brought into the idea. Then Flex got released and he was still with it. Slowly they seen the dream becoming reality. Then T.Z was released, he sat back and observed the gambling spot operation many nights then when Roxy finally had convinced the security, it was on! Redmack digging CiCi was just a bonus to the plan. Since Roxy and CiCi was already previous friends before the idea of hitting the spot was decided. T.Z didn't know how Roxy would take the idea of killing her friend at the end. Roxy didn't disappoint her bro T.Z. First word that came out of Roxy's mouth was "From the cradle to the grave, I'm with you no matter what!" Hearing that T.Z knew Roxy was still down for him at any and all risk. Cause the same applied with T.Z to her ad Derrick. "Derrick yo ass gone have to sleep on the sofa cause I'm too tired to drive you home", Roxy said as she yawned. "Bitch you crazy, you better sleep at the foot end then", Derrick told her. "Nigga I'll be damned if I lay my head next to them crusty ass feet of yours", Roxy spat turning her face into a frown. "Go lay in my bed Roxy", T.Z said. "You sho T?", "Yeah I'm good" T.Z said to her. "That's how you be a gentlemen Derrick" Roxy said pushing Derrick in the head playfully. "Y'all get this together I'll be back in a few" T.Z told them. "Going anywhere specific?" Flex asked, "Naw" I'm riding with you I ain't got shit else to do plus I need a ride home", Flex said. "Beep, beep", T.Z's car alarm pad sounded signal the auto-crank had been activated. T.Z and Flex headed out the apartment getting in the car.

Jax rode in the back seat of his platinum colored Rolls Royce Ghost checking his emails on his iPad 2. The rain from last night had finally stopped. Jax looked out the window as kids made there way to school on this Monday morning as he rode down Martin Luther King Jr. Blvd. "Not a concern in the world" Jax said to himself. "You say something boss?" asked Will. Will was Jax's personnel body guard, driver, and whatever other task Jax needed from him. Will had been working for Jax bout 15 years now so they were also friends. Will also handle a lot of business in Jax place for him. Jax never questioned Will's loyalty because he knew Will was genuine. "Nothing Will, You hungry?", Jax asked, "I know just the place", Will said as he drove the luxury vehicle through the slums of south Dallas pulling up at the famous hood food spot "2 Potnas". Even though the Rolls Royce stood out parked in front of the little family owned restaurant. Jax had no concerns because most nigga's knew who the street legend was even if you didn't know somebody around you did. South Dallas is where Jax started off from selling boy and girls pills. That was one capsule full of heroin and the other with cocaine. That was the late 70's then when crack hit in the late 80's. Jax never looked back. Will opened the door for Jax so he could get out. Jax stood next to Will's large 6'6 290-pound frame. "I see you cut yourself ", Jax said referring to the knick on Will's dark bald head. "That's what happens when you rush shave at 4 in the morning", said Will. "Say thank you to that crazy ass Redmack", said Jax. "I wanted to but you wanted me to stay in the car", Will said with his huge hands balled into a fist looking at them. "That's the reason why", Jax said smiling knowing Will's low tolerance for fuck up's especially costly fuck ups. Jax lead the way inside wearing a 3-piece brown Armani suit. All of Jax's suits where Armani, Gucci, Prada, some type of expensive designer with gators or croc's or a reptile covering his shoes. Everything around Jax describe money. Jax and Will took a seat. "May I help you?", the black woman asked looking to be in her mid 30's as she approached the table. "Steak, eggs, and coffee", Jax ordered. "Make it a double", said Will. "Oh I didn't know that was y'all Mr. Jax, Mr. Will. Coming right away", the lady said as she hurried off to get their food. "So Jax, how do you really want to handle this little situation?", asked Will. Jax crossed his legs and put his hands in the pyramid shape, "I'm giving Redmack 48 hours to come up with something to redeem himself", Jax responded. "What if he turns up empty?" asked Will. "Then I take control of the problem and Redmack won't have to worry about fucking up anymore" Jax explained. "That's the Jax I know", Will said with an evil grin on his face. The lady came back and sat two mugs of coffee on the table and headed back towards the kitchen.

T.Z drove down the familiar street of southeast Dallas better known as Pleasant Grove or the Greedy Grove with Flex riding shotgun smoking a blunt of kush. "Flex what's yo plans with yo cash?" "I'm not really too sure right now but whatever it is I better spend wisely cause ain't no telling when I'm see that type of cash again", Flex admitted. "The dope game nigga!", T.Z said with confidence, "yeah but these nigga's been out here on some bullshit with these outrageous prices then when a nigga is willing to pay the price they try and bird feed a nigga like a nigga a chump. "Shit ain't how it was before we went to the joint", Flex said. U remember Leto ? T.Z asked. "Leto, Leto....oh yeah, the old school S.A you use to play chess with every morning, the quiet dude, yeah I remember. What about him?", Flex asked. "Before I got out he gave me the number to his people. Dude name Felex, he say it's his nephew. He told me to call whenever I got settle but I didn't want to call like I'm asking for handouts so I figure now is the best time to move on this if we gone do it", T.Z explained. "T, real nigga shit, I'm with you, just let me know how much you need and I'm in. What about Derrick and Roxy?", Flex asked. "I'm pretty sure they in as well", T.Z said. "Let's get it", Flex said putting his fist in the air as T.Z dapped him up. "I'm make that call later today to see what the business is", T.Z said. T.Z knew if the dude Felex was as his uncle Leto pumped him up to be this could be an even bigger break for him. T.Z was really a hustler at heart, yeah, he could rob if it need be but the dope game was what he rather do. T.Z liked the constant flow of cash the dope game brought unlike being a jack boy. One thing about T.Z, he refused to be broke. He gone go and get it by any means.

After last night, T.Z kind of assumed that Flex would want in on the dope game. Even though $80,000 was a nice piece of change, it would be gone just as fast as it was got and Flex would need a steady income and a 9 to 5 was damn sure out the question. Flex lived with his baby mama in south Dallas off of Pine St. Flex baby mama was name Peaches, even though Flex was only 21 years old. His 5'6 reddish brown skin baby mama was 29, they had 2 girls together, Khadijah 6, and Kia, 2 months old. She had been Flex girl since he was 15 and she was 22. Peaches held Flex down doing his 3-year bid when he got caught selling to an undercover. She made sure Flex kept money on his books and on the phone for him to call collect and made the 2 ½ hour drive to the prison twice a month. T.Z had much respect for Peaches because a normal chick usually found a reason to fall off like T.Z's girl did. "I hope Peaches don't go off in yo mouth like a dentist for you coming home late", T.Z said joking. "Nigga she my bitch, I make the rules", Flex said knowing only one part of that sentence was actually true. "Aight then tough guy", T.Z said knowing the real truth that Peaches actually gave out the orders. T.Z parked in front of Flex's house, "Take however much you need and I'll come pick up the rest later", Flex told T.Z, "bet", T.Z said shaking Flex hand before Flex got out the car going into the house. T.Z watched Flex go inside the house even though T.Z was 2 years older than Flex, he would admire the younger dude for sticking with his family and taking care of them at all cost. T.Z had no kids; his closest family was his momma and an older brother but they took care of themselves just as he did. He really felt Derrick and Roxy was his brother and sister. T.Z promised the day he ever had kids he would try to be the best father possible. Roxy didn't have kids either, Derrick had two, Derrick Jr. 4, and DeErica, 3, by two different women. Blood test proved D.J was his but DeErica, he still wasn't sure but that's the cost when you raw dog hoes you just met the same night. T.Z pulled up at the red light on Malcom X and Hatcher behind the new Rolls Royce Ghost. "I need something like that", T.Z thought to himself looking at the half a million-dollar car. T.Z watched the big luxury vehicle glide off as the light signal turn green. T.Z trailed the Ghost for a few blocks since they were going the same direction.

T.Z animal instinct almost kicked in to keep following them. T.Z figured whoever was riding in that wouldn't have too much loose cash lying around. Their money would be in bank accounts, stock and bonds, shit like that so he headed home. "Boss could you see the face the driver of that Camaro?", Will asked already knowing what his longtime friend was observing. "Naw tint was too dark", Jax said, suspicious if the car was really following him. Jax looked at the piece of paper in his hand reading the numbers (BWM-521) in his head. Jax would get the license plates checked out to make sure it wasn't the FEDS or a stick-up kid trying his luck. For the last decade, the FEDS have been trying. pin a secret indictment on Jax but he always manages to stay ahead of the U.S. Government for some reason they haven't found out how either. "Stop at the first pay phone you see", Jax told Will. Will quickly turned the car in to the Church's Chicken parking lot on Bruton and Prairie Creek. Jax got out walking to the pay phone dropping 2 quarters in the slot, dialing the number; "Agent Scott" the female voice answered after two rings. "Loyalty before Royalty, Rags to Riches". "Death before Dishonor" the voice said finishing Jax's sentence confirming it was clear to talk. "I need a tag checked" Jax said looking at the paper. "Go head" she said "BWM-521" Jax said. "Got it" she said. "I'll meet you at Cheddar's at 7" Jax said hanging up the pay phone heading back to the car. "Who was that you called boss?" Will asked as he drove off. "Our little guardian angel" Jax said. "Hopefully she sends some blessings down as always upon us" Will said looking at Jax in the rear-view mirror. "We gone be fine" Jax said staring out the window.

CHAPTER 3

T.Z awoke out his slumber and reached for his iPhone 4 that laid on the coffee table the digital number read 5:42pm. T.Z stretched and yarned knowing it was time to get up and handle business. T.Z walked to his bedroom. Roxy was already gone so T.Z took a seat at the end of his King Size bed touching the screen on his phone scrolling thru the contacts. He stopped when he reached the name he was searching for then pressed talk on the screen. He put the phone to his ear as it rung several times "Hola" the woman answered in Spanish. "Speak to Felex" T.Z asked "Whose calling? "She asked "T.Z a friend of Leto" he said "Hold Please." T.Z. Waited bout 30seconds till he heard a man pick up the phone speaking Spanish to the woman. "Hello?" the man voice said in a deep cuban accent. "I was looking for Felex." T.Z told the man "This is I" Felex said." My name T.Z I got yo number from yo Uncle Leto he told me it was cool if I contacted you bout some business" said T.Z Yes, yes I remember hearing of you I thought I would have heard from you sooner." said Felex. Yeah, I had to get somethings in order first you know what I mean. Yes, I understand. When are you going to be available? Asked Felex, right now if need be. "Said T.Z "I like that meet me at Club Lipstick at 8:15 Felex said. How will I know who you are? "asked T.Z "Don't worry I'll find you. Goodbye now! Felex ended the call. T.Z looked at the phone ("What type of shit is that I'll find you.") T.Z thought to himself. He brushed it off though and thought about the meeting he had with Felex in 2hours. T.Z went to take a quick shower he wished he had time to let the hot water soak but it was always later for that. T.Z got out of the shower drying off at the same time. T.Z put on a set of silk boxers. He only wore silk boxers cause after being in prison he vowed never to wear another set of cotton boxers again. T.Z put on a pair of black Akoo pants with a black and red Akoo collar shirt and a pair of black and red Jordan's #13 to match. T.Z got his 9mm glock from out his top drawer tucked it inside his waistband then checked his self in the full-length mirror that hung against the room wall. He knew he was ready to roll. T.Z grab his red leather coat for the nippy end of October weather. "Beep-Beep" T.Z hit the auto-crank button on his alarm pad as he left out his apartment going to his car. Ace Hood Hustle Song played as T.Z phone rang. "Hello?" T.Z answered closing his car door. "Where you at Fam?" Flex asked. "Bout to go see whats up on that issue we talked about this morning. "T.Z informed him. "You need me to go with you?" Flex asked "Now I'm roll solo don't want to send the wrong impression. You know how S. A's be thinking. "T.Z said "Yeah I know they swear a nigga on some jacking shit." Flex said "I'm hit you on the horn when I'm finished!" "Aight be easy dawg! "Flex said as they ended the call.

Jax walked inside the restaurant taking a view of the people enjoying their meals. "You need a table sir?" the hostess asked politely "I'm sit at the bar." Jax told the lady as he walked towards the bar. He watched the big flat screen as the Dallas Cowboys played the Eagles on Monday night football. He forgot the game came on tonight because he would have called his bookie to place bets on his favorite team the Cowboys. Jax took a seat on the stool at the bar next to a woman in her 30's with shoulder length blonde hair dressed in a dark gray two-piece skirt suit "You here alone tonight?" Jax asked the woman "Only if its beneficial." she responded "Bartender let me get a crown and coke and a strawberry margarita for the lady." Jax ordered looking at the almost empty glass she was drinking out of, $15.50!" the bartender said. Jax gave her a twenty-dollar bill "keep the change!" Jax said "Wow! Big spender but next time I'll pay for my own shit!" She replied harshly dropping a twenty-dollar bill folded in Jax lap as she walked off. "Must be that time of the month." Jax told the bartender sliding the bill in his pocket "I hope so cause I would hate to meet her when it isn't that time then "the bartender said shocked at the lady actions. Jax watched the last 2 minutes of the 1st quarter finished his drink then headed out the restaurant. Will sat and waited patiently as Jax came out getting in the backseat of the Double R "Everything good boss?" Will asked "yeah you can drive off". Jax said to Will. Will backed out and left Cheddars Restaurant parking lot. Jax went into his pocket taking out the bill the woman drop into his lap unfolding it revealing a folded piece of paper tape to the money. ("No type of law enforcement car is registered to a Tiora Zander") Jax read the note in his head. ("4455 Pleasant Vi Drive Dallas, TX 75217") read the address on the back of the paper. The name and address was unfamiliar to Jax but he would keep the information just in case it was needed for later reasons.

T.Z step inside the strip club looking around at the light evening crowd enjoying their personal extravaganza the ladies put on for them. T.Z took a seat at the table in the corner of the club looking at his cellphone checking the time (8:03) He thought to himself wondering was one of the gents getting a lap dance was Felex. T.Z thought about calling him but decided not too!" Would you like a dance papi? "the Mexican girl asked standing in front of T.Z in just a G-String and stilettos. T.Z admire the woman physics as he looked her up and down "Maybe later!" T.Z said calming his manly urges T.Z watch the woman perfectly round butt jiggle as she strolled off across the club. "Excuses me sir would you come with me. "The waitress told T.Z "What?" T.Z asked confused "Mr. Felex is waiting "she told him T.Z got up and followed the woman to the back up the stairs to a secluded area which had to be a VIP

A man resembling a younger version of the baseball player Sammie Sosa was sitting on an extra-long couch between two white women also dressed in the strip club attire G-Strings and Stilettos. T.Z couldn't help but gaze at the woman breast because they both had breast implants. ("Damn I don't think they even make bras that huge.") T.Z thought to himself. "Have a seat!" Felex told T.Z. T.Z took a seat in a chair instead of on the couch next to one of the strippers. "Would you like a drink, lap dance, pussy? "Felex offered" Naw I'm good!" "T.Z said. "No! You're not gay are you cause I don't fuck around!" Felex said joking busting out laughing at his own joke with the strippers following his lead laughing as well. "Hell naw I ain't gay. I only came here for business so I'm keeping it that way. "T.Z said aggressively, "Will you ladies excuse us." Felex said sitting upright staring T.Z in the eyes looking serious. Felex waited until the ladies left the room before he spoke. "Listen here Mr. Tyrone Zanders I like your style so far cause you are right, business is business not pleasure so always remember that. I had to make sure you knew the difference before we even talked business. "Felex explained "I can understand that I see you did yo homework on me too. "T.Z. said "Always in this business. I know where Tiarro and Tony live I even know you pleaded guilty to shooting a man five times and he lived you were sentenced to four years in prison denied parole twice for being a menace to society. I know about your friends Roxanne Richmond and Derrick Shaw. Felex said revealing all the information he had on T.Z. "Keep my family out of this "T.Z demanded hearing his momma and brother name. "And they always will be only if you bring them in the situation by breaking the what you guys call it the G-Code these days. I only ask for loyalty & respect cause that is what I give by all means you understand. "Felex said "I can dig it . "T.Z said nodding his head in agreement. "Loyalty and Respect!" Felex said extending his hand for T.Z to shake on it. "Loyalty and Respect. "T.Z said shaking Felex hand to seal the deal of a new business relationship.

"My Uncle told me you were the last of a dying breed and my Uncle Leto word is usually bond. "So T.Z what are you looking for?" asked Felex "Best coke on the market and good green!" said T.Z "That can be arranged. Will this be on consignment or do you have the cash on demand?" asked Felex. "Depend on the prices you giving me if I'll have enough cash to cover it. "said T.Z "Understandable I'll give you the kilos of coke for $13,000 and the weed for $150.00 a pound if you C.O.D but on consignment $14,500 a key and $250.00 a pound. "Felex explain "T.Z thought about the proposition, He would be winning either way cause bricks were whole selling for $23,000 and pounds were up to $800 dollars a pound easy but T.Z decided to start his business venture off correct. "I'll C.O.D and take 14bricks and 70pounds." T.Z Said quickly doing the math in his head "That'll be $192,500! "Felex said showing his mathematics skills quickly as well. "When will you be ready for the transaction?" asked Felex. A.S.A.P! "T.Z said, Felex wrote an address down on a napkin "Be here at 9 tomorrow morning drive something a little more inconspicuous cause you will be riding to dirty to be driving that Camaro of yours. " Felex said extended his hand "by the way loyalty isn't just a word to me it's a way of life. "T.Z said shaking Felex hand then leaving the club.

Jax sat in the office of his 8,500 square foot ranch style home in Forney a country town 30 minutes outside of Dallas city limits, talking to his banker and broker. Two white guys that were brothers. Jim was the banker and Victor was the broker. While Will sat and listened in on the conversation. Jax had his legs crossed right over left and his hands in a pyramid shape as always. "So what you saying Jim you got to start charging me $300,000 dollars for every million I need washed through one of my business "Jax said "Yes! Because it's true your business are doing well and deed but they are not generating almost $15 million dollars every 2 weeks. "said Jim "But all my expenses take half of it." said Jax "actually only one third not half "said Jim "Jax there are many places I see fit we could invest in to help out. "Victor said giving his opinion" Draw up the plan and I'll think about it." said Jax tired of hearing the same thing about interest rates for various reason. "We'll contact you soon as we are finish. "Victor said as both brothers stood shaking Jax hand one at a time. "I'll show them out boss!" Will said as he directed the men out.

Jax sat alone in the office contemplating his next move. Even though he had financial adviser they were only that adviser Jax always made the final choice that would benefit him and his family best interest at the end. Jax was also far from a fool because he knew between the gambling spots and the drug game the type of money he was bringing in was getting harder to hide by the day. "Honey you still in here Jax wife asked opening the door. "Yeah Linda!" Jax asked in response. Linda was the mother of Jax daughter. Jax and Linda have been married for 19years now but together for 25 years. Linda was 49 but you could still see the beauty in her and the reason Jax fell in love with her so long ago. Linda stood 5'7 medium brown skin and still possessed an hour glass figure with long wavy hair bringing out the Indian breed in her. Linda came and sat in Jax lap kissing him on the lips. "Just let that life go baby the stress and worries are not worth it anymore. "Linda said knowing instantly the problem with her husband. Over the 25years Linda and Jax been together she has seen bout everything that comes along with being a hustler's wife but she always stayed by his side. Linda trusted Jax with her life she would speak on certain situation but let Jax have the final decision on the matter. "Yeah I know baby. I just got people who need me right now. "Jax told her. "I understand but your family needs you even more. Think about it baby. "Linda said before kissing Jax again then leaving the room. ("The life we lead") Jax said out loud to himself kicking his feet up on his oakwood desk. Will came back into the office and sat on the sofa. "Ring, Ring, Ring" "Hello?" Jax answered the iPhone 4 "Aye Jax this Red Mack." "What's up?" asked Jax "Remember that info you wanted on the three musketeer and the bitch! Red Mac said. "Yeah!" "Turn it on the news". said Red Mack. Jax grab the remote and turned it to the 10 o'clock news and listen to the report. Jax instantly recognize the burnt two Oldsmobile as the cars driven from the robbery. "I see it!" That's a start find some valuable information now. "Jax said ended the call. "who was that?" Will asked "Red Mack!" "What that sucka want?" Will asked "Somebody got double crossed. "Jax said "What you mean by that? "Will asked not understanding "Remember the three cats that worked security and the bitch that got to RedMack!" Yeah! There they go! Jax said pointing at the flat screen as the news show pictures identify the bodies found in the burning cars. "These streets will eat you up and spit you out!" Will asked now understanding what happen. Jax grinned thinking about how the nigga double cross them. As the news broadcast it was compelling Jax to want to get personally involved in finding the youngster behind the robbery even more.

CHAPTER 4

R oxy drove the rented navy blue 2011 Chevy Tahoe as T.Z rode shot gun with Derrick falling behind them in Roxy 2010 Pink Dodge RT Challenger on 22in Pink Ashanti Rims. T.Z took Felex advice and decided to just go rent a car for the day to be on the safe side. After the meeting with Felex yesterday T.Z gather his crew for a meeting to fill them in on what was about to take play. Like T.Z already figured Derrick and Roxy didn't hesitate to give T.Z $50,000 of their money from the lick to help purchase the drugs. That would cover the $192,000 including Felex $50,000 and T.Z own fifty. T.Z gave details to his crew about how Felex already knew about Roxy and Derrick and where his mamma and brother lived. Hearing all that Roxy and Derrick knew shit was serious when dealing with Felex before they even met him. T.Z felt it was best they met Felex to since they all was mutual business partners. Flex was unable to come cause his youngest daughter Kia had a doctor's appointment. Roxy followed the GPS direction as she parked in front of a brown building that had a sign sayin "Furniture for Cheap" posted on the top. Derrick parked next to them. "You ready?" T.Z looked over and asked Roxy "Always!" T.Z tucked his 9mm glock grab the duffle bag out the backseat and open the car door.

T.Z all black high-top Airforce Ones touch the pavement matching his all black Nike jogging suit with white stripes down the side. Roxy followed with her pink low top Airforce Ones Seven jeans a pink and white Aeropostale shirt and jacket to match. Derrick hopped out the Challenger in his white low top Airforce Ones True Religion blue jeans and a white long sleeve thermal with his rose god Franco chain with a cross covered in diamonds as the pendent. The trio once again headed into something on a mission for success. T.Z open the glass door covered in mirror tint as they all walked in "Hola?" the woman greeted the trio T.Z recognize the woman greeting as the woman who answered the phone when he called "Hi" they all greeted the woman back. "Mr Felex is in the back follow me please. The older Hispanic woman lead the way to the back where they kept the furniture that wasn't on display. "Your guest have arrived Mr. Felex" the woman said in her deep Spanish accent. "T.Z my friend, how are you? I see you brought company by two other men also dressed very casual along with Felex T.Z already knew Felex knew who Roxy and Derrick was and that T.Z wasn't alone. T.Z spotted the surveillance cameras on top of the building soon as they parked. "Yeah, I thought it would be right for you to meet my mutual business partners." said T.Z "I do agree!" said Felex "Roxy and Derrick meet Felex, Felex Derrick and Roxy. "T.Z said introducing them to each other. "The other member is not here because his daughter had a doctor's appointment." T.Z said Any man who doesn't understand that is not a man. Said Felex "Let's get down to business Tito go get the merchandise, Felex told one of the goons that stood next to him. The 6'4 250-pound Hispanic man who T.Z figured out by now were body guard for Felex help unstack the crates and open the first crate revealing

28

blocks of weed compressed together. "Each block is 10lbs" Felex said picking up one bell handing it to T.Z. T.Z inspected the block then handing it to Derrick. "Yeah this that Grade A Corn" Afghan you kids kill me wit with all these crazy new names. "Felex said smiling. The bigger body guard open the other crate revealing smaller blocks wrapped in brown paper with a Cuban Flag stamp on the brown paper. The trio had to hold their compulsory when they seen all the kilos of coke. "100percent pure Cuban finest!" Felex said picking up a single brick pulling out a switch blade from his back pocket. Felex dug the blade into the corner of the kilo pulling out the icy white powder with blue flakes. Want to test? "Felex asked the trio "Naw we dont fuck around. "T.Z said as Roxy and Derrick shook they head declining the offer "Good cause this white girl really can destroy your life. "Felex said "Here you go, T.Z said handing the duffle bag over to Felex.

Felex accepted the bag unzipping it looking at the stack of cash inside. "Do I need to count it?" Your Choice! That's 200 racks take the extra change as respect and thanks" T.Z said "Thank you my amigos Felex said handing the bag to the smaller body guard. "Pull your car around back for you can load up." Felex said T.Z nodding his head at Derrick and Roxy giving them confirmation it was okay to follow Felex direction. Derrick and Roxy left T.Z. Felex and his body guards alone while they pull the cars around to the back of the building. "You must really have trust in your friends. "Felex said asking T.Z "Trust Loyalty and Respect is all we give each other from the cradle to the grave." T.Z told Felex Very well. I will give them the same Felex said as he lifted the garage door that would usually be use to unload and load furniture through. "What the pink car for?" Felex asked the two body guards ease their hands into their suit jacket clutching their conceal weapons. "The pink car is my decoy car, I need its distraction for the Tahoe won't run into any confusion and if it do. Derrick go smash it into the police cruiser to make sure the problem is solved. T.Z explain easing the guard suspicion. Good Idea! Felex said hearing the backup plan. Roxy backed the Tahoe up till the rear doors were inside the garage door. T.Z open the back doors of the Tahoe, T.Z loaded seven of the ten-pound blocks of weed into the back of the Tahoe as Tito loaded the 14kilos of cocaine along side them. When they were finish T.Z put a blanket over the drugs then secured the back doors making sure it was closed. "My friend when you finish with that contact me on the same number as before okay!" said Felex "Aight" said T.Z "Have a safe trip my friend" Felex said, shaking T.Z got inside the Tahoe with Roxy still driving as Derrick followed in the Challenger not too far behind. T.Z knew the easy part was over, the hard part was making it home.

T.Z wasn't the only person getting a shipment in that morning across town in West Dallas. Jax was receiving his Black Gold. Bout 85percent of all heroin sold in the city was somehow related coming from Jax. Jax watched the bobtail truck pull into the vacant warehouse. As him and Will stood next to each other. Two of his top lieutenants Jerry and Cole got out the bobtail truck. Jerry was 38 years old and Cole was 42 both were medium brown complexion. You could tell the drug game was paying off by Jerry pop belly. Cole worked out on a regular so he was in shape. Jerry lifted the door up on the trailer revealing taped up brown boxes. Cole climbed up in the back of the trailer grabbing a box handing it to Jerry. Jerry used da key off his key ring to break the seal on the box. Jax picked up one of the kilos of pure tar heroin wrapped in saran wrap with a Cobra snake printed on a piece of paper stuck on top of it to symbolized that in came from the same person as always. Every three weeks Jax would get a shipment of half a ton of pure tar heroin in. Jax felt his time was over for him to be breaking down bricks and selling a couple at a time that what his lieutenants was for. If you wasn't purchasing 75keys or better Jax wasn't dealing with you head on. He knew too much bullshit came along with serving drugs on the lower level.

The people buying the kind of weight Jax served personally was the same people he been dealing with for years and knew their resume and didn't have to worry about no bullshit in the process. Everything was always bout business "How was the trip?" Jax asked Jerry knowing the eight-hour drive from Corpus Christi was a dreadful drive because of the quantity of drugs that were involved. "Hated it!" Jerry answered honestly. Jax knew Jerry and Cole hated the trips but they understood that when they took the position, Jax tried his best to get the drive shortened but his connect already told him it was hard enough just getting across the border so frequently now days especially with this war or drugs situation going on. So Jax had to settle with that then he was getting the Heroin for a 7 a key how could he complain "Sorry to hear that. Do I need to give you a permanent leave of absence then?"

Jax told him being sarcastic "Naw I'm good!" Jerry said thinking of the $100,000 dollars he receives from every trip not including the kilos Jax fronted to him at 25 a key for he could sell as well. "What about you Cole?" Jax asked. "You see I haven't said nothing that's this crazy ass nigga." Cole said putting all the blame on Jerry. "Since there's no more complaining let's get this shit unloaded its money to be made. "Jax said rubbing his hands together. Jerry and Cole unloaded all the boxes with Will help. Since Jax also stashed the dope on the warehouse along with cash no more than a million at a time, he didn't trust nobody else knowing where he kept his dope so Jerry and Cole had to do most of the labor from unloading the truck to making sure everything was accounted for. Up to cutting the dope as well. Jax and Will handle the financial end counting the cash making sure the cash was in order when re-up time came. Jax had a 3bedroom home through his real estate where nobody lived that he used for a stash house to hide his millions that couldn't be washed through his companies without being detached.

Only his wife Linda knew about that stash house and only reason she knew just in case something happen to him. Linda and his daughter would always be taken care of. Jax looked at all the boxes stacked remembering the first time he received the large shipment. He had told himself one straight year of this then he was going straight legit retiring from the dope game. That was 18years ago. Jax also was an addict, addicted to the heroin but not using it only distributing it cause every time he try to shake the monkey off it keeps calling him back. Yeah, he knew people in high places but that was only stalling the inevitable because there is no Mr. Invincible when it comes to the street life either one of two things would consume you the grave or the penitentiary and in Jax case it would be Colorado's Super Max Federal Penitentiary if he didn't break his addiction. Ring Ring, "Hello?" Jax answered his phone, "Hey Old Friend?" the man voice said. "Santo's what do I owe the honors of hearing from you. "Jax told him. "Making sure if it was okay to bring my new girlfriend over for dinner?" Santos said speaking in code. "Any friend of your is a friend of mine." Jax said speaking back in code. "I'll see you tonight round 7:30 then. Santos Said. "See you then old friend." Jax said ended the call. Santo's was was one of Jax loyal customers. Santos lived in Houston and would make the 3 ½ hour drive to Dallas. Santos would want 100 bricks of the heroin. Every time Jax thought about leaving the game alone calls like that make him remember why he haven't.

T.Z and his crew sat in the living room of him and Derrick apartment as T.Z assume his position as the orchestrator of what the crew would do with the drugs. Flex had made it back to meet up to see what T.Z plans were. "Y'all dig this its time to get money its four of us that means four different parts of the city that needs belong to us. It wouldn't make sense for all of us to set up in the same spot and get money now we got to network. Roxy you still got them I.D.'s from yo income tax scam shit? T.Z asked "Yeah I still got like six of them why?" she asked. "Cause we gone need them to get cheap ass rent houses or apartments whatever available just a front door to serve fiends out of, you understand. T.Z said as Roxy nodding her head in agreement. "Flex since South Dallas yo hood find a door to get rolling after 45 days put somebody else in there to work it. Then open another door. Roxy North Dallas that's all you do the same thing as I told Flex. Derrick, Oak Cliff make it happen. I'm work the Grove. Everybody cool with what I said? "T.Z asked" I'm cool with it but how do I suppose to make my spot roll? "Roxy asked" "the same way you make you Income Tax scam roll every year. Dedication and networking plus with the dope we got once people get word of it the shit gone sell itself. "T.Z said motivating his crew with words of ambition. T.Z only had one more problem that had to be fixed.

He was the only one that knew how to cook the crack. Flex said he experimented before but didn't never get it to lock up by himself. With the amount of coke T.Z planned on dealing with soon, he knew his crew would need to know on their own how to rock it up from straight dropping to whipping it stretching 36 ounces to 50 ounces. It was time for chemistry class as T.Z went under the kitchen sink pulling out a purple glass Pyrex pot and two large Pyrex glass measuring jars. "Time for class kids" T.Z said waving his hand for them to come over to the kitchen area. "Let me show ya'll how to really get rich. The pot is for the stove. The jars are for the microwave I'm show y'all how to do both so pay attention. Derrick get the digital eye and one of them bricks from off the table. "T.Z said as he turn the burner on top of the stove on medium high and adding about 2 cups full of water into the pot "T.Z said placing the Pyrex pot on top of the burner for the water to boil. T.Z. Took an amount of cocaine and sat it on the digital eye "27.3" the digital scale read. "For every amount of grams put a quater of that in baking soda! "T.Z instructing his crew as he got the baking soda out the kitchen cabinet. T.Z dropped the cocaine inside the now starting to boil hot water. Then measure out 13grams of baking soda. "This is why you never put a lot of water in the pot. "T.Z explain dropping the baking soda inside the boiling water with the cocaine causing a chemical reaction as the water bubble and fizzed up. "If the pot was even half way full the shit would have bubble over the tip. "T.Z said as they paid close attention seeing the chemical reaction. "Y'all see that" T.Z said as the cocaine and the baking soda combine start changing into a butter looking oil base. "Showtime now!" T.Z said holding the egg beater. T.Z picked the pot up off the burner and started whipping the egg beater

34

around in a continuing circular motion till he felt he pain in his wrist. "Turn the cold water on and put this stopper in the since just in case the cold water break the pot. "T.Z order as his wrist burned. T.Z swung the pot under the cold water shock the chemicals as he continuing to whip in the same circular motion explaining why "Ping Ping" the hard-round substance bounce around the inside of the glass pot. He stopped whipping relieving his wrist of the pain. He poured the water into the sink. T.Z extracted the damp golden color cookie shape substance out of the pot. "This is what change the world" T.Z said holding the now formed crack in his hand to display his work. T.Z place the dope on the scale "41.2" the scale read gaining four extra grams without even putting no extra cut on it "Who's next?" T.Z asked. T.Z and his crew stayed in the kitchen for almost 5hours learning how to cook crack from the stove top to the microwave nobody let the kitchen until everybody learned. Everybody caught on but it seems as if Roxy was born to cook though cause she got it the first try and most people never actually get it the first time around. Not even T.Z got it the first time when he learned back when he was 17 years old.

Meanwhile, RedMack drove his 2009 S550 Benz around the city going to talk to the families of Ape, Marcus and Black acting as if he was devastated and shocked by what happened to them since they worked for him. Asking who they hung with to help find information on the people who might have did it. RedMack wasn't looking for answers on the family's behalf only on his own cause even though Jax said he didn't believe RedMack was involved, He knew Jax didn't take fuck ups lightly so if answers didn't turn up in RedMacks behalf. He was sure it would be only a matter of time before Jax came at him. After visited three different families only significant thing RedMack turned up with is a number of a friend of Marcus. RedMack dialed the number on his Evo as he drove down Illinois Drive. RedMack listen to the phone ring a few times "Hello?" the man answered "Is this Fatboy? "Yeah!" who is dis? "Fatboy asked "This RedMack" he answered as if he was the Don "RedMack! What's good my nigga?" Fatboy asked as if he been knowing him for years. "Not too much I been fucked up since I heard what happen to Marcus ya dig." RedMack lied "Hell yeah me too!" Fatboy said sadly "I'm tryna find out who was behind the shit. "RedMack said "Let me find out when you do cause I'm on the same mission that was my dog "Fatboy said" "Where you at now for we can talk for a second?" RedMack asked. "Heading to Rudy's Chicken!" Fatboy answered "I'm around the corner I'll meet you there. What you riding? "RedMack asked "I'm in a Black Cut dawg "Fatboy said "See you in a minute" RedMack said ended the call. RedMack wanted to meet Fatboy to make sure he wasn't one of the other three niggas that he seen o the tape. RedMack was almost positive that Fatboy wasn't because he wouldn't have volunteered to meet up so easy unless it was a set-up again. RedMack refuse to be caught slipping once again, especially by the same group of niggas.

RedMack sat the 9mm Ruger in his lap as he pulled into the small parking lot of Rudy's Chicken. RedMack backed in next to the Black 1985 Cutlass Supreme. Fatboy sat inside the car with another guy as they bobbed their head to the music. RedMack rolled the passenger side window down to be seen behind the limo tint. RedMack signal for Fatboy to come get in. RedMack knew immediately that Fatboy wasn't apart of the robbery when he sat all 360pounds inside RedMacks car making it rocked when he sat down inside. "Whats good?" Fatboy asked instantly looking at the chrome gun that rested in RedMack lap "Tryna get some answers "RedMack said with a concern look on his face. "I heard that!" Fatboy agreed. "Had Marcus been fucking with any new niggas that you know of? RedMack asked "Hell Naw!" Marcus and me been cool since kids wasn't too many other niggas we fucked with beside A.C over there in the car. Fatboy told him. "What about Hoes?" RedMack asked some new bitch from the Grove named Roxy but she ran income tax fraud as hoe. "Fatboy told him" "What she look like?" RedMack asked "The bitch bad no doubt but Marcus acted like he was strung out behind some pussy. Matter fact I got a picture of the bitch in my phone of both of them together at my B-day party two weeks ago." Fatboy said as he reached in his pocket pulling out his Boost Mobile unlimited phone. Fatboy scrolled through the phone until he found the picture "Here it is." Fatboy said handing RedMack the phone. "Bitch pretty fine right." Fatboy said. "Hell Yeah!" RedMack said starting at the pictures with his blood boiling on the inside. He knew instantly she was one of the bitches from the robbery "What you say her real name is?" RedMack asked like he didn't know her face "Roxanna! I don't know her last name I just know she stay in Lake June Village drive a Pink Challenger on Deuces I remember going over there once. "Fatboy said. "She probably don't know shit either but I'll call you if I hear something" RedMack said handing Fatboy his phone back anxious to go pay Roxy a visit "Aight do that for me" Fatboy said as he rocked the car as he got out.

RedMack left the parking lot on a mission now he knew the whereabouts of one of them he could get the rest of the information he needed out of her. First, he had to make a call to Jax because he was damn sure the time limit was running out on him.

CHAPTER 5

T.Z drove down the streets of Downtown Dallas in his brand-new smoke gray 6.3 Benz leaving his loft he recently moved in. Four weeks had passed since he brought the drugs from Felex and you could see the difference T.Z had then stepped his game up to another level, but not just him his whole crew. Derrick also moved to a loft in the same building Downtown and coped him a white on white on 24's 760li BMW. Flex coped a Black 2001 AMG Benz G-Wagon and Roxy coped a Z8 Hardtop convertible BMW.

The trap houses they all open up started rolling instantly one cause they had the best quality drugs and wasn't stingy with it cause they were getting it for the low. Between the four of them they sold all the coke and weed in the first 2 weeks. Roxy whip game became amazing in the kitchen she was even out doing T.Z her teacher. T.Z now had two trap houses of his own with workers who he paid $500-week two people in each house. While he would only sell quarter bricks and up or whole pounds of weed the bust down hustla was only for the trap houses. T.Z and Derrick still paid the rent on their old apartments that was the meeting place for the crew when business needed to be handled or they just needed a place to chill.

T.Z pulled up at a 7-eleven to get some gas. As he parked he watched the greatest thing God had created walking towards a Cherry Red 328LI BMW. He quickly jumped out his ride showing off his platinum Franco Chain with the Texas Flag as the pendant. He had red ruby's and blue diamonds to make the colors of the flag. T.Z also had a Rolex watch with diamonds going around the face of it. "Hi you doing? T.Z asked stopping her as she open her door. "She stood bout 5'7 150pounds smooth brown skin as if she bath in special oils. Her wavy hair was pull into a ponytail hanging past her shoulders. She wore a pair of Gucci pants hugging her sexy tone thick legs and firm round butt with a black Gucci blouse that was cut in the front showing her C-Cup breast with some 4inch Gucci heels to match. "I'm good!" She responded looking T.Z up and down then glancing at his car. Tyrone but everybody calls me T.Z "he said extended his hand. "Yvonne" she said shaking his hand introducing herself. ("Damn she got it going on") T.Z thought to himself as the 31/2 Karat Diamond tennis bracelet ad matching platinum ring shine off her wrist and hand as he held her soft palm. "Can I get yo number for I can call you later?" he asked. "For what?" she said not wanting to give in to him to fast. To be honest she thought T.Z was handsome and his thug swagger made him even more attractive. "for I can get to know you cause I already want to marry you but I can't marry you if I can't call you." he said acting as if it was a joke but really serious. "I never heard that line before!" she said smiling showing her set of pearly white teeth. "Is that a yes then. "T.Z said. "214-555-1477" She said as T.Z stored the number in his cell phone. "Don't be having your baby mama's and girlfriends calling my phone either. "She said with attitude. "23 years old single no kids that means no baby mama drama! Just make sure yo man don't answer when I call. "T.Z said. "He might! Just talk to him instead if he do!" She said being sarcastic sitting down inside her car closing the door on him. ("Yeah I got to get her!") he thought to himself. She gave me a goodbye wave as she backed out the parking space. T.Z didn't give a damn about her having a boyfriend cause he was destine to make her his woman.

RedMack and Will sat inside the black Chevy Impala waiting on Roxy to come home. RedMack had been waiting on the right opportunity to get her but she was never home so he couldn't locate what door number she lived in but now since she brought a new car the Challenger is park out front most of the time. RedMack stalked her all yesterday to make sure his plans would go smoothly today. And to make sure it does, Will decided to come along cause if something went wrong and they were unable to get Roxy the police would definitely find RedMack body. Cause they only reason RedMack was still breathing was cause he call and told Jax he found one of the culprit and she would lead him to the others still nothing has been found out on the nigga's. Will was tired of the games. Will thought maybe RedMack was just to pussy to kill a woman. In these cold streets having a soft heart for a pretty face will have you lying in the morgue cause in the streets only the strong usually survive. RedMack and Will got out the car and casually walked across the parking lot to door number 160 where Roxy lived. Will pull out his lock picking tools to open the door. They already knew nobody wasn't there so that wasn't a concern. Will got the door unlocked and RedMack and Will went inside.

T.Z counted the cash to make sure it was $84,000 dollars as he served the Arkansas nigga four kilos at $21,000 a piece. T.Z young goons sat in the trap house with him strapped with artillery just in case the out of town nigga even thought about trying some dumb shit. T.Z played the robbing game when needed be so he damn sure knew not to be caught slipping. "It's all here you good my nigga!" T.Z told the man as he placed the four bricks of cocaine inside the duffle bag to leave. One of the young goon's name "G" walked the man to the door while clutching a Glock 9mm with an extended clip by his side as the other one sat by the door with the same gun and a AR-15 next to him watching the monitors that showed the front of the house. T.Z has the house burglar barred all the way around and when you step through the front door you were inside a small cage to get inside the rest of the house the cage door had to be unlocked and open. That was a defense not to get robbed and slow the swat team down whenever they decided to hit. All the trap houses the crew had were design that way. Instead of thinking about the $32,000 he just profited off the sell, T.Z mind was on Yvonne the woman he met early. She had been on his mind since early. T.Z looked at his cellphone debating on calling so soon but temptation he couldn't resist. He found her name then pressed talk on the touch screen. T.Z listen to the Nicki Minaj and Rihanna song "Fly" as he waited on her to answer "Hello?" the soft soothing voice answered. "I'm glad that nigga didn't answer yo phone." T.Z told her knowing that was her. "What? Who is this?" She said with an attitude like she didn't know who it was calling.. "I said I'm glad that nigga didn't answer yo phone." T.Z repeated talking slow being funny. "Don't you know how to call people phone like you got some respect for others?" she told him "I got much respect thats why I demand it cause I always give it." he said "Well you ain't demanding nothing over here." she retorted "Well I'm asking now would you mind going to dinner with me?" T.Z asked. She wanted to decline just not to give in to him but she couldn't resist the type of person he was "Aight! She accepted the offer. "What time will you be ready?" he asked "What time you coming?" she retorted T.Z could tell she had a smart mouth that usually would intimidate or get on most dudes nerves cause they didn't know how to handle her. "Where do you live at?" he asked. "Off of 75 and University Drive." she said. That was only bout 10 minutes away from his loft "text me the address!" he said "No I don't know you just call me when you exit 75" she told him "Aight I'll be there at 8:30 by the way be ready!" he said showing he could take control. "Okay! By the way I already ate McDonalds once today!" She said ended the call getting the last word in. He look at the phone smiling knowing he would have to bring his best game dealing with her. It was only 4:45 he still had a couple of hours to spare. He made a few more calls before he left the spot.

Roxy headed back to her apartment to pick up 5pounds of weed for this one dude name Mike she use to date. The crew never kept large amounts of drugs in the spot unless it was about to be sold right then because if the laws decided to hit they wouldn't have to take a major loss. Roxy had two females she recruited that use to prostitute she convinced them that what she had to offer was more safe and reliable she paid them $750 dollars a weeks plus they had a place to stay. Roxy took them from the track to the trap she would say. With two young 20-year-old females working the trap nigga's seem to come by more drugs just to show they getting money and trying to fuck but Roxy school the younger woman on not to mix business with pleasure. That's the main tactic Roxy use to get them away from their pimp saying one minute he pimping ya'll next he tryna play boyfriend mixing to much business and pleasure. Roxy zoom in her Z8 BMW jamming Mary J Blige song "25/8". "You ain't never lied girl!" Roxy talked to herself as she pulled through the gate of her apartment complex. Roxy dipped into the parking space turning the engine off jumping out. "Clak, Clak, Clak" Roxy Jimmy Choo heels sounded off the sidewalk as she trotted to her apartment in a rush. A cold chill ran threw her body as she unlock her door she shook the eerie feeling off as she open her front door.

T.Z stood inside his walk in closet fresh out the shower deciding on what he would wear it had been a few months since he been on a real date, most women T.Z met was a wham, bam thank you ma'am. That's the main reason he was single now because the average woman only arouse him sexual and he could get sex if he couldn't get nothing to eat, so a woman thinking sex would keep him around she was in for a rude awakening. T.Z popped the tag on a pair of tan colored Prada slack with a matching silk Prada button down long sleeve shirt with the matching Prada shoes. Roxy had just brought the outfit for him last week she thought it would look good on him and if she thought so he was sure Yvonne would to. T.Z put on his Rolex and twin pinky rings but decided not to wear his chain. He put on his Burberry cologne to seal the deal. He examine himself in the full-length mirror. He had to admit Roxy had him looking good. T.Z could get us to dressing like this on the daily Mob Boss Style. T.Z picked up his cellphone off the charger to call Roxy. He hit the speed dial number to call Roxy. He waited as the phone rung and went to voicemail. T.Z figured she would call back in a while he just wanted to thank her again for the fit he had on.

Roxy was frozen at what she was actually looking at as she step in her bedroom. "Foxy Roxy" RedMack said as he kicked back in her queen size bed changing the channels on her flat screen with the remote like he lived there. "What the fuck is you doing in my house nigga!" Roxy spat in anger "You couldn't have thought you was gone get away with robbing me, or did you? "RedMack told her. Roxy just remembered she left her pistol and cell phone in the car since she only planned on running in and back out the house. "FUCK!" she mumbled. She couldn't have seen Will sneak up behind her cause as soon as she tried to turn and run she was looking down the barrel of the silencer that stuck out from the end of his Bryco 9mm. "Fucked is exactly what you are!" Will said as he slammed the pistol into her head knocking her to the floor. Blood leaked out her head from the gash on her forehead. "Where them niggas at that helped you rob me?" RedMack demanded grabbing a fist full of her hair.

"Suck a fat long dick nigga!" She spat. "Bam Bam Bam" RedMack kneed her in the face several times then kicked her in the ribs several more. "AHH!" Roxy screamed as she was sure he just broke some of her ribs. Roxy laid cripple on her back with blood oozing from her nose, mouth and forehead. "Where they at?" RedMack demanded as he stomped Roxy half to death. Roxy was in a daze she wasn't able to decipher nothing RedMack was saying. "Pick her up and sit her in the chair." Will told RedMack. RedMack drugged her by the arm then lifted her into the lazy boy chair. Will grabbed a towel to wipe the blood out of Roxy eyes. In Will's years of experience in torturing people he could tell Roxy was going in and out of consciousness. "Roxy, Roxy can you hear me?" Will asked as she made a groggy sound "RedMack really wants to kill you but I didn't come here for that tell me the niggas name or where to find them and we gone" Will told her. "I...I...I... chew!" Roxy spit a glob of blood right in Wills face. RedMack instantly knocked her back on the floor. "Suck a dick huh!" RedMack said repeated her words as he unzipped his pants pulling out his dick. RedMack started urinating on Roxy swollen and bloody face. She was so injured all she could do was lie there and let the hot urine splash in her face. RedMack you crazy ma'fucker! But its time to end the games the bitch ain't talking!" Will said "You right!" RedMack said "Prrf, Prrf, Prrf" Will gave Roxy three bullets to the face instantly taking her young life.

T.Z was outside waiting on Yvonne to come downstairs from her condominium. Yvonne had been ready she just purposely made him wait outside to prove a point. She came out looking like a black goddess dressed in a Golden Colored Donna Karen dress with the back out and low cut in the front with some open toe Jimmy Choo heels and a Gucci handbag. She had the same bracelet from early on with a matching necklace. Even though it was dark outside T.Z could still see the diamonds and the platinum necklace shinning as she strutted to the car like a runway model. "I'm glad you was already ready" T.Z said being sarcastic since she made him wait 15extra minutes. "My bad!" she said "Gone have us miss our reservations." He said. "Mickey Dee's do reservations?" she said joking. Hell, yeah but you told me you already ate there once today so I choose Burger King instead" T.Z said as he even giggled from the joke. "Okay I'm sorry I started it, but seriously where are we going cause I am hungry" she said "Reunion Tower!" T.Z said knowing the five-star restaurant was one of the best in Dallas. 'I like that place but the view makes me lose my appetite since I'm scared of heights." Yvonne told him. "Don't trip I'll keep you safe." T.Z told her. They talked the 15-minute drive to the restaurant. T.Z valet parked his Benz then they took the elevator 40 stories up looking out at all the city had to offer.

The Reunion Tower was shaped like a huge ball at the top outside but inside the ball was a restaurant with tables that sat on a constant rotated floor giving you a view of the city from every angle. The elevator doors open welcoming them to the restaurant with a man playing a piano on the far end. "How may I help you?' the hostess asked "Zander!" T.Z told her. "Right this way the hostess directed them after making sure there name was on the list they took a seat at the table that rested on the slowly rotating floor. "Somebody will be here to help you in just a second" the hostess said placing a menu in front of each one of them. "So, Mr. Tyrone let me ask you something?" Yvonne said catching him off guard by calling him by his real name "What's that Yvonne" What do you do for a living?" she asked T.Z thought deep about the answer he was about to give her. "Hi my name is Krystal and I'll be your waitress tonight. Would you like something to drink?" the white lady asked. "Bottle of Cristal please. "T.Z said "Okay I'll be back in a second." the waitress said walking off. "Look Yvonne I'm be real with you a nigga hustle but I don't plan on making this a lifetime thing I just got out of prison less then 6months ago and I had to get back adjusted to society. Yeah, I know it's probably plenty of jobs that hire felonies but I ain't tryna be slaving for no 8.50hr.

I'll never accomplish my dreams stuck in a dead-end job so I do what I have to cause I refuse to be without or dependent on somebody else to feed me." he explain to her. "So, you telling me you haven't been out for at least six months she said. "Only five to be correct" she said "Looks like you doing pretty good for yourself then." she said surprising him with a compliment." the waitress place the bottle of expensive champagne in a bucket of ice and sitting two glasses on the table. "Can I have the fried shrimp for the appetizer." Yvonne ordered. "Yeah me too!" And the 12oz steak well done with mashed potatoes brown gravy and macaroni cheese for my main course. "T.Z ordered "I'll take the grill salmon with the same sides. Thank You! "Yvonne order as the waitress wrote down the orders. "Is that all!" the waitress asked they both nodded yes, the she left them. "You must like seafood." T.Z said noticing she ordered all seafood. "My favorite!" she said with a big smile. "What do you do Ms. Yvonne cause by the way the diamonds blinded I would think you hustle" T.Z said as Yvonne giggle "No I don't hustle. I attend SMU University I'm working on my master's degree in law and I do paralegal work on the side." she explain "I know paralegal work don't pay that good. That necklace cost probably what you make in a year's salary." he stated "Two years to be correct!" My father paid for it for me actually." she told him "Yo pops must be one of them big time lawyers that sell niggas out on a daily." T.Z said "No he isn't!"

The main reason why I understand your story because my father was just like you once in his life. A young black man with a dream." she explain to him. T.Z knew she was being honest staring at her beautiful brown bedroom eyes were sincere when she spoke. "Maybe I might need you to represent me one day in court." he said "I hope that day never comes for your Tyrone." she told him. Yvonne knew from the first moments she seen him that T.Z was a dope boy. She usually shy away from his type because she knew it wasn't any guarantees when dealing with a hustler one day he could be here the next in jail or dead but something about T.Z made her go against her better judgment. As their food was sat in front of them they talked about so much from previous relationships what high schools they went to and the people they hung with. T.Z found out Yvonne really was single and that she really was a down to earth person. T.Z felt his phone vibrating on his hip but seen it was just Derrick and didn't answer. Derrick called again then Flex. When he seen Derrick calling again he figured t had to be important. "What's good nigga?" T.Z answered the phone saying. "T where you at my nigga?" Derrick asked T.Z hearing concern in his voice "At the Reunion Tower on a date. What's up why you sounding like that?" T.Z asked. "Its Roxy she dead!" The words came out of Derrick mouth made T.Z heart and mouth drop. Yvonne assume whoever that was on the other end of the phone wasn't saying anything good. "WHAT?" T.Z spat loud enough to grab the people next to him attention. "Dead Dog!" Derrick said as T.Z could tell he was crying through the phone.

"Meet me at the apartment in the hood!" T.Z said hanging up "We got to leave now!" T.Z told her as he pilled 10 hundred dollar bills off his knot dropping on the half eating food. Yvonne didn't protest she followed cause by the look on his face she already concluded it was serious whatever that was going on. "Tyrone are you okay?" she asked as they rode the elevator down. T.Z looked up at her with tears in his eyes. "My friend Roxy I was just telling you about just died!" T.Z said as the tears streamed down his face. "I'm sorry!" Yvonne said hugging him until the elevator stopped. They got off and walked to the car not

49

wanting to wait on the valet man "I'll ride with you if it okay." Yvonne said He looked across the top of the car at Yvonne before he answered. "Yeah it straight!" he said as they both got in the Benz. The tires screeched as he sped out the parking garage heading for the apartment. T.Z mind race a million miles wondering what the fuck happen did somebody try and rob her spot did she get caught slipping leaving her spot? T.Z taught her never leave without her gun. ("If that bullshit as pimp nigga had something to do with it behind them hoes then for show he would pay for it with his life his mama life and his kids' life.") T.Z thought to himself as he weaved the Benz in and out of traffic to he reached his destination parking in two parking spots jumping out the car. When T.Z and Yvonne walked in the apartment both Derrick and Flex were sitting down smoking a blunt in silence "What the fuck you niggas just sitting around not tryna figure out what the fuck happen?" T.Z yelled at them "Look T" Look my ass you niggas just sitting here like the shit okay." T.Z scream as tears formed in his eyes until he finally broke all the way down crying. Derrick embraced him because he understood exactly how T.Z felt. "Let me holler at you in the room." Derrick whispered to him. "You can sit down. Flex don't bite unless told" he told Yvonne tryna make up for his outburst. T.Z close the door when they step in the bedroom. "T we already know who did this shit" Derrick said. "Who?" "They found Roxy inside her apartment while it was on fire but they say she had three gunshot wounds to her head so the fire ain't what killed her "Derrick told him. T.Z said exactly who did it when he heard "REDMACK" Derrick nodding his head in agreement. T.Z dropped his head knowing he was the main reason behind Roxy death but best believe he would be the main reason behind avenging

Roxy death as well. T.Z shedding a single tear on the right side of his face that would be the last tear of pain he would ever shed because the stakes just went up from get money to get money by all means necessary. Eat or get ate a piece of T.Z died that night with Roxy.

CHAPTER 6

RedMack sat at the bar next to a 28-year-old high yellow complexion woman having drinks inside the gambling spot as the workers cleaned up from the night crowd. RedMack had already convinced the lady to come home with him but little did she know only place RedMack was taking her was to a motel room. Between the Vodka and two X-pills she was on it didn't make it too much of a difference at this point. He probably could fuck in the backseat of his S550 if he wanted too! Fat as that ass was he wanted to enjoy her so the backseat back shot wasn't an option tonight. RedMack rubbed and caressed the inside of her thigh. Moving his hands up her short skirt until he felt her voluptuous pussy lips. Just as RedMack figured she didn't have any panties on. RedMack rubbed his fingers on her throbbing clit as his dick hardened inside his pants. RedMack couldn't stand the wait as he stood up escorted the woman to the front door "Lock up for me." RedMack said handing Ralph the bartender and longtime friend the building keys. RedMack and the lady got into his car parked out front as soon as RedMack started the car to drive off she leaned across the seat unbuckling his pants pulling out his already hard manhood. She licked the pre-cum that was already coming out then took all of him into her mouth as he drove. Redmack was so distracted that he didn't even notice the black Honda Civic that pulled out across the street behind him. RedMack cruised down

Lamar enjoying the head job he was receiving with one hand on the wheel and the other hand inside her asshole. RedMack had her skirt raised all the way up around her hips for he could get a good view of her bright round derriere as he drove and got head. RedMack needed to stop and get some condoms before he went to the motel so he pulled up at the gas pump at the Chevron when he came to a complete stop the woman really perform by making RedMack moan. He grabbed the back of her head and pushed it down as he bust in her mouth. RedMack instantly jumped as his driver door was jacked open "AHH!" the woman screamed as the two masked man yanked RedMack out the car on to the pavement. Everything happen so quickly RedMack never had a chance to reach for his pistol under the seat. "Hold up man take the money, the car, the bitch too!" Redmack hollered pleading for his life "Only thing I want is yo life nigga!" the masked man told him putting the .44Bulldog to his temple. RedMack had a confused look on his face. "Got caught with yo pants down again!" "the second mask man said referring to RedMack dick hanging out RedMack had full understanding of what was going on now "It wasn't me it was Will and Jax" RedMack said pleading for his life. "Tell Roxy I said what's popping" Boom, Boom!" the .44 Bulldog went off like a cannon sending brain fragments splattering everywhere. "AHH, AHH!" the woman screamed "You chose to suck the wrong dick tonight bitch" Boom Boom" the .44Bulldog blew two holes straight through the woman's chest. The store clerk was inside on the phone most likely with the police so they jumped in the Honda Civic where the masked driver was parked behind RedMack Benz waiting to drive off into the dawn of the morning. T.Z, Derrick and Flex took off their ski masked as they went to dump the stolen car and switch back to their own cars before the police caught the trail on them cause the store clerk got the license plates and the car description as well and in a matter of minutes the entire South Dallas would be swarming with police stopping every Honda in site. T.Z couldn't bring Roxy back but it sure made him feel a little better blowing RedMack's face off. He thought about the words RedMack said before he pulled the trigger. Will and Jax. T.Z heard all the street rumors about Jax and Will. T.Z had even seen the niggas a few times he was aware that RedMack worked for Jax from the start. That's how he knew RedMack might had been telling the truth but telling the truth still wouldn't save RedMacks life that day. Only thing bout Jax and Will they wouldn't be so easy to touch like RedMack it would take planning, patience and persistence to get away with murking them type niggas but somehow T.Z was gone get it done. He owed it to Roxy.

"This is a breaking new report an unidentified man and woman were fatally shot and killed early this morning around 6a.m. At this Chevron. Witnesses say two masked men pulled the male driver out the vehicle then shot him brutally. Then opening fired on the female victim killing her. Right now, detectives are still investigating trying to find the motive. Police say suspects fled in a Black 4 door Honda Civic if you have any information on what happened please contact the Dallas Police Department you can remain anonymous." the news reporter said as Will and Jax watched the news. They already knew who the unidentified man was by the S550 Benz with the plates reading "MAC RED" in the background. "The kid struck fast!" Jax commented "That he did" said Will. Will had already determined it was only a matter of time before he made sure Roxy body was found burning to send a message to the niggas and things went as planned as Will predicted. They would come straight at RedMack. Will took it as killing two birds with one stone. Roxy and RedMack were out the way and only one trigger had to be pulled. "Do you think the youngster know we were behind the shit?" Jax asked "Knowing RedMack pussy ass they do now." Will said. "Stay on alert just in case." Jax said "In case of what? You think this young nigga ready for war?" Jax told Will "the nigga ain't nobody!" Will said. "He might be nobody but nobody's become somebody's. And believe me Will the war has just started." Jax spoke the truth. Will respected Jax words so he stayed silent but he felt that T.Z wasn't even in his league to be considered a threat to them.

Later that day T.Z and Derrick met up with Roxy mother Ms. Richmond she was a splitting image of Roxy just older from skin tone to figure if you wanted to know how Roxy would look at 46 just see her mother. Roxy BMW and Challenger was parked out front of the 3bedroom house Roxy grew up in. As Derrick parked behind the BMW he remember getting the devastated call from Ms. Richmond saying they found Roxy inside her apartment dead. T.Z looked at the house remembering the days he use to sneak through Roxy window when one of her homegirls would spend the night to get some pussy. Roxy would lay in the bed playing sleep as he had sex with her friends on the floor. Some nights he would just come over and go to sleep on the floor alone he always made sure he was gone by 7:30 the time Roxy mother had to be at work 2hours early and came into her dark room to kiss Roxy goodbye and stepped on T.Z as he slept on the floor. Ms. Richmond went crazy cause she thought T.Z and Roxy were having sex with each other but after catching T.Z several more times and sitting down talking to them she learned they were more like brother and sister and not girlfriend and boyfriend. Realizing it was no keeping them apart Ms. Richmond start telling 15-year-old T.Z goodbye as she left for work. T.Z and Derrick got out of Derrick 750Li walking towards the front door. "Hi you guys doing?' Ms. Richmond asked opening the front door ahead of time to greet them. "We okay! How you holdin up ma? "T.Z asked. Since T.Z slept at Ms. Richmond house ate her groceries up she would say "you must think I'm your momma boy." Since then he been calling her ma. "I'm fine! Ya'll come on in sit down." she told them. Ms. Richmond was acting normal but they knew she was hurting on the inside of her only child being murdered and especially not knowing why. T.Z wish he could tell her everything from the gambling spot lick to killing RedMack but as good lady like Ms. Richmond couldn't and wouldn't even try to comprehend the situation "Ma you know I'm going to pay for all the funeral expenses just let me know the price." T.Z told her "Thank You!" she said hugging him tightly.

T.Z hugged her back cause she needed the comfort right now "Why, Why, Why they do that to my baby Tyrone?" Ms. Richmond cried in his shoulder "I don't know ma! I don't know!" T.Z told her as she continue to cry. "Excuse me I'm sorry for wetting your shirt Tyrone." She said half smiling wiping her red eyes. "Its okay its only my favorite shirt." T.Z said joking making Ms. Richmond smile. "this is what I want you to come get. I know Roxy wasn't a saint but she didn't deserve what happen to her either." Ms. Richmond said as she was handing Roxy chrome and pink grip .380 and iPhone 4 to him. "You sure you don't want to keep this stuff." T.Z asked "Naw I still got my trusty .22 revolver just in case!" she said T.Z laughed lightly "What's so funny?" she asked "You still got that thing." T.Z asked remembering the morning Roxy stole it and took it to school, Yes I do. There is no reason I need another one they all do the same stupid thing kill and hurt people" she said urging them towards the door to leave "Bye Ma!" "Bye Ms. Richmond." "Be Careful!" She told them as they walked towards the car getting in. T.Z powered on Roxy phone she had 71 missed calls a lot was from weird names of people he didn't know most likely customers of hers. T.Z took it upon his self to take over Roxy spot in North Dallas where she had Traci and Niki hustling at. The two ex-hoes Roxy knocked the pimp for. T.Z had already went there early to break the bad news to them and give them the proposition to work for him under the same pay and standards Roxy gave them. They accepted his offer having the same respect and loyalty that they gave Roxy if not more. T.Z would just keep her phone on and worked it as the customers called. T.Z could hear Roxy voice in the back of his head telling him not to sit around and bullshit cause she gone just get to the money even harder. Mary J. Blige going "25/8" played as Roxy phone rang a 903-area code and number showed on the incoming call ("East Texas") T.Z thought to himself "Hello?" T.Z answered saying "Where Roxy at?" asked the unfamiliar man voice "Who dis is?" T.Z asked "J.J!" he said. She not around right now this her brother what's good?" T.Z asked "I was heading to the gym out there thought I might lose 14 pounds or so." "J.J told him speaking in code "How long it's gone take you to get here?"

T.Z asked "2 ½ hours.!" "Call me when you 10 minutes away I'll give you the direction to the Gym but you know membership 900 a month. "T.Z said telling him the price. "For real that's what's up better then paying $1100 like before." J.J said surprising T.Z he thought Roxy been charging the same price. Everybody else in the crew was. "Talk to you later." T.Z said ended the call. Derrick look at T.Z like who was that "That was some nigga from East Texas I told him 900 a pound he was excited cause Roxy been charging him $1100 a pound. "T.Z told Derrick "That sound like some shit Roxy would do tax the shit out of a nigga." Derrick said laughing. "You right about that." T.Z said agreeing.

Four days later T.Z, Derrick and Flex sat on the first row next to Roxy's mother, aunts, uncles, and cousins for Roxy funeral. The services were held inside the Gospel Tabernacle Baptist Church. T.Z and Derrick split the entire funeral expenses between them as promised. T.Z looked behind him through his dark tinted Gucci shades at all the different people some he knew and others he didn't. Who came to pay their respect to Roxy, Since the fire actually started with Roxy body the chrome casket had to remain down and locked for nobody could see her badly burnt body. Ms. Richmond had already broken-down crying once as she entered the church viewing the casket from a distance.

It would be a hard task for Ms. Richmond to get through this funeral. The church choir begun a song T.Z had never heard before since T.Z and Flex were Muslim it wasn't to many church songs they did know. Only time either one of them came inside a church was for occasion as this one. T.Z listen to the different people sobbing some of who he was sure that didn't even know Roxy. The choir mellowed out to a light hum as the dark skin tall slim older gentleman who had to be the pastor of the church, took the podium to deliver the eulogy. "Let us bow our heads in prayer." the pastor said then started to pray.

"O Allah, forgive those of us who are alive and those who have passed away, those present and those absent and our young and elderly, the males and the females. O Allah, those whom you keep alive from among us, make him live according to Islam, and those whom you wish to die from among us, let him die in the state of faith AMEN!" T.Z and Flex repeated the same prayer silently to themselves as the preacher prayed. "In Jesus name, Amen!" the pastor said ended his prayer. T.Z mind thought the day when he was release from prison and Roxy and Derrick was waiting outside the front of The Walls Penitentiary in Huntsville, TX for him in Roxy Pink Challenger. He remembered the huge hug and wet kiss on the cheek she gave him. He could still feel her body on him and lips on his face. "It's Okay!" I'm Gucci!" T.Z jumped as he heard Roxy voice saying her favorite word "I'm Gucci" meaning she okay. T.Z looked around making sure his mind wasn't playing tricks on him but maybe it was because the only person talking was the pastor the other noises were sobs. T.Z mind went back to when he was 17 years old and Roxy boyfriend use to get mad at her cause she was always spending time with T.Z over him. Her boyfriend name was Wayne Simmons. One day Wayne told her "you and that nigga got to be fucking cause ya'll always together." "if we was I damn sure wouldn't be wasting my time with yo little dick ass!" she spat. Roxy hit his soft spot cause Wayne was the pretty boy type every girl would love to be seen with him but after sex they would slowly leave him cause it was true Wayne had a little dick and he knew it. That's why he always made sure all his girls got whatever they asked him for. Wayne was furious when Roxy said that he hit Roxy

59

with two jabs to the face busting her lip and giving her a black eye. Later that day when she got home. T.Z and Derrick seen her face asking "What happen?" "Wayne hit me!" Roxy said. T.Z didn't ask why cause it didn't matter to him rather Roxy was in the right or wrong he had her back. "Come on!" T.Z said getting in the driver seat of her 1996 Toyota Corolla. Derrick got in the passenger seat Roxy in the back and went to Wayne house. Soon as they got their T.Z got the tire iron out the trunk and walked to Wayne front door. Soon as the front door open revealing Wayne's pretty boy face, T.Z smacked him with the tire iron splitting the side of his face making him drop to the ground. T.Z kicked him in the face until blood was all over T.Z white Reeboks'. If Derrick and Roxy wouldn't have been there, he probably would have beat Wayne to death. T.Z ended up getting arrested for aggravated assault with a deadly weapon. Derrick and Roxy came up with 10 percent of $50,000 to bond him out two weeks later. T.Z ended up getting 5 years' probation for the case but violated by shooting a dude catching another case that's why he coped out for 4 years in prison. As the pastor came to the closing of the eulogy. T.Z, Flex and Derrick and three of Roxy uncles stood up and went towards the casket, three on each side. T.Z stood at the front on the right side with Derrick and Flex behind him. Roxy oldest uncle stood across from him with her other uncles James and Chris. T.Z placed his left hand on the side of the casket. "NOOOO! NOOOO!"

Ms. Richmond shouted out as the casket lifted up to be carried out to the awaited hearse. Three stretched Lincoln Town car Limousines waited out front with the hearse to drive the family to the grave site. T.Z, Derrick, Flex and Roxy uncles rode in one limo. While Ms. Richmond and the rest of the family rode in the other two. None of the men spoke a single word the 10minute ride to Lincoln Memorial Cemetery. Everybody in the limo seem to be caught up in their own deep thoughts. The limos came to a stop after entering the gates of the massive cemetery. As T.Z stepped out the limo observing all the headstones that laid on the grass. He remembered the last time he was here, a homeboy of his got killed. 2 weeks after T.Z was release from prison. T.Z homeboy name was Ryan Smith, he was found shot 16 times in his Charger the police never found out why. Ryan was also in the game. At the top of this game but somebody quickly put a stop to it. That's how these streets were one minute you on top of the world, next week you six feet under it. ("Cold World!") T.Z thought as he carried the casket to the grave. T.Z kissed his hand then touched the top of the casket after they sat it on top of the harness to be lowered into the earth. T.Z went and stood by Derrick and Flex as the crowd filled around the grave to watch the casket be lowered.

The pastor made one last final prayer for Roxy soul then the casket started to descend into the ground. People walked up and dropped a single red rose on top of the casket as it went down. T.Z stepped up after the last person reaching inside his Black Armani suit pocket pulling out two white roses "Assalam, 'alaikum wa rahmutullah!" T.Z said turning his face right then left then dropping the roses in the grave. The crowd began to disperse as T.Z stood in the same spot looking down at the casket "she's in a better place." Ms. Richmond said placing her hand on his back breaking the trance he was in. T.Z turn and gave Ms. Richmond a hug. "I miss her!" T.Z said to Ms. Richmond as they hugged "Me too! Me too!" She said letting the embrace go looking him directly in the face. T.Z remove the sunglasses from his eyes looking Ms.

Richmond in her red puffy eyes preparing himself for the question that he figured was coming. "Do you know who is responsible for this Tyrone?" T.Z dropped his head remaining silent taking a deep breath. "Will they be able to hurt anybody else?" she asked. "No!" T.Z answered coldly. Ms. Richmond understood the lifestyle he lived so hearing that she walked off hoping she wouldn't have to attend his funeral next. Derrick and Flex walked up next to T.Z "You going to be aight my nigga?" Flex asked looking down at the casket in the ground. "Yeah!" Come on let's go the limos waiting on us. Derrick said "Ya'll go head I'm chill!" "T.Z told them. "How you gone get home?" asked Flex "I'll call somebody to come get me or a taxi." T.Z said. Derrick and Flex understood he just needed sometime alone so they respected his wishes. "Aight fam!" Call me if you need me" Derrick said "Me too" Flex said "You know I will!" T.Z said. Derrick and Flex heading to the limos leaving T.Z alone by the grave. T.Z squatted down over the open grave. "Damn Roxy I told your hard headed ass to always have yo strap on you. Oh yeah I got that hoe RedMack too!" I Love you save a place for me up there." I Love You too!" he heard Roxy voice say "Excuse me!" the man voice said from behind startling him as T.Z jumped up.

"Felex!" Felex stepped up next to T.Z making a cross symbol on his chest then kissing his hand "How are you my friend?" Felex asked "I'm holding up. What are you doing here? "T.Z asked wondering "Paying my respect remember loyalty and respect is not just words it's a way of life." Felex repeating T.Z words from the first time they met. "I appreciate it and I know Roxy would too!" T.Z said "No problem! What happen to Roxanna was a tragedy do you know who was responsible for this?" Felex asked "Yea I know!" What is being done about it? Do you

62

need for my people to lend a helping hand?" Felex asked "One of them is taking care of already but the other two will be a little harder to get too" T.Z explained "Who are these guys you speak of?" "Jax and Will!" T.Z said "Jax and his hitman Will yes I know of them. You are right Jax is a well-respected man you could label him a made man if he was Italian killing Jax and keeping your own life is a very hard task for a man to accomplish but the hitman Will he's fair game." Felex told him. "So you tryna tell me Jax is untouchable" T.Z said "No my friend. No man is untouchable not even myself. I am only saying a lot of repercussion and retribution would be taken for killing a man of his standards. " Felex explained "I understand but he gave the green light for killing Roxy and I truly believe in an eye for eye, tooth for a tooth, her soul for their soul." T.Z said "I understand completely my friend I'm make a few calls to see what I can find out for you." Felex said "I'll be very thankful for it." T.Z said "Are you going to sit out here all day?" Felex said "Naw!" Would you mind dropping me off at my car? "No problem!" T.Z took one last look at the casket then walked off towards Felex car.

Jax sat alone in his 2010 Cadillac Escalade Ext Truck looking at the bizarre sight through his binocular as he sat far off undetected. ("Felex") Jax thought to himself. Watching the youngster talking to Felex then getting inside Felex Maybach brought a whole different meaning to the situation. That's the main reason Jax choose to come on this little mission by himself cause Will hot headed quick to pull the trigger ass would have probably shot the funeral up not conscience of who was there. Jax knew Felex had more power than him but they each showed each other the utmost respect in the streets. There interest never conflicted with each other so he knew Felex wasn't behind all this. Jax knew coming to the funeral would be valuable on his end but now he had to figure out how was Felex connected to the youngster. "I told you Will this is War!" Jax said out loud to himself.

T.Z rode in the backseat of the Maybach with Felex as Tito one of Felex's guards drove and the other rode shotgun. "T.Z I understand you are upset about Roxanna and I know you want vengeance and there's no stopping that. All I ask is that you think rational and prepare yourself mentally cause jumping headfirst into something can make a situation worse then it was or should have been. I can tell you are a warrior but remember this war will take more mentally fight then physical if you want to come out victorious at the end. Felex told him T.Z nodded his head in agreement to the words of wisdom Felex shared. Ace Hood song "Go and get it!" played as T.Z phone ringer "Yvonne!" name displayed across the screen. His mind been so caught up in what happened to Roxy he never called Yvonne back after dropping her off that night after their date. "Hell?" he answered saying "Hi are you Mr. Tyrone?" Hearing her soft voice made T.Z feel a little better already. "I'm good. What about you?" he asked "Trying to figure out why you haven't call me after you ran that weak ass game to get my number in the first place." she said "I see you haven't changed but my bad I have been caught up getting all these funeral arrangements together." he told her. "I can understand that, How was it? I know it was sad but did the services turn out okay?" she asked "Yeah everything was good. What you bout to do?" "Nothing!" "Let me get back to my car then I'm call you maybe we can finish our date." he said "Call me and well see!" she said ended the call. "New Girlfriend!" Felex said smiling "I hope so!" T.Z said thinking about Yvonne as the Maybach glide down the street.

CHAPTER 7

T.Z walked through North Park mall in his white V-neck Polo Shirt and White and Red Plaid Polo Shorts and white Polo Shoes for the first of Spring Weather. Derrick had on some Paris blue jean shorts with a white tee and some white and gray Jordan #13's with his platinum 4 row chain and six row bracelet that match. T.Z also was rocking his jewelry to the fullest as well. T.Z had even went and got his grill re-done to 8 platinum teeth at the top with VVS diamonds and two at the bottom on each side tooth with VVS diamonds. It had been almost three months since Roxy funeral. The crew was doing even more numbers than before and it showed by the expensive cars they drove and the shopping sprees. Their names were even started to ring in the streets as the three young niggas having lots of cash. T.Z and Yvonne was spending a lot of time with each other as well. Even though after almost two months of dating they still hadn't had sex T.Z respected her wishes so he never tried to force her to do anything plus he had a line of groupies ready to bend over on command so he wasn't tripping off no pussy.

His main concern was getting money at this exact moment. He took

Felex advice by not rushing into anything and making a costly mistake and by costly that meant his life or somebody else's who meant something to him. T.Z also knew he would have to have his paper right also just in case cause never know he might have to leave the country. Cause T.Z found out from Felex that Jax had more then the Mexican cartel on his side but also the D.E.A as well. That's why T.Z felt every move he made on Jax from now on had to be strategically calculated before doing it. Even if Jax couldn't personally get to him he could alert the D.E.A on him and that's a battle T.Z would have a hard time winning against the U.S Government. They walked with their hands full of shopping bags from various stores. It was 5:50 and they had been in the mall since 11:00 that morning. The crew had plan on going out tonight to have a little fun cause they been so busy on the grind they seldomly went out anywhere. "You bout ready to go?" TZ asked "Hell yeah I been waiting on you to say something." Derrick said to him. They headed out the mall to Derrick's brand new 2011Black Corvette on offset 22in Forgiato's on the back and 21's on the front. They loaded all the shopping bags into the car then got ready to leave. Derrick started the 750-horse power motor getting ready to leave the mall. Derrick pulled the American Muscle out into traffic smashing the gas pedal down, going 0-60in 3.5 seconds "I Love this shit!" Derrick said whipping the Corvette in and out between cars. "I hear you but if you don't slow the ma'fucker down we ain't gone be able to enjoy it!" T.Z said looking at the speedometer reading 130mph and steady increasing. "You scared of a little speed nigga!" Derrick said. "Naw just yo reckless as driving that's all." T.Z grabbed his phone off his hip to call Flex. He hit the speed dial then listen to the phone ring waited on Flex to pick up "Leave a message!" he heard Flex voicemail come on then hanging up T.Z wondered what was up with Flex cause usually he would answer the phone.

Flex sat inside the white Pontiac G6 he brought for his baby momma with a plate in his lap and a fifty-dollar bill rolled up snorting lines of cocaine. Flex seen T.Z calling him but decided to just let the voicemail pick up. Even though T.Z didn't have a clue that Flex had started snorting coke. Flex felt if he answers the phone T.Z might find out. Flex knew it was the coke that had him tripping but lately Flex had been tripping all the way around really tripping fucking off all his money with nothing to show for it only thing Flex had was 15grand 10bricks and 20pounds of weed. And after selling all that money would be needed for he could re-up with T.Z and Derrick. Flex felt to ashamed to tell T.Z the truth about his money dilemma after how T.Z help put him on with Felex. That's the main reason Flex was about to do what he did the best, rob. Flex was parked in a parking lot of a grocery store waiting on the dude name Ken to arrive. Flex figured it wouldn't be too hard to get him since they then conducted business a few other times in the previous weeks so Ken wouldn't be expected any shady shit on Flex part. Flex sat the plate down on the passenger seat as he spotted Ken pulling up in his Green Acura Legend. Flex was glad Ken by himself as he looked inside the car as the Acura parked next to him. Flex took a deep breath trying to calm down from the adrenaline of what was about to take place and from snorting almost a gram of coke within 30minutes. He for out the G6 with two duffel bags zipped up. Flex sat in the passenger side of Ken's car not closing the door completely "What's good Flex?" "Slow motion right now got a few other moves to make that's all" Flex said trying to keep the small talk to a minimum. "I can dig it!" Here you go then." Ken said reaching on the backseat floor picking up a duffel bag handing it to Flex. Flex unzipped the bag and took a quick peep at all the greenbacks then zipped it back up. Flex sat the bag with the cash on the ground outside the car then stood up pulling out his .45 Rugar from his wristband pointing the fun at Ken. "Don't move, Don't say shit nigga if you don't want to die." Flex said as Ken put his hands in the air with a scared and confused look on his face. Flex reached and grabbed the keys out the ignition putting them in his pocket and taking Kens Galaxy phone as well. Flex closed Ken's car door while still aiming the .45 at him picking up the bag full of money getting inside the G6 driving off. Just that quick Flex was $214,000 dollars back of the good plus he still had all his drugs. That's why Flex like the Jack game cause even though it was more risky the money came faster and easier to him. Flex knew Ken would probably still check the two duffel bags he sat in the car leaving behind, but when Ken open the bags revealing only old phone books then Ken would fully understand he just got.

T.Z sat on the floor inside his walk-in closet with his safe open putting the red rubber band around the wad of cash identify that was a ten-thousand-dollar wad. He had all his five, tens, twenty and twenty-five stack color coordinated by rubber band colors. Black bands mean five thousand stack, Red means ten thousand stack, green means twenty thousand stack, regular color means twenty-five-thousand-dollar stack. T.Z found it was easier to keep track of whenever he needed to get some money out of or how much he had saved. In the short time he been dealing with Felex, T.Z already had over million saved up including his spending habits. T.Z made sure he left 4stacks with black rubber bands sitting out to take with him when he went to the club before he close and locked the large firesafe. He looked at his phone and seen it was already 9:30pm and Derrick and Flex would be at his door in a minute. T.Z popped the tags on the clothes he put each piece on then removing his durag showing his crisp taper fade and deep bee hive waves. He even had a pair of Gold Versace frames with clear non-prescription lenses to put on. He put on his chain and bracelet and black Cartier watch. He had never been a self-centered person but looking at himself in the full-length mirror. He considered his self as a broke bitch fantasy and rich hoe dream. He heard Ace Hood song playing knowing his phone was ringing "Yeah!" he answered saying "You ready or what nigga?" Flex asked "Yeah!" I'm downstairs in the parking garage." Flex said. "Aight here I come."T.Z said ended the call. He grabbed the stacks of money stuffing his pockets then headed downstairs to the parking garage. "No this nigga didn't!" T.Z thought to himself when he seen the doors up in the air on the 2011 Benz SLS AMG. T.Z knew that was a quarter million easily spent. He walked a full 360 degrees around the vehicle "When you get this?" T.Z asked "When I missed your call early." Flex said "How much you pay?" T.Z asked really not concern about the price but how he paid for it. They let me drop 200 thousand and called it even." Flex said cocky "Don't tell me yo silly ass gave them folks $200 cash!" T.Z asked getting upset. "Hell, nawl nigga you already know I'm paying notes you bet not tell nobody." Flex said laughing trying smoothing his lie out hearing T.Z getting upset about the dumb decision he made. "Bout to say nigga you gone get us sent back to prison you'll come off easier stealing the ma'fucker then paying cash with dope money!" T.Z said "Damn bitch no you didn't do the game like that!" Derrick said excited stepping off the elevator into the parking garage with Dot next to him. Dot was Derrick young protege. Dot was 18 years old 5'9 slim built with a brown complexion. T.Z like Dot as well he knew the youngster had a lot of potential to make it in these dirty streets. If Dot wasn't so loyal to Derrick T.Z would have recruited Dot to come work for him. "Yeah I knew we would need something fast to keep up with the vet." Flex told him "Let's find out cause forgot my shit a Callaway GS SC 606 edition nigga not that stock bullshit." Derrick said hitting the auto start button on his key pad. T.Z got in the passenger side of the SLS as Flex drove while Derrick got in his Corvette with Dot.

T.Z looked over at Flex sporting his all brown Gucci fit adorn with expensive jewelry thinking did Flex really make a huge mistake that might alert some unwanted company better known as the F.B.I! Flex pulled the 563 horses out the parking garage with Derrick following behind them. Flex got on I-35 heading North rocketed the SLS from 0-60mph in 3.6 seconds. Derrick was right next to them speeding in his corvette bobbing his head to T. I's song "Ridin' Round & Gettin' It!" Flex slowed down when he seen the speedometer hit 153mph. Not wanted to feel the results of a fatal or bad accident but Derrick being the need for speed freak he was push the gas pedal down to the limit racing off "I swear that nigga retarded. T.Z said watching Derrick continuing to build up speed. The brake lights on the Corvette lit up as Derrick slowed down to make the Walnut Hill exit to get to the club. Flex exited not too far behind. Club Beamers was one of the hottest clubs in Dallas so the parking lot was filled to the max when they drove up. "This ma'fucker packed!" Flex said looking at the long line standing outside the door "Hell yeah!" T.Z agreed. Derrick and Flex pulled their expensive cars right in front of the door for the cars could be valeted. The people standing in line head turn when they seen the doors on the SLS go up like wings. Flex and T.Z heard the various compliments as they emerged from the Foreign vehicle. Derrick looked at his red bottom shoes and matching Gucci pants and straighten out his gray collar Gucci shirt when he got out his car Derrick also had on his platinum Fraco chain with a platinum Jesus face covered in diamonds. As Dot had on Derrick old gold chain that he gave him. Also, with a pair of red bottom shoes black 501 Levis and a red polo collar shirt and red polo hat. They paid the valet man $400 dollars a-piece to park and an extra 100 to have their cars sitting out front waiting when the club was over. "You get them passes?" T.Z asked Derrick about the V.I.P passes to walk straight on him not having to wait in line. T.Z dropped out 7,500 dollars for a table on the second floor of the club for him and his crew early when they left the mall. "Yeah!" Derrick said going on in his back pockets pulling out four passes giving one to everybody then keeping one for himself.

All four of them strutted towards the entrance as if it was a red carpet laid out front. They all showed their passed then let the bouncer scan them with the wand making sure they didn't have any weapons on them. Even though the club was big it still was wall to wall packed with a line still outside. T.Z lead the way through the club headed up stairs to where their table was. They showed the bouncer their passes and he placed a green wristband on them indicated they were allowed upstairs. They went upstairs and found their table taking a seat. It was still a lot of people upstairs but the crowd wasn't wall to wall like downstairs. They took in the view of all the sexy ladies dancing and walking around the club it had to be a 4 to 1 ratio of women to men. "What you guys drinking?" the light skin waitress asked of the loud music. "4 double shots of patron!" Flex shouted. "4 bottles of Moet too!" Derrick shouted smiling at the lady "Is that it" she asked "And yo phone number." Derrick added. She smiled and walked off not commenting on Derrick's request. "Don't nobody go for that 1980's

Nintendo as game no more." Flex said laughing. Derrick gave him the middle finger. "T.Z isn't that Bri-Bri over there." Derrick said pointing. Hell, yeah that's that slut!" T.Z said remembering like it was yesterday how she disappeared on him after she came and visited him when he was still in the county jail. T.Z went to court one morning and the District Attorney offered 20 years and said he wasn't up for no negotiation. Bri-Bri was T.Z girlfriend at the time he caught the case so she was in the courtroom for support. Later that day she came to visit him complaining how it was hard out there for her by herself. At the time T.Z had only been locked up 3months. Even though he understood what she meant he still tried giving her encouraging words. Like most young females in Bri Bri position the words had little or no impact at all. Bri-Bri put a hundred dollars on his books and now was the first time since that day he seen her. "Here ya'll go." the waitress said with a tray in her hands placing the double shots of patron on the table then the four bottles of Moet "We ain't gone need them glasses, thanks tho!" Flex told her "That will be 1000 dollars!" Derrick pulled out a knot of money pulling off eleven hundred-dollar bills "Keep the change!" Derrick said handing her the money. "You keep this!" she said reaching in her pocket handing him a napkin then walking off. Derrick open the napkin and it read "Carmen 214-55-3130!" I guess she still play with her Nintendo!"

"Nigga it cost you hundred dollars you probably could have gotten some pussy for that much!" Flex said Only pussy you getting for hundred dollars is that base head from them dope fiends you be serving nigga!"

Derrick said with everybody laughing "Here come yo bitch T!" Derrick said "That ain't my bitch!" T.Z spat looking directly at Bri-Bri as she strutting over in her stilettos laced around her thick calf muscles with some white apple bottom shorts that showed the bottom of her yellow round fat booty cheeks, with a red and white halter top apple bottom shirt cut short to see her belly button ring with kinky twist in her head. Bri-Bri still looked better than ever but after what she did he would feel less than a real nigga taking her back especially now that he was on top. "Hey T" Bri-Bri spoke standing across the table from him. "Pop!" T.Z open his bottle of Moet sending the cork flying across the room "What's good?" T.Z said after taking a swig of the champagne "I guess you still mad at me?" she said. "Am I still mad, you left me alone in a cell to rot so why should I be mad?" T.Z said sarcastically. "Can you come over here so we can at least discuss this in private?" She said "Dig this, these are the people who stayed on my side when my back was up against the wall so whatever that need to be said can be discussed right here." T.Z told her. "T. I'm sorry I couldn't handle knowing you might get 20 years." she pleaded. T.Z smiled showing his platinum and VVS diamonds "Bye Bri" T.Z said. "But T!" she begged. T.Z reaching in his pocket pulling out a hundred-dollar bill "Now we even!" T.Z said standing up grabbing her hand placing the money in it then sitting down. Bri-Bri understood what the money meant cause a hundred dollars is what she gave him then walked out of his life. Bri-Bri walked away from the table heartbroken cause even though she fell off on him while he was locked up she never fell out of love with him. T.Z watched Bri-Bri walk off it hurt him to do her that way because he could tell she was still in love but the life he lived he could always get him sent back to prison and he knew what she would end up doing if he went back so he rather not even play himself for a fool trying believe different. T.Z looked at his initial still showing on the back of Bri-Bri thighs as she walked off. "Damn T that's the chick you use to tell me about when we was locked up?" Flex asked looking at Bri-Bri ass with lust in his eyes. "Yeah that's her!" he answered "You might should have forgave her since she look like Rhianna with a Nicki Minaj ass!" Flex said "I know yo tender dick would have T.Z said know exactly what Flex was thinking seeing the way he was eyeballing Bri-Bri the entire time she stood there talking. T.Z thought about hitting that ass for old time sake but he knows the emotion that would come along with it. Come on Dot let me show you how to snatch some of these hoes up." Derrick said standing up with Dot following behind him. "I can dig that!" Flex said standing up walking out to the floor with his Moet bottle in hand also. T.Z wasn't the dancing type so he stayed sitting at the table taking swigs of the Moet.

Flex eased through the crowd on the dance floor to the opposite side of the room where the restrooms are located. Flex went inside the gentlemen's room going in a stall locking behind him. He sat down on the toilet quickly itching for a hit of the coke that was in his pocket. Flex took the 8 ball of coke out his pocket opening the bag. He scooped a small amount on to his house key then snorted it. He felt the drain going down his throat instantly as he took a few more bumps giving him his temporary high. Flex sat there for a second enjoying his high then wiping his nose making sure no evidence showed of him getting high before he exited the restroom. T.Z smiled as he watched Dot and Derrick on the dance floor doing the south Dallas swag dance. "T.Z what's good fam longtime no see." The tall slim black as ace of spade man said. "Slick! What's the damn deal nigga?" T.Z said shaking his hand. "Surviving in these treacherous streets!" Slick stated "I heard that my nigga!" T.Z said "I heard about Roxy sorry to hear that the streets gone miss her." Slick said Hearing Roxy name always put a pain in T.Z chest thinking about what happen to her. "Where you be at now nigga?" T.Z asked "I'm in East Dallas hustling by where the old projects use to be. I got a spot rolling hard over there. "Slick confirmed what T.Z was already wondering "What you selling?" "Green, powder packs, work and wack one stop shop." Slick told him "What type of pricing you paying for the green and work?" T.Z said "I'm getting the pounds for 950 a piece and a quarter brick for 55hundred!" T.Z said putting his phone number in Slick phone. Call me tomorrow nigga we gone get paid believe that!" T.Z had been knowing Slick since high school. Slick was two years older than him but one thing T.Z knew about Slick the nigga was a true hustler the nigga could sell whatever he got his hands on and wasn't scared to venture off to different hoods to set up shop. They sat and conversated for a while catching up on things that's been going on and happen while T.Z was on lock. T.Z had to take a double look to make sure he saw right. Yvonne was walking across the club with some dark skin chick. "Aye, Slick I don't mean to leave you but I got to go holla at somebody!" Slick looked right in the direction of Yvonne knowing who T.Z was talking about seeing the beautiful woman. "Go handle yo business nigga I'll call you tomorrow!" Slick said.

Yvonne walked through the crowd in her open toe Dior heels and Dior one-piece silver skirt acting like she never seen T.Z over there sitting at the table with the dark skin tall guy talking. She stops walking and made small talk with some guy who she didn't know that was asking for her number just for T.Z could see as he headed her way "Damn baby I been looking for you!" T.Z said wrapping his arm around her waist pulling her close to him making the other dude stop in mid-sentence then walking off "Why you do that? We were talking!" Yvonne said acting as if she really cared about the conversation the stranger was making. "Fuck Him! What you doing here anyway?" T.Z asked "Ummm.... Cause I'm grown first of all on top of that you ain't my man or my daddy." she spat "Ain't my fault I ain't either one!" T.Z said. Even though they spent a lot of time together they had never actually made it official that they were a couple. Mainly cause T.Z never asked but Yvonne was growing tired of just the being friend's thing. She wanted him to herself to call her man. That's the main reason she came to the club to peep him out. He had already informed her early doing the week that he would be here so she just happen to decided to come as well. "Anyway, let's not even go there!" She said giving T.Z a crazy look. "Who is she?" T.Z asked switching the subject "This is Lisa we go to school together. Lisa meet Tyrone!" Yvonne introduced them "Call me T.Z!" "Nice to meet you!" Lisa said I got a table over here let's go sit down!" T.Z said leading the way to the table. Bri-Bri was standing watching the scene unfold in her face, yeah it was true she left T.Z while he was locked up but she still felt as if he was hers and no other woman needed to be with him, she spent 3years with him dealing with the phone calls from different females, nights she didn't know where he was or when would he be home so for him to dis her in front of his crew Bri-Bri couldn't take it.

T.Z talked with Yvonne and Lisa having a few more drinks until Derrick, Dot and Flex joined them back at the table. T.Z had finally convinced Yvonne to come back to his loft but Yvonne had already assured him that he still wouldn't be getting no pussy from her tonight. T.Z felt Derrick nudging him on his leg. He looked at Derrick like what cause he was deep in mid conversation whispering in Yvonne's ear. He followed Derrick eyes looking in the opposite direction at Bri-Bri and two of her homegirls heading towards them. T.Z sense trouble when he seen them headed straight for him ("Here this bitch come.") T.Z thought to himself "T we need to talk right now!" Bri-Bri demanded "Don't come over here with that bullshit Bri.!" T.Z warned her. "What's bullshit is you all over this bitch in front of me!" Bri-Bri shouted pointing her fingers "Excuse me, what you say?" Yvonne said standing up. T.Z stood up stepping in between them. "Damn Bri get on with that dumb shit that's why I don't fuck with you now!" T.Z shouted at her! "FUCK YOU and that dumb bitch!" Bri shouted next thing you seen was Yvonne grab the empty Moet bottle reaching around T.Z hitting Bri-Bri across the face making her stumble and fall. One of Bri-Bri friends attacked Yvonne from the side as Lisa jumped up swinging at the other girl. It was a real live brawl going on with T.Z in the middle. T.Z instantly went to actions grabbing the chick that attack Yvonne and pushing her across the room freeing up Yvonne. Bri-Bri charged at Yvonne with blood coming from her mouth from getting hit with the bottle. Bri-Bri and Yvonne engaged each other throwing blows "Got damn you niggas help stop this shit!" T.Z shouted at Derrick, Flex and Dot as they stood back and watched. Derrick grabbed Lisa as Dot grabbed the other chick she was fighting. Flex grabbed Bri-Bri from behind putting his piece on her fat ass stopping her while T.Z pulled Yvonne away. The bouncers came running over trying to see what was going on, I'm kill you bitch!" Bri-Bri screamed! "You ain't gone do shit bitch look at yo face hoe. These bitches can't fade me!" Yvonne shouted as T.Z forced her away and down the stairs Derrick and Lisa was right behind them. The bouncers started clearing the section out "Let me go!" Bri-Bri shouted at Flex "Calm down, calm down I'm just making sure you okay!" Flex said in defense letting her go. Bri-Bri and her homegirls made sure they were okay besides a few scratches and Bri-Bri mouth and broken stilettos' they were all okay. The bouncers came over to Bri-Bri and her homegirls telling them they had to leave. It was almost two o'clock so the club would be closing soon anyway so it didn't matter to much that they had to leave.

"You alright!" T.Z asked looking at Yvonne face she was red but had no scratches or bruises on her. Lisa had a scratch on her neck but she was okay as well. They stood in front of the club waiting on the valet man to pull Yvonne car around. "Yeah bitch what's up now, ain't no bottles out here!" Bri-Bri shouted as she came out the club. "Bitch its whatever hoe!" Yvonne spat taking her Dior heels off standing bare foot ready to fight. The club had start letting out so a crowd was gathering around to see the cat fight! "Get on with that bullshit Bri you already got yo ass whooped once tonight!" T.Z shouted turning his head in the direction he heard the dude yell from "Let them hoes fight nigga!" the dude said again making sure T.Z heard him "Nigga me and you can fight since you want to see a fight so bad!" T.Z said making everybody focus on them now. "You ain't said shit!" The brown skin 6'3 190 pound said as T.Z ripped his button-down Versace shirt off tossing it to Yvonne "No T" she said grabbing his arm trying stop him but he yanked away throwing up his guards ready to fight "I wish you would swing!" Dot said pointing the 9mm right at the side of the man head coming out the crowd. Soon as they walked out the club Dot went to Corvette parked in the front getting the pistol out the car "Nigga you about to lose your life over some bullshit!" Dot told him with his trigger finger centimeters away from the hair trigger. T.Z thought about letting Dot put the man brains on the concrete as the dude stood froze in fear. "My....my...my bad let me make it!" the dude pleaded for his life T.Z shook his head signal to Dot not to kill him. Only reason T.Z spared him because of all the witnesses that stood watching in anticipation to see a murder. "Pussy as nigga!" Dot told the dude backing back lowering the gun. "Uuh!" the man grunted as T.Z hit him with two jabs to the chin dropping him "Let's go!" T.Z said waving his hand at Dot, Derrick and Flex and grabbing Yvonne by the hand. Derrick and Dot got in the Vet as Flex got in his SLS parked behind Derricks Corvette. "Where's the valet man with your car?" T.Z asked not seeing her BMW328i. "My car is right over here." Yvonne said hurrying over to the white 4 door Porsche Panamera opening the driver door even though they were trying to leave before the police got over to see what was happening. T.Z almost froze when he seen Yvonne open the door to the Porsche. He got in the backseat as Lisa got in the passenger seat. Bri-Bri stood and watched all three cars pull off leaving the parking lot. She reached in her back pocket to get her car key feeling a napkin that she knew she didn't have. Bri-Bri took the napkin out reading the short note. "I know you don't know me but call me A.S.A.P (2)555-1091. From the guy who was holding you back! Flex!" Bri-Bri had to think about it to make sure she wasn't tripping cause so much was going on at the time. ("That nigga that grab me was T.Z homeboy!") Bri-Bri thought to herself knowing she was correct. Bri-Bri watched the taillights of Yvonne Porsche disappear ("This could be useful") Bri-Bri thought putting the napkin back in her pocket heading to her car.

T.Z ended the call with Flex letting him know Yvonne would take him home. "You might should have told him to drop you off! "Yvonne said not wanted to lock eyes with T.Z in her rear view as she drove "Oh yeah!" I thought you was spending the night with me?" he said "I was until I ended up fighting your bitches all in the club." Yvonne spat "First off them are not my bitches and I haven't seen or spoken to Bri since I been out of prison!" T.Z told her "Whatever Tyrone!" Yvonne said "That's how you gone act?" T.Z said with no response back from her. "Lisa you want to come to my house or you still going home?" Yvonne asked "I'm still going home girl." Lisa said knowing her friend wanted to still spend the night with him but she knew how stubborn Yvonne could be so she gave T.Z another chance to try his luck after she would get out the car and Yvonne and him could talk alone. Yvonne drove and dropped Lisa off at the apartment in North Dallas not too far from the club "She likes you don't give up so easy on her." Lisa told T.Z as he got in the front seat when she was heading inside her apartment. T.Z nodding his head as he sat down closing the car door. T.Z looked at Yvonne three broken nails on her right hand where French tips use to be as she gripped the steering wheel of the foreign vehicle "So when you get this?" T.Z asked looking at the plush interior "I been having this!" she said non-nonchalantly not taking her eyes off the road. "My bad about tonight if I could have did anything different to avoid the shit from happening I would have!" T.Z admitting being honest. Yvonne smacked her lips like yeah whatever as they rode in silence the rest of the way. Yvonne pulled inside the parking garage T.Z didn't see Derrick's Corvette so he knew him and Dot probably went to an after-hour spot. Yvonne parked in a visitor's parking spot and waited on T.Z to get out without even looking or speaking to him. "That's how its go be!" T.Z said opening the car door "Umm!" "Aight then!" T.Z said snatching the key pad off the console and pushing the crank button cutting the engine off then jumping out the car leaving Yvonne sitting there. "Give me my damn car key!" Yvonne spat getting out the car. T.Z continue to walk to the elevator when the door open pushing the button for the 10th floor. Yvonne started running when she seen the elevator about to close but T.Z press the open button right before it close for she could get on. Yvonne breathing was heavy from the short sprint trying catch the elevator. They stood face to face as the elevator closed and went up "You gone le-"

T.Z pulled her close and started kissing her interrupted her sentence with the passionate kiss she couldn't do nothing but kiss back as his tongue enter her mouth sending sparks flying threw her body. He rubbed his hands down her back to her soft derriere cupping her back side in his hands "Ding!" the elevator signal as the doors open. She stops the kiss then grabbed his hand and pulled him to his door. T.Z unlocked his front door soon as the two stepped inside closing the door they engaged right back into the passionate kissing T.Z thrusted her in the air holding her up by her butt as she wrapped her legs around him making her skirt rise exposing her ass cause she had on a Victoria Secrets red G-String. He carried her into the bedroom placing her on the bed gently as he stayed on top kissing her neck and unzipping the back of her one-piece skirt. Yvonne slid the skirt off revealing her matching bra and panties. He began to unstrap her bra exposing her big dark brown nipples as he sucked and nibbled on them. Yvonne reached for his belt buckle unlatching it then unbutton his pants pulling them down. T.Z manhood was ready sticking straight out his boxers. Yvonne put her hands around his thick long meat and began to massage it going back and forth. T.Z worked his hips in the same motion as Yvonne hands went. T.Z pulled her panties off making her release her grip from his manhood. T.Z took a look at her fat shaved pussy lips as she laid with her legs open inviting him in. He removed his muscle shirt then went deep sea diving into Yvonne aqua flow. He could see cum already running out as he licked her clit and inserting two fingers in her vagina, as he worked his two fingers in and out of her. His tongue went even faster around on her clit. Yvonne moaned louder and louder until her juices skeeted out into his mouth and on his fingers. T.Z had her in heaven right where he wanted her as he flipped her-over in the doggy style position licking her from her pussy to her asshole. She rotated her hips and ass in his face. T.Z seen the precum oozing out as he prepared to enter her. Yvonne moaned out as the head of his manhood went in, it had been 5 months since Yvonne had some real dick in her.

As T.Z began to put his pound game down Yvonne moan out in pleasure mix with pain. "Fuck me T!" she cried out matching each thrust he made in her. "This my pussy from now on!" T.Z said as he smacked her ass cheek "It's yours baby!" It's yours!" she shouted "You gone act right huh!" he said smacking her ass harder "I'm act right. I'm sorrrry!" she screamed as he deep stroked her putting it all the way in then out then back again. Yvonne moaned as she came back to back while T.Z continue to go to work. Then T.Z went deep as possible hitting her walls making her moan then exploding all inside her until every drop was release in her. T.Z pulled his manhood out looking at the cum from Yvonne covering his manhood and even some on his pubic hair. He was even surprise on how wet Yvonne got. T.Z sat on the bed catching his breath. Yvonne mounted him as they naked bodies perspired from the hot sex! She kissed him on the lips then his chin "You my woman now." she kissed him on the lips again giving him confirmation that he was right. She got up walking towards the bathroom T.Z watched her voluptuousness body as she walked right before she entered the bathroom she licked her tongue seductively around her lips, signal with her same finger in her mouth sucking it seductively. T.Z got up and followed behind her into the bathroom.

CHAPTER 8

T he sun shined down on Jax as he stepped on the stairs exited the private jet carrying two suit cases with Will behind him carrying two suitcases as well. Jax covered his eyes with his Versace glasses cause his eyes hadn't yet adjusted to the bright Mexico sunlight. A Mexican man waited with the trunk open to a Black Rolls Royce Phantom parked a few feet away from the jet. They handed the man the suitcases then took a seat in the backseat of the Phantom as the man loaded the suitcases in the trunk then getting inside the driver seat leaving the private air strip. Jax looked out the window as the man drove the expensive vehicle through the slums of Juarez. Jax and Will looked at the little Mexican kids knock on the window asking for money as they sat behind the limo tint. Jax pulled out a thousand dollars dropping the money out the window as the driver pulled away. The group of 15kids tussle over the money that Jax tossed out like loose change. Will looked at Jax knowing kids no matter what race has always been Jax weakness. That's why Will didn't have none cause the life he lived having a weakness could determine if he seen another living day or not. After riding through the city then travel in the open country roads viewing all the pasture. Jax and Will knew exactly where they were headed cause they had been down these roads before. The Phantom turned off the main road on to a dirt road if you never been there before you would think you were headed to nothing. The dirt road curved behind a mountain then sloped down on the way down you could see a mansion sitting down at the bottom with barn houses behind it with about 70 acres of land with all type of cattle grazing the land. It even had a man-made lake behind it for the animals. The Phantom came to a stop in front of the mansion. The driver hurried and got out to open the door for Jax and Will for them to get out. Jax viewed the armed guards patrolling the roof and front doors as he exited the vehicle. A dark brown skin Mexican man overweight for his 5'6 frame came out the front door escorted by two more guards armed with AR-15's. He had a cigar in his mouth puffing on it. "Welcome back to Mexico!" the short man said embracing Jax then Will in a brotherly hug. "Thank you, Pedro," Jax said greeted him "Come!" Pedro said leading the way into the mansion with the guards following behind Jax and Will lost. Pedro lead them into one of the 7 living rooms that was in the mansion that was occupied with three expensive Italian couches and Italian rug laid in the middle of the floor. Pedro sat on one couch and Jax and Will sat together on the other with two armed guards standing behind Pedro. The driver came placing the suit cases down on the floor two at a time. "What's in the bags?" Pedro asked already knowing the answer. "A gift!" Jax said smiling. Pedro signal for one of the guards to open the bag. The guard open a suitcase revealing stacks of money "Each suitcase has 5million!" Jax told him. "Lleva El Dinero Para El Cuarto De Atras." Pedro ordered the guards in Spanish to remove the suitcases "like something to drink?" Pedro asked as his housekeeper enter the room

"Doesn't matter!" Jax said "Grace! Trece Tequila!" Pedro order "So Pedro what is it that we needed to discuss.! Jax asked sitting in his signature style. "As I'm sure you have heard a few of the border patrol have been arrested for that reason because they were caught making deals with undercover F.B.I agents posing as Cartel members." Pedro said "Yes I heard!" Jax said. "Those guys were our mules to get the shipments across the Texas boarder and until we get somebody else on the inside the shipments will have to come through the California and Arizona boarder for now if you want your same shipments without any problems." Pedro said. Jax knew the drive alone was a risky drive but crossing state lines would make it worse and trying to get across the border without a inside plug with a half-ton of heroine was like counting the odds on shooting yourself with a shotgun in the head and living. "Just give me the meeting place and my people will be there.!" Jax said "I knew you wouldn't back out!" Pedro said as Grace handing them their drinks. "I only asked one favor though!" Jax said. "Tell me!" Instead of a half-ton every three weeks make it a full metric ton every 1st of the month." Jax asked "Done!" I'll let you know where to send your people to pick up the delivery. Hopefully things will be back to normal real soon!" Pedro said taking a sip of tequila. Jax raised his glass in agreement then drinking some.

Back in the states Flex sat on the toilet in the bathroom with the plate full of cocaine snorting coke till his nose bleed "Got damn Flex you been in there for an hour!" Peaches his baby momma knocked on the bathroom door screaming. "Hold the fuck up!" Flex yelled as he snorted the line then putting the plate underneath the sink. He stood up looking at himself in the mirror. He could see the drug having taking effect on him. He was losing weight face sinking in and eyes were blood shot red. Flex opened the bathroom door with Peaches standing right there with her hands on her hips frustrated. "I thought you said we would go out to dinner if I got my momma to watch the kids." Peaches said "Damn why you rushing me just chill!" Flex said brushing pass her "Every time you start putting that shit in your nose you get to tripping acting like a dope fiend!" Peaches said. Why did she say that cause Flex turned around grabbing her by the throat slamming her against the wall "Bitch what you call me?" Flex growled threw clench teeth tightening the grip around her throat cutting her air circulation off. "I can't breathe!" Peaches hardly said as he gripped tightened. She tried pulling his hands but his grip was too tight. Peaches felt herself bout to blackout. Peaches hit Flex in the balls making him grunt and let go dropping him to his knees. Peaches tried to take off running for the front door but Flex grabbed her by her ankle making her fall face first.

Flex got back in control of the situation by dropping his knee in her back then pulling her neck backwards by her hair punching her in the side of the face as she cried and begged him to stop. Flex dragged her into the bedroom by a fist full of hair. "Nooo Flex you hurting me!" she kicked and cried. "I'm teach you to stay in a bitch place." he said before smacking her across the face several times. They had argued and fought before but never like this. This wasn't the man she loved this was the devil. Flex had no remorse for the beating he was giving her. Peaches had a mouth full of blood and two black eyes not to mention the many bruises that hurt her body as well when Flex got finish with her. "This bitch then blew a nigga high!" Flex said out loud to himself leaving Peaches curled up on the floor in the fetal position crying "You bet not move either or I'm go back upside yo fucking head." Flex yelled as he headed back to the bathroom to retrieve the plate that held his coke. Flex got the plate and snorted a line. "The type of girl I love, one who doesn't talk back and gives me nothing but pleasure." Flex talked to himself as the cocaine better known as a white girl drain down his throat boosting his high right back up. Ring, ring, ring "Yeah!" Flex answered his phone. "Is this Flex?" the feminine voice asked. "Yeah! Who dis?" Bri-Bri!" When he heard her name he instantly perked up remembering her fat juicy as jiggling when she walked. "Uh what's good?" he asked "Shit you tell me you the one gave me yo number." she said "I'm trying coming see you. "he said "That's cool I stay in Buckner Village you know where that is?" she said "Yeah ,Yeah I'm leaving South Dallas, I'll be out there in a few." he said. "Call me when you enter the apartments" she said "Aight bet!" he said then ended the call. The plan was starting to fall in place. Flex could tell Bri-Bri was the average gold-digging hoe from the hood looking for a captain save -a-hoe!

Pedro, Jax and Will walked on the land in the back of the mansion heading to the barn with the horse stall. As they enter the barn a trainer was grooming one of Pedro Champion thoroughbred race horses "His name is Wild Clown he runs 2 minutes 33seconds in a 1-1/2 mile. His name is Lucky B Triple Crown winner twice." Pedro said pointing to another horse. "I paid two million dollars for him just to breed him with her crazy Sally also Triple Crown Winner I paid 4 million for her." Pedro said pointing at another horse. Pedro showed off his other horses as well before they left out the barn heading over to his huge garden that contain carrots, cabbage, potatoes, tomatoes, snap beans, onions, bell peppers, green peas and head lettuce. "When you live so far out you don't have time to be going to grocery stores plus when you grow it yourself you know its rope to perfection." Pedro told them. "Yeah maybe one day I can retire and live like this!" Jax told Pedro "The option is yours but you a city man Jax you would get tired of the peace you get out here." Pedro said. Jax know that was probably true but somedays he does feel like getting his family and moving them off a distant place. I'm not sure yet!" Jax said "Well whenever you ready let me know I'll have my people build you a house from the ground for cheap." Pedro told him "I'll think about it!" said Jax "The same goes for you Mr. William!" Pedro said. "Thanks but no thanks I love the city I love the life style I probably wouldn't change for the world." Will told Pedro "I hear you but remember when you always live by the sword be also prepared to die by it." Pedro told him "Always!" Will said. "Pedro let me ask you something?" Jax said "Go ahead." "What's going on with you and Felex people?" Jax asked "That's a strange question, why do you ask?" Pedro questioned "because I might have a little situation on my hands that might need to get solve and I'm not sure how or if any deep Felex might be in it." Jax said. Will knew exactly what Jax was talking about and since he was known as Jax muscle he felt disrespected by Jax asking Pedro when Will said he could already handle the problem. "Well right now we are at a truce with the Cuban Cartel all their product comes in threw the eastern states mainly by water while we go through the western and Texas. Felex and his brother Mario are the leaders of the Cuban Cartel in the states. Mario is in Miami and Felex in Dallas. And if something bad end up happening to either one a lot of dead bodies would start being found until answers come up." Pedro told him. "I see I'm pretty sure it won't go that far" Jax said. "I hope not as well cause there's already enough wars going on inside on our own organization so let me know if you need my help solving your situation without started another international war." Pedro said. No thanks the situation is not a problem at all and believe I will personally handle it Will spoke out before Jax could talk. Jax looked over at Will hearing the defensiveness in his voice. "Very well then but remember Jax I'm in your corner and I'm always a phone call away." Pedro said giving conformation of his friendship to Jax. "thank you and the same for you." Jax told Pedro

Bri-Bri came down the stairs of the apartment in some black tights Aeropostale shirt and some flip flops to talk to Flex. He sat hanging his red bottom shoes outside the Benz SLS AMG with the driver door in the air. Kids in the apartments complex stop and pointing at the expensive car marveled trying guess the price of it. Flex remembered the days of his childhood when he used to do the same thing "How you doing?" Bri-Bri asked as she approach the car. "What's good?" Flex asked as he took in the view of her print through the tights. Bri-Bri knew what he was staring at the typical guys do. So, she did a 180 degree turn acting like she was looking at her apartment for he could get a good view of her ass as well. ("Damn!") Flex thought knowing she couldn't have no panties on cause there was no line showing. "I'm aight!" she responded turning around. "I'm glad you called I was thinking about you!" Flex lied then standing up saying "Oh really sneaking your number in people pants is something you always do huh?" she asked "Hell naw!" I just didn't like how T.Z did you and a pretty woman like you deserve nothing less than the best." Flex stated "What and who might that be?" she said "Me!" he answered. Bri-Bri wasn't nowhere near simple minded or green to the game but looking at Flex and his ride she figured he could be very resourceful so she played into his simple game. "Oh is the right!" And what can the best do to keep a woman happy?" she asked "Give her the world" Flex told her "That sounds good but I prefer actions baby" she said "Let's go inside and talk" Flex said "Come on!" Flex grabbed his 9mm from under the seat tucking the gun in his waistband then closing the car door. Flex followed behind Bri-Bri as she led the way to her apartment. On the stairs she bent over on purpose acting like she hit her toe putting her ass in his face. ("I knew it!") Flex thought to himself as he caught a glimpse of her butt crack when she bent over revealing no panties. Flex picture himself hitting Bri-Bri from the back watching her ass jiggle as she walked up ever stair making her derriere jump as she went up the stairs giving Flex a little show. They entered the one-bedroom apartment that Bri-Bri lived in alone. Flex walked in the nicely decorated apartment looking at the various pictures. Flex thought about how he was doing his homeboy behind his back but Flex tried to justify the situation telling himself. T.Z didn't want her so she's up for grabs. "See anybody you know." Bri-Bri asked knowing exactly what picture Flex was looking at. She had more pictures of T.Z but that was the only picture she keeps out after T.Z got locked up. "Naw!" he said sitting down on the couch. Bri Bri grabbed the remote turning on her 60in flat screen T.V as rap videos came on. "How do you know Tyrone?" she asked sitting down next to him "We were cellies in prison together." "Oh! How long you do?" "3years 2months!" he said. "What did he use to say about me?" she asked "You a no good bitch and a lot of some more shit. But fuck all that I ain't trying discuss him I'm focused on you." Flex said "Okay! Where is your girl at?" I ain't gone lie I got a baby mama but we on bad terms." "How many kids you got?" she asked

"Two!" Khadijah 6 and Kia 6months my two angels." Flex said "I'm sure you know but I'm 24 with no kids and no man." she said "Damn maybe I can help change the no man part and the other one later down the line." Flex said "Hopefully!" she said. It was true Bri-Bri was single but she had many friends but they only stayed friends as long as they paid her bills and took care of her wants as well cause even though Bri-Bri worked at Wal-Mart she demanded a lot of things outside her financial means as Gucci, Louis Vuitton, Bulgari, Prada, and Burberry right now she was on a mission to upgrade her 2005 Chevy Malibu without coming out of her pockets to do it. Flex was her target to make it happen plus Flex was handsome so she felt she was winning all away around "You smoke?" Flex said "Yeah!" "Roll up then!" Flex said as he took out 14 grams of the kush weed from his pocket with a box of Gracia Vagaz Cigars handed them to her. As he continues to watch Tyga video "Rack City Chick" bobbing his head to the beat as she rolled the blunt. "You got a lighter" she asked as he reached in his pocket retrieving a lighter handing it to her. Bri-Bri dried the blunt moving the blunt across the flame to make sure the green leaf cigar stuck. She put the blunt in her mouth then sparked the opposite end. She inhales the weed smoke blowing it out in her nostrils "Cough, Couch" Bri-Bri choked taking a long puff then passing it. "Be easy!" Flex said as the coughing made tears come to her eyes "What's that?" she asked "Kush!" I told you only the best for the best. "Flex said bragging taking long deep puffs showing no signs of choking cause his lungs had adjusted to the high quality weed. They sat and talked while smoking two back to back blunts of the Kush. Flex could tell Bri-Bri was high cause her eyes was Chinese. Flex was as little high but he needed a bump to put him where he needed to be "Can I use yo bathroom?" he asked "It's in the room!" she said. Flex got up and went to the bathroom locking the door behind him sitting on the toilet. Flex took out the package of cocaine opening it then sticking his house key in the package then snorted the coke off the key. He took three different hits then sat back and allowed the white girl to take effect. He put the package back in his pocket standing up looking in the mirror. He put a little toothpaste in his mouth the rinsed it out. He washed his hands then looked around the bathroom making sure he didn't leave any traces. He seen everything was good so he flushed the toilet to act as if he just finish using it then left out. Bri-Bri was laid flat on her stomach across the couch with her eyes shut. The coke had Flex hormones raging as he looked at Bri-Bri ass walking into the living room. Flex couldn't resist himself anymore as he eased on top of her from behind seductively licking her ear lobe and neck. "Umm!!" Bri-Bri moaned feeling the sexual sensation on her neck. Flex made sure his pants were sagging when he laid on top for she could feel his swollen manhood on her ass when he got on her. Flex made sure the tip of his manhood was right on her pussy lips print showing from behind under her butt cheeks. Bri-Bri bit on her bottom lips as Flex kiss on her neck and back. Flex raised the back of her shirt up kissing and licking down her spine until he reached her butt cheeks. Bri-Bri raised up on all fours giving Flex a complete view of her big yellow booty cheeks. Flex even seen T.Z initials tattoo on the back of her thighs as he went head first into Bri-Bri ass licking her anal making her toes curl then pussy. Flex turn her over making her lay on her back pushing her legs in the air as he licked her clit. "Oh! Right there!" She moaned while grabbing his head in pleasure. Bri-Bri closed her eyes as she felt herself creaming in his mouth. Flex pulled his swollen manhood out. Bri-Bri seen the pre-cum already dripping out even through it wasn't bigger then T.Z dick it was far from little. Bri-Bri raised up grabbing his dick and spitting on it without placing her mouth on it. Then jacking him off going faster and faster. When she felt the blood rushing to the tip for him to cum she wrapped her free hand catching all the cum in her hand. Bri-Bri wasn't an amateur at what she did. She knew if Flex fucked that first night it would be a slim chance he would ever comeback so she had to give him a little taste but not the whole meal cause he would come back for what he didn't get the first time and she could play that to her advantage cause she understood niggas like Flex do about anything for a fat ass and some pussy("Sucker!") Bri-Bri thought as she walked to the bathroom with her butt showing to wash her hands and vagina making him marvel staring at her back side as she left the room.

CHAPTER 9

T.Z drove his Camaro as Derrick rode shotgun with him. T.Z had to go by his traps to pick up his money from his workers. T.Z always had a set amount of money he should receive from each spot and every Friday he would pay the workers a thousand dollars. He bumped up the payments on all his workers when he took over Roxy spot. Even though they probably wouldn't find out he didn't think it would be fair for them females to be getting paid more then his young gorillas and they worked just as hard if not harder. Each spot only had a max of two workers so two thousand a week was chump change to the money they were making. T.Z pulled in front of the duplex house that he turned into a trap bout 3 weeks ago also in the Grove. The burglar bars open and Kobe was 16years old you could still see the lil boy features in his bright skin face as he stood only 5'6 125pounds soaking wet. T.Z let his car window down as Kobe pulled the brown paper bag from his pants handing it to T.Z through the window. "That's the whole7500" Kobe said as T.Z looked inside the bag. T.Z grabbed the plastic grocery bag off the floor in the backseat containing a quarter brick worth of coke and crack and 2 pounds already in dimes and twenty packs. "This is as 12,000 dollar pack y'all should be done in about 3days

95

top!" T.Z said handing Kobe the grocery sack not even worried if Kobe would try something slick. "Aight T., Derrick!" Kobe said heading back in the duplex. T.Z wasn't worried about Kobe or none of his workers doing any foul shit one cause he had all the resume from where their momma lived to Granny's and brothers. He would never drop off more then $12,000 dollars' worth of drugs at one time anyway so if a nigga felt like losing his life over 12 stacks or his people life then that's his mistake. Then T.Z didn't force anybody to work for him he always let the young dudes know whenever they felt like venturing out on their own just let him know there would be no hard feelings in fact he said they could even cop their own shit from him at a playa price. He commended the niggas who wanted to be their own boss. A lot of niggas didn't know how to be a boss so they rather get bird fed instead even though T.Z was feeding them good.

T.Z drove off from in front of the trap house headed to East Dallas to meet up with Slick. Slick had called T.Z yesterday but he was laid up with Yvonne all day and decided to only do her yesterday and nothing else so he told Slick he would come by today and take care of him for Slick wouldn't think T.Z was doing like most niggas do lie! "Damn nigga where you going now?" Derrick asked realizing T.Z wasn't heading to the old apartment they shared. "Drop this off to Slick!" T.Z said pointing his thumb toward the backseat. "Slick, Slick black ass Slick?" Derrick said. "Yeah Nigga!" "When you see that crazy ass nigga?" Derrick asked. "At the club the other night when I was at the table by myself. Damn I thought I told you I must have forgot." T.Z said "That's cause Yvonne had yo mind all fucked up nigga!" "Nigga must be serious!" T.Z said "I am serious nigga!" You wanted to knock Bri-Bri out yourself when she called Yvonne a bitch I seen your face Nigga!" Derrick said laughing. "Cause that was some hoe shit Bri pulled especially after what she did when I got locked up!" T.Z said "Yeah I guess you right but what's up with you and Yvonne anyway?" Derrick asked looking at T.Z as he smiled showing his platinum grill "That's my baby now!" "That's my baby now! Sweet tender dick as nigga!" Derrick said mocking him jokingly. T.Z pulled inside the recently built townhouses grabbing his cellphone off the clip on his hip calling Slick. He waited as the phone rung." Hello?" Slick answered "I'm pulling in front of your door!" T.Z said "Aight come in!" Slick said ended the call. T.Z parked the car then grabbed his glock 9mm from under the seat putting it in his waistband even though Slick was an old homeboy of his he could never be to safe just in case. "We going inside!" T.Z told Derrick as he turned off the engine. T.Z grabbed the other grocery bad he had left sitting on the back-seat floor before they got out the car closing the door. Slick stood in the doorway of the townhouses as they headed to the door. "What's good niggas?" Slick asked "Slow motion!" T.Z said "Nigga what you doing out here in the East!" Derrick asked "Getting at this cash its plentiful out here! Y'all niggas come in" Slick said leading the way. Derrick closed and locked the door behind him.

T.Z looked around at the well-furnished house that had family pictures posted here and there "Sit down" Slick said "Who crib is this? T.Z asked looking around curious "Mine! Well my baby momma and kids live her too!" Slick said. "Nigga you be hustling out this bitch?" T.Z asked "Hell naw!" My spot right around the corner I thought it would be better if you came over here." Slick explain answering the question T.Z wondered about. Slick meant business that's why he invited T.Z over to his home instead of his trap to show he wasn't on no fuck shit and was ready to do business. "I told you I would bless yo game Slick and I'm loyal to my word I just ask you stay loyal to yours." T.Z said "I can do that!" Slick said "Here! That's a whole brick and 5pounds I need $18,000 for the brick and $4,000 for the pounds. How long it's go take you to get rid of all that!" T.Z asked Slick looked in the bag surprise to see all the contents inside "I'm busting everything down so no more than 2 weeks!" Slick said "Get your money but its plenty more where that came from this well don't go dry so there no reason to try and make dollar for dollar on every gram." T.Z explain letting him know the faster he finish the more dope he could get on consignment from him. "I'm keep that in mind" Slick said "Well I'm let you get to the money cause we bout to head out." T.Z said as he stood up "Good looking out T.Z!" Slick said shaking his hand "Anytime call me when you finish!" T.Z said as him and Derrick headed to the door to leave. T.Z and Derrick got back in the car leaving Slick house "A T. I was gone ask you who 4 door Porsche was Yvonne was in at the club them Forgiato's was nasty on it." Derrick asked. "Hers and she got a 328i she so ma'fucking spoil she still got the pony her daddy brought her for her 16th birthday." T.Z said "Damn for real!" Hell, Yeah she probably got just as much in her bank if not more then I got in my safe." T.Z told him. "Well at least you don't got to worry about her hand being out!" Derrick said "You right about that but shit everybody pulling out new whips I'm have to find a way to get me something else cause I'm not gone be able to lease nothing else to expensive in my momma name again and I damn sure can't use my name. T.Z said "Yeah you right bout that. Why don't you call Felex he might can help you out you know he plug in to about everything under the sun he probably could help you meet the president if you wanted to." Derrick said joking "That's a good idea I'm a call him and see" T.Z said dialing Felex number.

Back in Dallas, Will drove a Black Dodge Ram 1500 truck around the grove on the hunt for answers. Will didn't appreciate how Jax made him look like he couldn't do his job by finding and taking out the youngster. Jax told Will how the youngster was somehow connected to Felex but it didn't matter to Will cause anybody that stood in Will's way on his mission would suffer the consequences for befriended the youngster. Lately Will felt as if he old friend Jax was getting weak for the game cause never have they let an adversary survive this long against them when a problem occurred. Will pulled the Ram truck into the apartments Roxy lived in when she died. The building that Roxy lived in was still burnt up with yellow crime scene tape on the building. Will drove slowly in the apartments. Will stop the truck letting down the window "Hey come here" Will shouted to the window to a teenage boy "Who Me?" the brown skin boy with an air fro asked. "Yeah you come here!" Will said as the boy walked over to the truck. "Whats up?" "What is your name kid?" "Everybody calls me J-Baby!" "Let me ask you something J-Baby who stayed in that apartment over there?"

Will asked pointing to the burnt apartment. "Roxy did!" "Where she at now?" Will asked already knowing the answer to his question. "She died some hoe ass nigga killed her!" J-Baby said. "Hoe as nigga them harsh words youngster." Will told him. Well its true Roxy was good people every time her and T.Z seen me or one of my dawg they would bless our game with some dollars." J-Baby said. T.Z I don't think I know him!"

Will said "Everybody knows T.Z he drives the Black 63Benz and Camaro SS on 22's" J-Baby said "That must be her boyfriend." Will said as he played the youngster for more information. "hell naw!" that's his sister or cousin." J-Baby said. "Okay now I know who you talking about." Will lied just to agree with him. "I told you, you knew him." "You was right but thanks for the help J-Baby." "What's your name ole school for if I see T.Z I can tell him you was looking for him." J-Baby said. "I'm old friend of Roxy and him name Mr. Wilson that's Randy Wilson!" Will said raising his window up driving off. Will gave the youngster a fake name just in case he did run into T.Z not to alert him. Will was pretty sure, sure enough to be his life that T.Z was the name of the face he been looking for. He would keep this valuable information to himself for right now cause he felt if he told Jax. Jax would say wait and do things strategically cause this war. Will felt he was a one-man army and could end this war quickly and on his own. It seemed to Will as if Jax didn't have faith in Will anymore but after this either one or two things would happen. Jax would trust Will judgement again or somebody would have to step-down and Will wasn't for early retirement. Ring Ring "Hello?" Will answered his phone "I have the address and name" the man voice said "What is it?" Will asked "Rochell Richmond 444 Pleasant Dell Dr." the voice said. "Aight!" Will said ended the call. Will had a friend of his that work for the county morgue pull Roxy information and see who identified the body next to kin. Will figured it had to be her mother now he had the address to pay her a visit. Will decided to drive by the house since it was around the corner from the apartments. Will rode past the one-story house viewing the pink challenger and the BMW Z8 parked out front Will knew he had the right address. ("If you want war I'm bring it to your front door!") Will thought as he drove by. Then driving through the alley checking out the back of the house.

T.Z pulled up in the parking lot of the car lot that had a sign saying "Gomez Extravagant Motors" From all the different foreign vehicles parked T.Z knew Felex sent him to the right place. T.Z and Derrick got out the car walking towards the office building as a hispanic man walked out meeting them." Hello?" How may I help you?" Felex sent me to you he told me you the man to see if I needed a ride. T.Z said "Yes, yes he told me some friends of his would stop by. What exactly are you looking for luxury or speed" Hector asked. "A little of both mixed in one." T.Z said. "Follow me" Hector lead the way "Over here you have the 2011 Bentley's from GT Super sport Coupes to the 4 door Continental's over here you have your Porsches from 911 Turbos to 4 door Panamera then you got the 2011 Maserati Granturismo and Qualttroporte and the Ferrari's are here this is the Spider F1 2008 these are the new 2011 Ferrari Californias we even have Lamborghini's from the new Gallardo's to Murcielago's and whatever we don't have here we will get it if you want it.

For example, let me show you this only since your Felex friends cause he asked for nobody to see it." Hector walked over to where a two-car garage was lifting it up "What the fuck is that?" Derrick asked amazed doing a circle around the two cars parked. "The white one is an Aston Martin one 77 only 77 made the silver one is a Pagani Huayra." Hector said "Can I look inside?" Derrick asked opening the door to the Huayra sitting behind the wheel. "That is Italian leather interior with 700 horsepower and a AMG 12 cylinder turbo charged engine 0-60 in 3 second flat 220 which means you would need a Nascar to beat it." Hector told them. "How much is it?" T.Z asked "Both cars are 1.8million a piece." Hector said "That's a little too much for me." T.Z said "Understandable but I can tell you need something exotic something you don't see on the road everyday am I right?" Hector asked "Yeah you are right but that!" T.Z agreed "I know just the car but it doesn't arrive until next week the GT Venom!" Hector said "Never heard of it!" T.Z said "Yeah that's a bad ma'fucker I seen it on the internet supposed to be like a Lotus mix with a Viper." Derrick explain "Correct!" Hector said "I'll come check it out when it comes in." T.Z said "Okay. Write your number on the back of this." Hector said handing him one of his business cards and a pen. "Getting the car paid for isn't the problem which I'm sure you know but I have nobody to sign for it." T.Z explained as he jotted his name and number down! "Yes Felex already fill me in on your little dilemma and don't worry I will handle that, the car will remain in the car lots name into you decide otherwise so it will also be your choice to lease it or cash out either way you will have no legal problems. I guarantee you that." Hector explains. "I take your word!" T.Z said "Then I will see you next week" Hector said extended his hand "Next week!" T.Z said shaking the man hand. "expecting to do business with you as well." Hector said shaking Derrick hand "Oh you will believe that!" Derrick said looking at the Huayro. T.Z and Derrick walked back to T.Z car. T.Z looked at all the foreign vehicles contemplated on which vehicle he would buy if he didn't like the GT Venom. He felt like a grown kid inside Toys R Us with a choice to get one favorite toy "Did you see them whips." Derrick said as they got inside the car "I had no choice I was right next to you." T.Z said sarcastically "FUCK YOU, you know what I meant." Derrick spat "Stop saying silly shit then nigga" T.Z said laughing driving off. "Nigga pull up in that one -77 or better yet that Huayra Ma'fukers ain't gone know what the fuck that is." Derrick said excitedly "Hell Yeah but almost 2 million dollars damn nigga can buy a helicopter for that much." T.Z sad "Fuck it I'll come through the hood jumping out a candy painted black hawk on these niggas really giving the streets something to talk about. " Derrick said joking "Your silly ass probably would do some silly ass shit like that and wondering why 6 months later you in the Seagoville Federal Prison trying cop a plea-deal." T.Z said shaking his head side to side at Derrick. "Shit a nigga ain't trying to do a day behind them walls.! Derrick said "I ain't trying to do no days behind no walls at all. That's why I stress make smart moves. Like Flex my intuitions keep telling me he made a bad move buying that SLS" T.Z said "What makes you think that?" Derrick asked "Cause I ask how he got it. First he said he drop 200g's cash then he changed his story to paying payments something tells me he wasn't lying" T.Z explained. "I'm tell you like this only reason I gave this nigga a pass in the first place was cause of you but the nigga proved to be a genuine nigga and I dig the nigga style but if the nigga get hot by the feds and show any signs of breaking I'm dead him before he get a chance to tell cause you already know we stick to the G-Code." Derrick told T.Z "We gone stick to it to the casket drop believe that but I'm keep a close eye on him just in case" T.Z said looking at Derrick nodding his head in agreement.

Ms. Richmond laid sound asleep in her bed but a noise she heard in Roxy old room woke her. She thought maybe she was just hearing things cause when she tried paying close attention to see if she would hear something again she didn't. She looked over at the digital clock on the dresser that read "2:54am" in red ever since Roxy death she been taking anti-depression pills with a night cap to go to bed. Ms. Richmond decided she might as well have another drink since she woke up. She got out of her bed wearing nothing but an extra-long T-shirt. The anti-depression pills were still having an effect on her cause she went to the kitchen, a light blinded her until her eyes adjusted to the light. She grabbed the bottle of Zinfandel out the cabinet and headed back to her room turning the kitchen light back off as he walked down the dark hallway back to her room she look in the darkness of Roxy old room ("Wasn't the door closed") she thought maybe just hallucinating as she wobbled to her room. AH-! Ms. Richmond scream was muffled by the huge gloved hand covering her mouth from behind in the darkness soon as she stepped into her bedroom. The wine bottle was snatched out of the hand as she was lifted off her feet in a choke hold. "If you want to see the sunrise then you better shut the fuck up. You understand." the unidentified man order. "Mmmm Mmmmm!" Ms. Richmond mumbled scared for her life now sober out of fear. The man carried her over to the bed dropping her down. Ms. Richmond fell on the bed looking up at the large frame man in the pitch-dark room only light was from the clock so it was too dark to even make out the man's face. Ms. Richmond crawled backwards towards the headboard. "I don't have anything please!" she begged as she began to cry as the man grabbed her ankles force fully pulling her back closer to him. Smack, smack the man back handed her across the face twice busting her lips. Then he wrapped this massive gloved hand around her neck choking her and slapping and punching her in the face continually with his loose hand. " AHH!" Ms. Richmond cried out but her screams fell on deaf ears. "Where the fuck is T.Z? The man demanded Ms. Richmond was so confused when she heard the man asked about T.Z "What about him?" She asked back sobbing "Where is he?" the man ask punching her in the face again? He lives downtown in some lofts She shouted out. "Which ones?" He demanded giving her body blows breaking her ribs. "AAHHH! I don't know I swear to God. I don't know. Ms. Richmond cried out in pain in the darkness "What's his real name?" "Ty Tryone Zan Zanders "she stuttered saying. As the man punched her several more times soon as Ms. Richmond thought the torture was over it wasn't. The man forced her bruised and beat up body on to her stomach. She was so badly injured all she could do was lie there as she heard the man unbuckling his pants. She felt some kind of liquid being put on her anal "AHHH!" Ms. Richmond screamed as she felt the man large penis penetrating her forcefully ripping her apart all she could do was take the pain as the man had his way with her until he finished raping her then beating her the rape felt as if it lasted for hours but the digital clock only read 3:20 when she heard the man leave the room leaving her sodomized, tormented and injured.

"Here he come now!" the man in the passenger side of the car pointed as he watched the silhouette of the large man jog down the street getting in a Dodge Ram truck driving off. "You got now motherfucker!" the driver said pulling off following the Ram truck.

CHAPTER 10

T.Z sped down I-35 as his Camaro SS zoom reading "115 mph" on the digital dash board. T.Z was at home sleep when he received the phone call from Roxy Uncle Charles telling him Ms. Richmond was in the hospital. Ms. Richmond was still taking Roxy death hard so T.Z hope Ms. Richmond didn't do or try to do any harm to herself. He tried asking Charles what happen but all he would say was come to Parkland hospital to the ICU ward. T.Z had tried calling Derrick before he left the apartment building but Derrick had his ringer going to voicemail, then Derrick Corvette wasn't even park in the garage so he knew Derrick wasn't even home. The sun was just rising as T.Z parked in the no parking zone jumping out his car in a pair of red Jordan basketball shorts, white t-shirt and red and white Chris Paul edition Jump man's. Jogging through the automatic opening doors to the elevator. The button to the ICU floor was already lit up signal somebody else was already on that floor in the elevator. So many thoughts ran across his mind as the elevator climbed. The elevator doors opened as it reached the ICU floor two other people got off the elevator with T.Z as well. T.Z trotted toward the reception desk. T.Z seen Roxy family sitting down in the waiting area before he could ask the lady behind the desk a

106

question. "James, Chris where is ma?" T.Z asked walking towards them. Chris, Ms. Richmond youngest brother stood up walking towards T.Z "Pow!" Chris swung a right hook hitting T.Z in the mouth busting his lip. Chris threw another hook but T.Z seen it coming and duck it then pushing Chris backing up throwing his guards up out of reflex but surprise at Chris action. T.Z honestly didn't want to fight Chris but he had no choice but to defend himself. Chris threw two wild punches at T.Z but T.Z weaved the first one and block the second one counter it with a left jab connecting to Chris chin. Robin, Chris wife tried stepping in between the two men stopping the fight but being only 5'1 115 pounds the effort was almost useless. James came from the other side grabbing T.Z trying to slam him to the floor catching T.Z off guard cause T.Z was focused on Chris. "Break it up, break it up!" The tall white man said grabbing T.Z as Charles grabbed his young brother. James, they heard the commotion from inside Ms. Richmond room. "I got your bitch ass nigga!" Chris spat at T.Z "Nigga fuck you get me now" T.Z spat back. "You better hope that nigga find you before I catch you slipping." James said T.Z frowned up with a confused look on his face. "WHAT YOU SAY NIGGA?" T.Z asked as the hospital security came to help break up the fight. "Would you walk over here with me for a second sir?" the tall white man asked. T.Z was so focus on Chris and James he didn't pay the white man no attention. "Sir!" the white man said. "What!" T.Z shouted out of frustration. Then T.Z took a good look at the white man dressed in blue slacks, black dress shirt and blue tie knowing exactly who he was especially with the gun holster on his hip. "I'm detective Gary Simmons with the Dallas Police Department." the tall white man introduce himself extended his hand for a handshake. T.Z gave the man a cold stare looking him up and down walking off without saying a word. "I'm not here for you I'm trying to help find the suspect who hurt Ms. Richmond." the detective said as T.Z walked off. His words made T.Z stop "Ms. Richmond was beaten and raped!" the detective said T.Z hated that he had to go against the code and talk to the police but he had to for Ms. Richmond sake. "Who did it?" T.Z asked "I'm not sure but I thought maybe you could help me though." Simmons said. "How can I help?" T.Z asked "By telling me who your enemies are or who might be out to get you." Most of my enemies are still in prison where I met them but how does that play into this?" T.Z wondered "Cause whoever was behind this assault was asking about you." Simmons said surprising T.Z. Now he understood why Chris and James flipped out on him and why James said that to him. ("Naw it can't be them") T.Z thought to himself. I'm not sure, all this is a shock to me as well. " T.Z said. "How bout this here's my card let's talk again real soon. Make sure you find me and I don't have to find you." Simmons said handing T.Z his business card. T.Z read the card then turned to leave "Mr. Zanders!" What do you know about a one-eyed Jack?" Simmons asked freezing. T.Z when he heard Jack "What you say?" T.Z asked looking back "One eye Jack what you know about that?" Sorry not too much I don't play cards why you ask that?" T.Z asked "Cause the suspect left a Jack of Spade at the crime scene." Simmons said "Couldn't tell you!" T.Z said walking off with his blood boiling for revenge cause T.Z knew exactly what it meant. Detective Simmons watched T.Z leave he knew T.Z had a clue who was behind this. He also knew Roxy was just murdered and T.Z was like her brother. So, the person who assaulted Ms. Richmond was probably looking for T.Z to get back at him for whatever he done against Roxy killer. Detective Simmons had been on the force for 16 years, 7 as a detective and he was familiar how these street wars went and ended like most do in a lot of blood and bodies being found and crying family members asking why that had to happen to their love one's but Detective Simmons would get to the bottom of what happen to Ms. Richmond even if it meant bringing T.Z down as well.

T.Z removed the paper towel from his busting lip looking at the blood staining the paper towel as he exited the hospital. T.Z grabbed the parking citation off his windshield before he got back inside his Camaro "Can this day get any fucking worse." T.Z said out loud to himself, starting his car leaving the hospital. T.Z hated that he didn't get to see Ms. Richmond but he wasn't sure if she would want to see him anyway after what happen. T.Z wondered how long would this tit for tat game go on between him and Jax until one of them was got first or to everybody around them was gone and it wasn't nobody else was left to harm. T.Z was getting even more upset as he thought about the situation as he banged his hand on the steering wheel out of frustration. Drake verse on the song "Motto" played as T.Z phone ringer as T.Z drove "Hello?" he answered "What's good dog?" Derrick asked in a sleepy tone voice "Bad news!" T.Z said making Derrick wake up hearing that "Bad news what you mean?" Derrick ask "Where You at?" T.Z asked "At Pauline house." Pauline was one of Derrick's many women who he would sleep with random nights out of the week. "I'm on my way over there to holla at you bout it". T.Z said. "Aight call me when you out front." Derrick said as they ended the call. Pauline lived off Jim Miller and Loop 12 so it would only take him about 10 minutes to get there.

T.Z tried to call Flex as well but only got the voicemail he figured Flex was probably still sleeping. T.Z needed to inform his crew on what was going on so they could be aware and not get caught slipping cause T.Z was sure anybody who associated themselves with him might be in trouble.

T.Z parked in front of Pauline house before he could call Derrick to tell him he was out front. Derrick came walking outside in some blue jean shorts white Air Forces and no shirt smoking a blunt. Derrick got in the passenger side of the Camaro "What's up?" Derrick said closing the car door. "These hoe ass niggas then got at Roxy momma! T.Z said "What!" Derrick said shocked "These niggas beat the shit out of Ms. Richmond then to top it off they raped her" T.Z explained "How do you know it was them?" Derrick asked "Cause the nigga who did the shit was asking about me then to top it off the nigga had the nerve to leave a Jack of spade like a calling card saying I did it nigga fuck you!" T.Z said as Derrick remain quiet taking deep pulls from the blunt then passing it to T.Z "So what's the plan cause a nigga ain't standing for that shit!" Derrick said. "The hard part is finding the nigga Jax and when we do find him it has to be K.O.S worry bout the consequences afterwards." T.Z explained "Kill On Sight!" Derrick said repeated T.Z words I know the shit might be reckless and end up being costly but it has to be done. T.Z said "No its gone be done cause Roxy would roll over in her grave if we didn't!" Derrick said

Jax stood next to Cold and Jerry giving them the final instruction on where to pick up the ton of heroin from. They would catch a flight to Tucson, Arizona meet up with Pedro men then drive back. Instead of the heroine being inside the back of a trailer as before it would be stashed inside a model home being hauled as the load along with two fake escort cars signal a overload. Jax would pay to get the escort cars ship back to Tucson along with the diesel truck as well. Jax also raised their pay to 130,000 a piece as well. Jax wish the men a safe trip as they left headed for the airport. Jax was wondering where Will was at cause he hadn't heard from him since early the day before. He could tell Will took the conversation he had with Pedro in Mexico the wrong way as if he couldn't handle his job but that wasn't the case. Jax was just making sure the actions he took didn't start a international war but somethings on that level Will didn't never seem to understand. Jax knew that was Will down fall and wouldn't be able to succeed in controlling a empire. Jax looked at his Rolex watch checking the time remembering he had appointment to be at. Jax got behind the driver seat of his Escalade truck heading to his rendezvous alone.

Will walked through the doors of the county morgue and down the hall wall. "Aaron!" Jax called to the average height older dark skin man as he stood over the body of a young black woman doing a autopsy. Aaron looked up at Will then remove his mask revealing is gray goatee "Hi you doing Will?" Aaron asked as Will approached him. "The normal making sure you stay in business as always. Will Said "As Always!" Aaron said "What happen to her?" Will asked looking at the woman lying dead on the table "Her name is Kelly 20 years old police say her ex-boyfriend had a fatal attraction couldn't let go. Looks like she died from asphyxiation by some type of cord." Aaron explained "Shame! I actually came cause I needed your help again!" Will said. Aaron gave Will a weird look remembering the last time he showed up in person asking for his help.

Will had two dead bodies wanting them cremated. "No not that again!" Will said knowing what Aaron was thinking "Then what?" Aaron asked "I need you to find all the information?" Aaron asked "Alive!" Aaron logged on the computer then using the Dallas County database entering "Tyrone Zonders" almost 200 names came up to shorten the list Aaron changed the race to African American and age from 21-26 the list shorten to 13 names. "Can you see the faces? Will asked "Only if they got a Texas I.D or a Criminal Background." Aaron said. "Let me see the pictures." Will said Even though Will never seen the tape from the gambling spot robbery so he really had no exact face to remember thanks to Jax wanting him to wait in the car that one morning. Aaron flip through the different pictures. "Stop!" Will said looking at the picture he knew that was T.Z he remembers the face being on a picture inside Roxy apartment. "Print everything you got on him off!" Will said. Aaron went to print as the printer went to work printed out two sheets of information on T.Z. Will grabbed the papers out the printer reading how many times T.Z been arrested and the day he was release from prison. He had no cars or houses or apartments in his name but the sheet had information on his mother her name the three cars she sign for which included a Benz and a Camaro SS. A house she paid mortgage on and a loft she rented out downtown. Will was for sure now that was him and knew exactly where to find him at. Will gave Aaron 10 crispy hundred-dollar bills for the help "Thanks!" Aaron said putting the cash in his pocket "No Thank You!" Will said leaving the room putting the paper work inside his pants pocket. Will got back inside his Ram truck pulling the information back out to read it over. Will knew exactly where the new lofts were located at but the only problem he remember they had a door man that would only let you up if you come through the entrance of the building but the parking garage had a elevator that he could ride without being seen but would have to follow another car just to enter the gate unless buzzed in by a resident. "Knock, Knock" Will raised up looking at the Hispanic man at his window. "Jumper cables" the man asked in broken English. Will put his finger up signal hold up as he sat the papers on the seat. He glance in the rear view mirror looking at the other Hispanic man standing by the navy blue 01 maxima with the hood up. Will open the door to his truck getting out "Whats wrong?" Will asked stepping out his truck "Battery dead!" the man said pointing to the maxima with the hood up. Will walked over to the car with the man. Soon as Will got close to the car he went into his waistband pulling out the snug nose .357 revolver "BOOM!" Will knocked the Hispanic man off his feet with the close-range head shot "BOOM BOOM!" Will fired two more shots barely missing the other man who stood next to the car the entire time. "Tat, tat, Tat, tat" the 9 mm bullets sprayed Will truck and broke his windows sending glass shattering everywhere. Will ducked his head down as he started the motor in the Ram truck. Will had a built-in gun holster under his seat with a XP 9mm in it. Will release the gun from its holster with his adrenaline pumping. Will felt as if he was Josey Wales off the Western as he fired a shot through his broken back window. "I live for this kind of shit!" Will shouted out the window as he fired hris shots. Will wished he had the time to kill the man since that was what they came to do to him this was the third time in two days he spotted the same car following him at first he thought it might be T.Z but noticing they were hispanic. He figured it wasn't with him then the Feds came to mind but when the man knocked on the window asking for a jump he was sure they were hitmen. Will had to leave cause the police would be there shortly since they were in the parking lot of the county morgue having a shoot out. Will put the truck in drive making the Ram tires screech as he smashed the gas pedal leaving the parking lot. Will was a expert in killing, so for him to become somebody else's prey he didn't take it kindly that was a direct insult to him. Will wished he could have had the chance to put the barrel of his gun down the man throat to find out who sent them to kill him but Will had to act fast or probably would have got killed by the men. Will was puzzled on who might have sent the men Pedro was on one of his list but Pedro men would had shot on site the first time they seen him not waste time trailing him. Then his old friend came to mind would Jax hire somebody to kill him but if Jax wanted him dead Jax would kill Will personally to keep it confidential so many thoughts raced through Wills mind as he drove the shot-up truck away.

T.Z sat in the La-Z-Boy chair watching Kobe play "Call of Duty: Black Ops" online on the Playstation 3 as he smoked a blunt of Kush by himself since Kobe didn't smoke "What's wrong big bro?" Kobe asked looking over at T.Z staring at the wall. "Mo money, Mo problems!" T.Z said exhaling the smoke out his nose. "You straight keep playing yo game" T.Z told Kobe as they both seen the guy walking up to the house on the monitor. T.Z grabbed the .40cal off the table and went to the side patio door sliding it open meeting the man before he got there "What you need?" T.Z asked through the burglar bars and screen "Two twenties of hard!" the man said looking around then sticking his money in the small hole in the screen. T.Z reached on the table getting two red 15 by 10 baggies then handed it through the same hole. T.Z closed the patio door back then came and sat back down sitting the two balled up twenty-dollar bills on the table for Kobe to put with the rest of the money to keep the money count in order when it was time for T.Z to come pick it up. There were always days T.Z would come sit in the trap and serve customers like he use to do once daily. "You said Mo' Money, Mo' Problems but money makes problems go away a lot easier." Kobe said "I use to feel the same way until I found out some problems just can't be paid for! Just got to be handled ya dig!" T.Z said "Well if you ever got a problem that need to be taken care of just let me know cause I ain't tripping you my nigga T.Z and I'm with you. Kobe said T.Z looked at Kobe and smiled admire the courage he had "I'll remember that!" "now get the door it's your turn" T.Z added grabbing the game controller out of his hand. Kobe grabbed the same .40cal as he went to the patio door to serve the customers. It was almost 4:00 in the evening the 99 rush was about to began so traffic was bout to start moving back and forth from the duplex house. Drake verse on the song "The Motto" Played as T.Z phone rang "Hello?" T.Z answered his phone "What's good hustler?" the man voice said over the line "Ain't shit talk to me G.G" T.Z said to him. "I'm tryna find the best 25pound bag of dog good they sell" G.G said speaking in code "Nigga have you tried the store?" T.Z said "Oh my bad ain't this the customer service department of Wal-Mart" G.G said. "Ha ha funny nigga!" I got some of that premiere one shit in the green bag just give me bout a hour then I'll meet up with you" T.Z said speaking back in code. "That's a bet!" G.G said as they both ended the call. T.Z was gone sit in the spot with Kobe until his other worker got there at six but G.G needed 25 pounds of weed that was 22,000 dollars waiting to be made. "Kobe?" "Whats up?" I got to make a run so you on your own hold shit down! T.Z said "Always!" Be Easy Nigga!" Kobe said. "Fo sho!" T.Z said waiting on the last customer to drive off before he left out the front door.

Jax sat behind the Oakwood desk talking on the phone as Will walked into his office now changed into a Brown three-piece Gucci suit. "Tell them I like the way they did the restaurant and thanks for the hard work. Aight then later." Jax said ended the call "Where you been all day?" Jax asked Will as he stared directly in Jax eyes trying to read him like he did most people. Only problem Jax wasn't most people he couldn't be read like a book cause he barely displayed any type of emotion. "The usual shoot outs in broad daylight!" Will said sarcastically watching how Jax reacted to the comment. Your here now so it must wasn't to hectic" Jax said not knowing Will was serious. "I guess so!" What I miss?" Will asked switching the subject cause discussing the matter wouldn't get the answers he wanted. Will would have to just wait until the next hit come cause Will assume whoever sent them two guys. They had people at their disposal so more would come cause the first two were amateurs in Wills eyes. "I went and met up with Victor to check out the restaurant before it open this weekend." Jax said I forgot you said that was this morning the shit slip my mind." "Its not big deal everything went well. Where have you been anyway?" Jax asked curious of Will whereabouts "Following up on a few leads" Will said "Few leads on what?" "Listen Will don't stress yourself over that. He will get dealt with when the time comes but right now isn't the time so let's focus elsewhere like on this shipment coming in from Tucson, Arizona Jax said "In Mexico it seem like a issue." Will how long have we been doing this together 12 plus years have I ever undermined you by getting outside help? No, I haven't so don't never call yourself second guessing me as well" Jax added as he stood face to face with Will. "My apologies! Will said extended his right hand "Accepted!" Jax said embracing him in a brotherly hug. Today's events flashed through Wills mind as Jax let go of the embrace. Will had a good idea that his old friend wasn't behind the hit on him but he still had to stay on alert and be cautious.

T.Z was headed back to the trap house to meet up with G.G he had the 25 pounds of weed inside two duffel bags on the backseat floor of the Camaro SS. He could still feel the cut on the inside of his lip from early when he got punched at the hospital. T.Z wanted to still go see Ms. Richmond to check on her. He decided he would go up to the hospital whenever he got finish with G.G. T.Z parked in front of the duplex grabbing the two duffel bags as he got out the car walking towards the front door. Kobe was already opening the door and unlocking the bars for him to come in. Quick the other youngster who T.Z had rotated hours with Kobe was now there. Quick was 18 years old light skin and bout 5'9 him and Kobe would take turns working the spot 12hrs a piece a day it didn't matter to T.Z which 12 they worked, he left that choice up to them just as long as the spot was open 24hours a day. "Hello?" T.Z answered his phone soon as he heard Drake voice coming from his phone. "I'm bout to pull up" G.G said "Aight park behind my car and come in." T.Z directed Kobe grabbed the .40 cal as Quick sat on the couch with the AR-15 across his lap. They both knew a big transaction was about to take place if somebody was coming inside instead of getting served through the gate. T.Z had his personal Glock 9mm tucked on his waist with the 30-round extended clip hanging outside on display to be seen as he went to the door. T.Z didn't think G.G would try anything slick but, in the game,, you could never be to safe. Kobe and Quick watched the monitor making sure G.G was the only one person walking to the door. The camera's outside the house gave four different views of the house on a 4-way split screen so they had the heads up on anybody approaching the house ahead of time. T.Z open the door unlocking the bars for G.G. Could come in "What's good hustla?" G.G asked coming in with a duffel bag in hand "Slow motion!" T.Z said closing the gate locking it then the door. "Slow motion better than no motion believe that" G.G said T.Z lead G.G. Over to a flip out table with four fold up chairs around it. With his back turn towards Kobe and Quick. The two young goons kept a close eye on G.G as he sat down across from T.Z. T.Z unzipped one bag removing a pound from the bag handing it to G.G to look at. G.G examined the Ziploc bag opening it sticking his face into the bag to get a good smell of the weed "Yeah, Yeah I'm loving this!" G said sitting the pound on the table then picking up his duffel bag unzipping it showing T.Z the dead president "Whats that?" T.Z asked "22racks!" G.G said taking the stacks out the bag sitting them on the table "Each wrap is two thousand dollars!" G.G added placing 11 different stacks on the table. "Come here Kobe" T.Z said "Whats up big bro" Kobe said walking over "Run this through the counter" T.Z said pushing the money off the table back into the bag. Kobe pick the bag up and went into the kitchen G.G you still out there in North Dallas getting it huh? T.Z asked making small talk while he waited on Kobe to finish. He could hear the money counter flipping through the bills "Yeah its good out there the money plentiful. You need to get a spot out there G.G. said not knowing T.Z already had one. "I might have to look into that. Why you don't be fucking with the work?" T.Z asked "I have before but weed always been my thing the dope carry too much time when you get jammed up" G.G explained.

"All this shit carry too much time if you ask me" T.Z replied "True that G.G agreed "Hey T its 22,050 dollars" Kobe shouted from the kitchen. Keep the change it ain't shit but fifty dollars" G.G said Right on!" Here is the rest of the shit" T.Z said unzipping the second duffel bag showing the pounds of weed to him. G.G counted the Ziploc bags full of weed making sure it was all there. "You want to weight them out too?" "Naw I trust you but can I keep the duffel bags since you got mine?" G.G asked "Yeah its cool" T.Z said as G.G zip the bags back up preparing to leave. They both stood up walking to the door. "Good looking out!" G said "Anytime just get at me" T.Z said shaking his hand then opening the door for he could leave. T.Z closed and locked the door behind him.

Later that night T.Z crept down the hallway of the hospital since it was passed visitation hours in the ICU ward plus he never found out what room Ms. Richmond was in. T.Z knew the hospital had surveillance camera's so he didn't want to do nothing that would draw attention to himself. T.Z eyes caught a glimpse of the word Rich on a chart. He made no hesitation and eased inside the room closing the door gently behind him. The room was dim as he enter. As he got closer to the bed T.Z looked at the bandages on the sides of Ms. Richmond use to be pretty face. Her face was badly swollen and bruise. T.Z could even see hand impression marks around her neck. It hurt to see her laid up in a hospital with I. V's coming out of her with all kinds of other contraption connected to her keeping her alive knowing he played the star role in helping this come about. "I'm sorry ma!" T.Z said holding Ms.

Richmond hand T.Z closed his eyes saying "Allah most gracious, most merciful I asked that you strengthen us and protect us from the curse one. I also ask that you bring my ma back to full health through her hard times and allow her to overcome in the name of Allah the most high. Amin!" T.Z said a short prayer for Ms. Richmond. T.Z felt her hand tightened as his but her eyes never opened. T.Z kissed her on the forehead the only spot that didn't have a bandage on it then left out the room.

Detective Simmons sat in his unmarked Impala watching T.Z get inside his Camaro SS in the hospital parking lot. Simmons knew it would be only a matter of time before the men that attack Ms. Richmond caught up with T.Z or he found them first regardless Simmons would have em and T.Z got caught up in the cross then that would only make his arresting record look better now that he finally had a trail on T.Z all he had to do is sit back and wait the rest would fall into his lap. T.Z pulled out into the night as Simmons trail behind him not to close.

CHAPTER 11

"**E**very ma'fucking day you complaining about some hoe ass bullshit damn just shut the fuck up sometime!" Flex spat at Peaches as she smacked her lips storming into the bedroom. Flex wanted to go teach Peaches not to be slamming any doors around the house but at the moment he ad other business he needed dot see to. Flex left out the house getting I his Benz G-Wagon truck he had to met up with T.Z in bout an hour to drop off his share of the cash to re-up but the only problem Flex was 150 thousand short it didn't seem like it to Flex until re-up time came that he had been blowing that much cash constantly. That's the cost when you live everyday like a rockstar snorting powder and tricking. Flex had collected all the money from his two trap houses and old all his product as well and all the money he had was $350,000 dollars cash. He thought about just lying to T.Z and Derrick telling them something came up he had to pay for but he knew they would ask a hundred questions because at the low as prices they were coping at you could still handle business, we good an still have money left over. That's why early today Flex mad a call to a loyal out of town customer of his, Flex call Nate telling him he had a fresh shipment coming in tomorrow but he needed to get rid of the bricks he already had. He lied and told Nate if he come cop them today he would sell each one at $14,000 a key when he usually charges 22 a key. He lied saying he only had 15 left so Nate agreed to the deal thinking he was winning. Nate was coming down from Oklahoma were here sold the bricks for a easy $28,000 a piece. Nate had called Flex bout 20 minutes ago telling him he had a check into the Intown Suites off I-35. Flex drove to the motel plotting how he was gone rob Nate he was planning from the start to do him like he did Ken but he forgot Nate didn't like to conduct business in the open he was the paranoid type who always thought the Feds was watching him. Right now, Flex already had his mind made up that Nate had to be got cause he had no bricks to sell him and he couldn't let that money slip by him. Flex parked his truck in the parking space right below the 2nd floor room. Flex took out his little baggy containing bout a 8-ball of cocaine dipping his pinky nail into the bag then snorting the powder he did that bout 3 or 4 more times. He lit up a Newport short go mellow the high and how his now pumping nerves. He took a long drag of the Newport then dropping it in the ashtray then getting out the truck exhaling the smoke into the air. Flex went to the back of the truck opening the rear of the truck back. Flex went up the flight of stairs then walking to he reached door 215 "Knock, Knock" Flex took a deep breath as he knocked on the door. "Flex what's up baby boy!" Nate said as he open the door inviting Flex inside. The brown skin Nate stepped aside as Flex walked inside the room. Flex eyes went directly to the other dark skin man who sat on the bed reading a Donk, Box and Bubble car magazine. Flex looked at Nate like who is he "That's my kinfolk Ro he good." Nate said closing the door. Flex wasn't expecting for nobody else to here except Nate naw he might have a problem on his hands especially if the nigga strap to. Flex could smell in the air that hey just finished smoking some wack, dip, P.C.P whatever you prefer to call it. Nate went and sat down at the small table inside the room close to the door leaving Flex standing up. "You got the cash." Flex said getting straight to the point. "Nigga you got the dope!" Nate retorted. "Naw nigga I just like to walk around with a big as suitcase in my hand." Flex said sarcastically "That's why I like you D-Town Niggas cause y'all funny as fuck" Nate said smiling ("I bet you ain't gone like me in 10minutes") Flex thought to himself. "Yo, Ro get the money." Nate told him as he reached under the bed pulling out a Louis Vuitton bag tossing it to Nate. Ro got up to go to the bathroom. That split second was the little break Flex needed to gain the upper hand soon as Nate unzipped the expensive bag showing Flex the green stacks. Flex made his move reaching in the back of his shirt pulling out the 9mm "Don't say shit nigga!" Flex growled between clench teeth pointing the barrel directly at Nate's temple. Nate had the deer and the headlights look of being shocked and froze. Flex yanked the bag out of Nate's hand. "Wha-" "Pop"!" Flex got startled by Ro voice putting a bullet in the side of Nate's head "Pop, Pop!" Flex fired two shots in Ro direction as he dove back into the restroom. Flex took both of Nate's phones that sat on the table as he hurried out the door running to his truck getting in. "tat, tat, tat, tat,!" Bullets come flying into Flex hood and windshield good things Flex had bullet proof windows on his truck cause the bullets were coming straight down at him. "Tat,Tat,Tat,Tat!" Ro sprayed the Tech-9mm at Flex truck as he backed out and sped off. Flex wasn't planning on killing Nate but he didn't hear Ro come out the bathroom and his first reaction was to pull the trigger. With a dead body and an eye witness the situation just got worse cause he just got the police involved but only lead he thought they had was Ro. When he felt he was far enough away he tossed both of Nate's phones out and would also destroy them later as well.

T.Z sat inside his Benz 63 on the phone talking to Yvonne "So baby I ain't go get to see you until later on tonight!" T.Z complained "Hopefully not too late. It shouldn't take to long for me to go over to the county jail and speak with Mr. Walsh." Yvonne said. "Damn baby cant he wait until tomorrow" T.Z said. "Baby the man been waiting 20 years for this day coming up." Yvonne said "So one more day shouldn't hurt." T.Z said What about on your release day they would have told you to wait one more day cause somebody forgot to get a paper sign." Yvonne said "Yeah I guess I understand." T.Z replied. "Plus baby you know I told you I been working on this 107 case for 2years now and I'm finally getting this man exonerated." Yvonne said "Ain't the Innocent Project of Texas taking most of the credit though?" T.Z asked "Not really but they are also playing a major role in helping this work out for Mr. Walsh!" Yvonne said. So, you go be on TV with him on Friday? T.Z asked "Yep looking gorgeous as always!" Yvonne said "Well baby I'm proud of you for real the system needs more people like you!" T.Z said "Thanks Baby I'll see you tonight!" Yvonne said "Aight!" T.Z said ended the call. Derrick got out his 760Li as he parked next to T.Z carrying a duffel bag getting in the passenger seat of T.Z Benz. "What's good dog?" T.Z asked "Ain't shit! You?" Derrick asked "Chilling. I went and see Ms. Richmond the other night T.Z said "How is she? What she say?" Derrick asked "She was sleep when I got there but she beat up pretty bad dog." T.Z said "Damn!" Derrick said dropping his head "Where the fuck is this nigga Flex at? I told this nigga to be at the apartment at 5:30pm" T.Z said getting frustrated dialing Flex number "Hello?" "Where you at nigga?" T.Z said to him soon as Flex answered. "I'm coming in the gate right now!" Flex said as T.Z pressed the end button on the screen "Nigga be bullshitting I sear!" Derrick said sarcastically "Flex parked the SLS AMG next to Derrick BMW and got in the backseat of T.Z Benz with the same Louis Vuitton bag he got from Nate in his hand "What's good y'all?" Flex asked "Slow Motion" Derrick said "Waiting on your slow ass nigga!" T.Z said putting the car in reverse backing out.

Detective Simmons took pictures of the two unidentified men getting inside the car with T.Z carrying duffel bags which Simmons figured had to be drugs or money because of the expensive foreign cars they were driving. Within the one day Simmons had been following T.Z he had already concluded T.Z was a drug dealer after seeing T.Z pull in the garage of the loft downtown and leaving out in a Benz only two lifestyle paid for a $2,000 a month loft and Benz for a young black man. He either was a rapper or a trapper and Simmons had a good idea T.Z didn't rap. Simmons ducked down in the seat as he watch the Benz back out the parking space his unmarked Impala SS to trail them. Simmons pulled out the apartments not tryna lose them as he watched the Benz get on 175 headed west. Simmons rode the emergency lane going around cars until he reached the ramp to get on the highway. Simmons use the police interceptor motor to get bout 100 yards away from the Benz as the luxury AMG V-12 motor sped down the highway gliding in and out of traffic.

T.Z parked in front of the furniture store that Felex owned and all three men got out with their bags in hands. Walking into the furniture store "Hola Seniors?" Maria greeted them. "Hello?" they all said back. "Come, Come!" Maria instructed them to follow her. She led them into Felex office where he sat behind his Red Oak Wood desk talking on the phone "Luego!" Felex said hanging up the phone. "What's up Felex?" T.Z asked taking a seat in a chair "I'm fine! And you?" Felex asked "We Good!" T.Z said "Let's get down to business then shall we" Felex said "Here's my $500,000!" T.Z said sitting his bag on the desk. "500!" Derrick said sitting his bag on the desk. "500 tho!" Felex said sitting the Louis Vuitton bag on the desk. "1.5 million all together then. I'll have your product in the morning if that's not a problem." Felex said "Naw its cool T.Z said "A slight problem occurred and it won't be delivered to the morning." Felex said "That ain't no problem!" Derrick said "Yeah we ain't tripping. "Flex said very well. Did Hector take care of you like I ask him" Felex said "Yeah he said he had some special car coming in next week for me to look at." T.Z said. "Yeah that sounds like Hector. He is a very reliable man you have my word on that." Felex said "Around what time do you want us to come back tomorrow?" T.Z asked "Don't worry for your inconvenience I'll have it delivered to you instead. I'll call you later tonight for the address and it will be there by 9:00sharp tomorrow morning." Felex said "Aight!" T.Z said standing up shaking Felex hand "See you guys later!" Felex said shaking Derrick and Flex hand. Felex lead the way out of his office back to the showroom floor as the three left the building walking back to T.Z car. A reflection hit T.Z eyes catching his attention he couldn't tell exactly where it came from but it was on his right side. T.Z turned his head looking in that direction "What's wrong?" Derrick asked catching the look on T.Z face.

"Nothing!" T.Z lied saying knowing exactly what he saw. Then men got in the Benz and T.Z drove off (I see you ma'fucker!") T.Z thought as he drove past the empty unmarked Impala SS("That was a close call!") Detective Simmons thought as he raised up. Simmons seen the reflection of the lens of his camera hit T.Z eyes catching his attention he wasn't for sure if T.Z seen him or not. Simmons understand T.Z was neck deep in the drug game especially when he seen the three exited the furniture store without their duffel bags. "What started out as a assault investigation ended up leading to a continuance criminal enterprise bust thanks to Detective Gary Simmons" Detective Simmons could already see the news headlines and the promotion along with it. He knew he just stumble upon every detective dream case by accident. Simmons was determined to bust this thing wide open.

T.Z thought about what he just seen. Somebody was taking pictures of them leaving Felex store. He wasn't sure on who it was could the D.E A. or just D.P.D but either one T.Z wasn't trying to face them in court. He wondered was they just watching Felex or were they watching him and his crew or everybody. How long have they been on to him so many questions ran across his mind as he drove back to the apartment constantly checking his rearview mirror making sure he wasn't being followed. T.Z pulled into the apartments parking next to Flex SLS "Hey y'all make sure y'all watch yo backs extra close." T.Z told them "That's why I keep my extended clip" Derrick joked "Naw I'm serious. I know I seen somebody taking pictures of us leaving Felex store." T.Z said "That's what you seen?" Derrick said "Hell yeah!" T.Z said "They may just be watching Felex he said he had a slight problem all of a sudden." Flex said "Yeah could be true but if they on to Felex and we fuck with him we just as guilty when it comes to the Feds." T.Z explain "So what you want to do then?" Derrick said "Keep yo eyes open for the next few days if shit look fishy then we close up shop until everything cools down you niggas have enough cash saved up to survive decently for at least a year or two" T.Z said "A year or two!" Flex said. "I'm not saying chill for that long maybe a couple of months but you should have that much put up by now." T.Z said Little did T.Z know Flex barely had enough to live for the rest of the month without his habits included. "Yeah Im Good!" Derrick said. "I'm aight too!" Flex lied. "Well its agreed upon if shit start getting hot in the next week then we chill until shit blow over cause all our money gone go to lawyer fees if the FEDS don't take it all when they hit us." T.Z said "Remember that" T.Z added saying Flex got out the backseat getting into his car. Things were getting worse and worse for Flex he was already paranoid bout him getting jammed up for killing Nate now he might be under Federal Investigation. Flex always thought when a person was getting money he had less problems but now he had serious problems. Problems that could put him in prison for life. Flex left out the apartment complex and parked around the corner after hearing the news about him being watched he needed a hit of the white girl that seem to help ease his problems.

T.Z and Derrick sat in the car talking about the seriousness of the situation and how closing down the spots they had around the city would hurt stop hustling period would hurt financially but them were the precautions they would have to take to stay free. "Damn T soon as as this shit start getting good it's like a nigga got to quit." "Yeah I can dig it but that's why people say get in make your money then turn legit and get out cause this shit is only temporary." T.Z explain "Have you thought about going legit?" Derrick asked "I got a few ideas in mind. What about you?" T.Z asked "I would like to but on the real all a nigga know is these streets shit I can't think of anything legal I really want to do" Derrick said "It got to be something nigga!" T.Z said "Maybe a car accessory shop or rim shop" Derrick said. "A idea is a good enough start to accomplish something" T.Z said "What you thing about doing?" Derrick asked "Probably Real Estate and clothes shop just to start off." T.Z said "Handle your business cause clothes and a house is something I'm always gone need for the low.!" Derrick said laughing

Detective Simmons sat at his desk reading over the files he looked up "Tyrone Zonders born 7-31-88 arrested for Aggravated Assault with a deadly weapon on 10-03-05 received 5years probation, arrested again for aggravated Assault on 09-04-06 plead guilty on both charges receiving 4 years TDCJ time released on 09-13-10. Xavier Johnson A.K.A Flex born 11-5-90 arrested 02-10-07 delivery of control substance to a undercover officer and unlawful carry weapon pleaded guilty on all charges receive 3 years TDCJ time released 12-30-09 on parole. Derrick Shaw born 08-13-88 only arrested for Justice of the peace unpaid tickets "Simmons looked at the mugshot of the three men tryna piece the puzzle together on how they were tied to Rosa Domingas the owner of the furniture store where they dropped the bags off to. She was a 68year old Hispanic woman with NO background not even a traffic citation. "I have to be overlooking something" Simmons told himself. Times like this is when Simmons wished he still had a partner cause two heads were better then one after Simmons partner Ralph Fritz died in a fatal car accident on a hot pursuit after a rape suspect. Fitz sped the unmarked Crown Victoria on I-175 tryna make the deadman curve doing 120mph losing control hitting the guard rail flipping the car over several times. Simmons was in the passenger seat during the accident only sustaining a broken arm and two fractured rims on his left side. While Fritz had several contusions to the brain with internal hemorrhaging from the brain. Fitz was in a coma for about 2 weeks until his body couldn't hold on no longer. Simmons thought about the tragic accident that occurred almost 2 years ago. Since that day Simmons has been working alone. Simmons read at the bottom of T.Z file "Telford Unit" then looked at the bottom of Flex file "Telford Unit" Simmons notice that they both were incarcerated at the same prison doing the same time. He could find the importance of the information but remember it just in case it was needed for later purpose.

CHAPTER 12

Jax watched the 62in flat screen admiring the work his daughter was doing for society even though Jax fill the streets up with poison everyday he did a successful job at raising his child as she stood among the bunch of high paid attorney's and politician. "she all grown up now." Linda said also watching the TV sitting next to him. "yeah it seems like yesterday she started her first day of kindergarten." Jax said "Before you know it she'll be getting married having kids!" Linda said as Jax gave her a whatever look. "Hopefully not no time soon she needs to finish college first." Jax said. "Of course, but she is a grown woman as well." Linda said. "Ummm!" Jax mumbled. Jax knew he had a beautiful daughter any man's dream girl but he didn't like to think about some random guy being with his baby girl that's one reason he spoil her to the fullest for she wouldn't feel like she needed a man just to take care of her like the average young woman thought. Jax could count on one hand how many boyfriend his daughter then had since she started dating and to Jax none of the guys were good enough for his baby girl but to Jax Jesus Christ probably wouldn't be good enough for her either ask him. "Honey one day you gone have to let go and let her make her own decision" Linda said "I do let her make her own decision. I just make sure she makes the right one." Jax said "Honey we raised a great child any parent would be proud of you but you gonna have to let up. Linda said "Let up my ass I don't need none

of these knuckles headed boys pulling up on their big rims tryna fast talk my child. It ain't gone happen long as its blood running through these veins." Jax you couldn't tell him amount his family.

Yvonne walked out the courtroom with Mr. Walsh next to her and the Innocent Project of Texas Committee on her other side as the media from the local new channels and newspaper approached them with microphone pointed and camera rolling "Mr. Walsh how does it feel to be set free after serving 20years for a crime you didn't commit." "I'm just thankful mostly especially to Ms. Yvonne Goldstein for just picking up my appeal out the kindness of her heart and the Innocent Project people for supporting her when she presented my case to them." Mr. Walsh said "Ms. Goldstein What is your outlook on this situation?" The prevailed for Mr. Walsh an innocent man can go go home to his family." Yvonne stuttered getting caught up in her words as she seen the familiar face moving behind the crowd of reporters blowing her a kiss "I'll be back!" Yvonne whispered in Mr. Walsh ear as the president of the Innocent Project of Texas stepped up to answer question from the media. "What are you doing here?" Yvonne asked curious "I remember you telling me you would be looking gorgeous so I couldn't miss that." T.Z said looking Yvonne up and down as she wore a Gray Gucci suit for woman with black pin stripes and gray close toe Gucci heels with her hair in a genie ponytail. "I must admit you look like you belong on the corner of G.Q magazine. "Yvonne said noticing the Navy Blue and black

3 piece Armani suit T.Z wore with 1 carat cuff links. "Armani" Yvonne said recognizing the brand without looking at the tag "Come here crazy girl." T.Z said hugging her smell the Chanel #5 perfume she wore arousing his hormones. "I see somebody is happy to see me." Yvonne smiled looking down at his pants. "I didn't come here for that!" T.Z smiled saying as he buttons his suit coat up to cover his print. "Are you sure?" Yvonne teased "Well not the only reason. I came to take you to lunch are how you sophisticated folks call it brunch" T.Z said in a England Accent. "I might already have plans" Yvonne said

"Oh you do!" T.Z said "Naw I'm just playing baby let me finish up here then I'll be ready Yvonne said then walked off. Yvonne strutted extra hard as she walked off cause she could feel T.Z eyes staring at her. T.Z smirked watching Yvonne walk off as he checks the time on his black Richard Miller watch "10:50am" He said to himself realizing the court proceeding only took a hour to finish. T.Z didn't like being around courtrooms or jails cause it gave him a eerie feeling knowing at any giving moment he could be back in that position again. "No, no not my child! An older black woman cried walking out a courtroom on the opposite end of the hallway. T.Z put his head down shaking it side to side knowing another young brother just lost his life to the system after hearing a mother cries "you ready baby?" Yvonne asked getting his attention. "Yeah come on!" T.Z said leading the way. They walked past the sobbing mother as she sat on a bench both T.Z and Yvonne remain quiet as they passed her "Baby you got one of your law firm cards on you?" T.Z asked as he stopped "Yeah, why?" she asked. "Let me have it" he said holding his hand out. Yvonne opened her Louis Vuitton clutch retrieving the business card handing it to T.Z, He turned around and walked towards the sobbing mother. "Excuse me ma'am" T.Z said "yes" the lady said looking up at T.Z with red puffy eyes. "I'm not tryna be nosey but what's wrong?" he asked "my son went to trial by judge on a murder charge and received 85 years for something he didn't do. The lady broke down crying saying. T.Z knew going to trial by judge you might as well pleaded guilty and went open plea instead cause a nigga was shit out of luck going trial by judge. "May I ask why he do that?" T.Z asked "Listen to that damn no good public defender." she said. "What's your name ma'am?" "Ellan Jones!" "Well Ms. Jones here's a number to a good appeal attorney." T.Z said handing her the card "I can't afford to hire no lawyers." she said tryna hand the card back. "Don't worry about the cost just call and ask for Yvonne Goldstein tell her Tyrone referred you and I'm handle all expenses." T.Z said shocking the woman as her eyes widen looking at him as if he was an angel from God, answering her prayers. "Thank You Young Man!" "No problem" T.Z said walking

away "That was so sweet of you" Yvonne said. "I just understand that's all by the way how much are you going to charge me?" T.Z asked "Technically I'm not an official lawyer until I take my bar test at the end of the month so I can't charge but I can work on the case but for you consider that my first case I take pro bono after I pass my test this month." Yvonne smiled saying as they headed out the courtroom.

Derrick drove down Ledbetter in his 760Li bobbing his head to Two Chains and T.I song "I'm getting it" headed to meet up with one of his customers name Lil D. Lil D was one of Derricks loyal customers Lil D was from Oak Cliff and was known for getting money and busting that pistol at niggas at the drop of a dime even though him and Derrick were from different hoods and he was about 10 years older then Derrick he still showed major respect for Derrick. Derrick pulled up at Big T Plaza and pulled over by the rim shop were Lil D said he would be. Derrick parked next to Lil D Black 745Li on Chrome 22in Lexani rims. He watched the miniature Slim Thug walk to his car. If Lil D had been 6'5 instead of 5'5 you would swear he was the rapper Slim Thug. Lil D had long braids and a platinum grill just like Slim Thug. The reason Lil D was known for busting that pistol cause he suffered from the lil man complex he would take the smallest things offensive and flip out thinking you taking his height as a weakness. "Whats up baby boy?" Lil D asked getting inside on the passenger side "Ain't shit whats popping I mean whats good D" Derrick said rephrasing his words remembering Lil D was a five deuce Hoover Crip who acted as if he was in 1987 in the heart of L.A California." You lucky you my nigga Derrick" Lil D said smiling "You threw off D for real." Derrick said "Thats how it be when you been smoking wack since 13!" Lil D said "Come get this cash nigga!" Lil D saying as he pressed the trunk button on his key pad popping his trunk. They both got out and went to the trunk of Lil D 745Li. A blue and black backpack sat in the trunk. Lil D picked the bag up handing it to Derrick as he unzipped it "How much?" Derrick asked "147,000!"

Lil D said Derrick pressed the trunk button on his key pad popping his trunk. He opens his trunk tossing the backpack inside then picking up a black leather duffel bag inside his trunk. "Thats ten all together so you owe me 63stacks." Derrick told him letting Lil D know that he fronted him 3keys "Aight!" "Holla at me in a few days." Derrick said closing his trunk. "I want you to meet somebody before you go" Lil D said "Who?"

Derrick asked suspiciously placing his hand on his waist next to the 9mm hid under his shirt "Scary ass nigga that ain't what I mean." Lil D knowing from years in the streets what Derrick was reaching for. "Who then?" Derrick said "Follow me" Lil D led the way up to were care were getting rims put on. "This my kinfolk Ken Ken. Ken Ken this Derrick. "Lil D introduce them to each other. Derrick looked at Ken Ken then at the 1972 Chevy Caprice painted candy powder blue with the top town exposing the all-white ostrich seat that had 10in screens in the headrest with the word "OAK CLIFF" stitch in the seat squatting on a set of powder blue 28in Giovanna's "That's yo whip?" Derrick asked "Yeah!" Ken Ken said "That ma'fucker sitting right!" Derrick said. "Yeah my kinfolk need a reliable plug and I know you stay on like a light switch." Lil D said "Believe that!" Derrick said "Yeah cause my last connect did some bitch shit and robbed me but that didn't stop shit plus I got a $20,000 price tag on his head."Ken Ken said "Who is this clown ass nigga?" Derrick asked "A nigga that call himself Flex!" Ken Ken said. "Who?" Derrick asked double checking making sure he heard correctly "Flex! Why you know the nigga?" Ken Ken asked. "The name sounds familiar thats all" Derrick lied "If I hear something I'll call D and let him know" Derrick added saying "Aight!" So, it's cool if I call you when I need something then. Ken Ken said "Yeah get my number from D and holla at me whenever you ready. I'll play you up on the same prices. "Derrick said as he went back to his car to leave. Derrick was surprise at what he just heard. He knew Flex would jack a nigga if need be just like he would but since they start dealing with Felex it hadn't been any reason to. Unless Flex was just a grimy nigga like that but Flex never made himself to be grimy like that if so Derrick would need to watch out for the nigga his damn self cause them type of niggas leave they own homeboys stinking somewhere time start looking bad enough. Derrick drove down the street tryna put the shit together but it wasn't added up. It had to be something missing Derrick didn't know he dialed T.Z number on his cell phone but the voice mail answered.

T.Z stood in the parking lot of the Frank Crawley courthouse giving Yvonne a kiss as he drops her back off at her car after they finish eating lunch together "Call me later!" T.Z said "Okay!" Yvonne agreed as T. Z close the car door for her as she got in T.Z got back in his Benz seeing he had a miss call from Derrick as his phone sat on the car charger. He dialed Derrick number back " Hello" Derrick answered on the first ring "What's good dog?" T.Z asked "Man this shit crazy bro." Derrick said "What you talking about?" T. Z asked "It's this old school nigga that I know he introduce me to his fam name Ken Ken. The nigga Ken Ken tell me his old connect robbed him and he got a tag on the nigga head." Derrick said "So and what that got to do with us?" T.Z said "Here's the crazy part the nigga connect name was Flex" Derrick said "Flex who T.Z asked confused "Nigga Flex, Flex!" Derrick said "But that don't make no damn sense Flex don't got no reason to be robbing a nigga for a couple stacks." T.Z said "That's what I thought but it can't be more then one nigga name Flex selling chickens in the D." Derrick said "Something can't be right that shit don't add up" T.Z said "That's why I said shit crazy" Derrick said "How much he said he got hit for?" T. Z asked "He didn't say but he did say he got 20racks on his head." Derick said "Nigga offering 20 thousand for a street his he must have got hit had by Flex" T.Z said "Thats exactly what I'm thinking as well." Derrick said "I'm catch up with Flex then I'll get back at you." T.Z said "Aight then!" Derrick said ended the call. Derrick was right shit was crazy but T.Z would figure out what really went on.

It had to be Detective Simmons lucky day cause on his way out of the court building after sitting and testify on a grand jury

indictment hearing all morning he sees Tyrone Zonders standing next to a 328i BMW kissing a woman. Simmons could tell by her attire she had to work for the legal system somehow. Simmons call the plates in on the BMW and found out the car was registered to a Yvonne Goldstein who happen to be a paralegal for a big-time law firm. Simmons wondered what a young beautiful lady what a promising future was doing with a no-good drug selling thug like Tyrone ("This is steady getting more interesting") Simmons thought to himself. Simmons wanted to follow T. Z to see what other kind of information he might stumble upon in the process but decided not to cause after almost getting his cover blown the other day he know T.Z would probably be looking and checking for someone tailing him and Simmons didn't want to alert T.Z and end up losing the opportunity to take down a entire criminal empire doing his own investigation.

T.Z had call Flex and told him he needed to meet up with him right now. Even though Flex was tryna make up excused why he couldn't right now. T.Z wasn't hearing or accepting no for an answer. T. Z told him he would be waiting in his living room when he got there then. Flex didn't want T.Z to see Peaches face how he been abusing her on a daily basis lately. T.Z stayed out of people personal relationship problems but T.Z didn't condone beating up women and Flex felt he was too old to have

T.Z preaching to him about how to handle his woman. T.Z pulled up at the carwash on Martin Luther King where he was supposed to meet up with Flex at. T.Z sat inside his Benz behind the limo tint watching the local dope fiend wash cars as he waited on Flex. After T.Z waited for about 15 minutes or so Flex come whipping his SLS into the carwash parking crazy next to T.Z jumping out leaving his doors in the air getting in the passenger seat of T. Z car. "What's up nigga?" Flex asked "Chilling!" I needed to holla at you bout some shit" T.Z said "What's up?" Flex asked sniffing wiping his nose. "You know a nigga name Ken Ken?" T. Z asked looking at Flex as the question caught him by surprise. "Don't lie bro!" T.Z asked looking at the

expression on Flex face. When he heard Ken Ken name. "Yeah!" Flex admitted dropping his head in shame "How much you hit the nigga for?" "200racks!" Damn! Why and you eating out here." T.Z asked "Cause shit was personal!" Flex lied saying "What you mean by that?" "The nigga knew not to holla at my baby momma but did it anyway behind my back dirty macking my name to her. She told me and for that type shit the nigga lucky I let him live" Flex explain telling a bold face lie. "Understandable. The nigga got 20racks on your head what you want to do about it or let it ride out cause you think the nigga bluffing?" T.Z said Flex thought about it for a second then said "He ain't bluffing!" "Done deal you already know what the business is then next time let me know before you pull a move like that on a nigga for I can have the heads up on shit." T.Z said "You right my bad dog!" Flex said "Remember we in this shit together fam blood in blood out!" T.Z said as they dapped each other up. "Let me ask you this. How you know the nigga Ken Ken?" Flex asked "I don't! Derrick do through somebody that re-up from him"

139

T.Z said "I hate to get Derrick caught up in the mix of my bullshit like that!" Flex said "I'm holla at the nigga and see what he say then we move from there." T.Z said matter of fact let me call this nigga. T.Z dialed Derrick number and waited as it rung. "Hello?" Derrick answered "Where you at dog?" In the Cliff Why, what's up?" "I need to chop it up with you" T.Z said "Meet me at the apartment. Your ever talk to Flex "Yeah he next to me right now" T.Z said "Is the shit true?" Derrick asked "Yeah!" "For real" Derrick said surprised. "That's what I need to holla at you about the nigga Ken Ken foul!" T.Z said "Enough said I'll meet you at the apartment!" "Derrick said ended the call.

CHAPTER 13

Flex walked through Neiman Marcus inside the Galleria Mall with Bri-Bri as if they were a in love couple. Bri-Bri had finally used her finesse skill to get Flex to front the bill on her a shopping spree. Bri-Bri walked with her hands full of shopping bags along with Flex also carrying the other bags she couldn't hold. Bri-Bri had spent close to $17,000 dollars of Flex money and the most he ever got out of her was a few hand jobs and licking her clit. Flex figured the little shopping spree should get him what he wanted. Flex didn't take it as tricking his money off he called it a small investment regardless of how he looked at it Bri-Bri still was coming out on top at the end cause she had days she gave her goodies to niggas for free but with niggas like Flex in her life she wouldn't never have to fuck for free "Oh baby look at that watch!" Bri-Bri said excitedly as she pointed at the Christian Dior watch "and it's on sale for half price 35 hundred!" Bri-Bri told him "3500 for that watch!" Flex said "Please baby I promise this is the last thing then we can leave." Bri-Bri whined knowing she was pushing it 'Aight!' Flex said as he put the shopping bags down and counted $3,500 dollars out handed it to Bri-Bri for she could pay for the watch but little did Flex know she would keep the receipt and return the watch to get a cash refund later on in the week after wearing it probably once or twice. At times she couldn't understand how T.Z even befriended a nigga like Flex. To Bri-Bri Flex and

T.Z were two niggas who had only one thing in common to her everything else they were totally opposite. Bri-Bri walked back over to Flex "Thank you baby!" she said before kissing him on the lips as he tasted her strawberry lip glass. "You ready to go now?" Flex asked ready to get back to her apartment knowing for sure that he would get to hit that ass this time. "I guess so!" she said as they headed for the mall exit. Bri-Bri came to the conclusion that she would have to give him some today if she wanted to keep draining from that well cause after spending 20grand the nigga expected more than just a thank you and she didn't want to expose her hand making him look like a complete sucker that he was plus he was working with a nice piece down there so Bri-Bri still would be winning all the way around if Flex knew how to use it. They got inside Flex new 2011 CTS Coupe painted pearl white on 22in Dub rims. Since Flex G-Wagon was in the shop getting fix from Ro shooting holes all in it and Flex didn't like driving his SLS every day or his baby mama car so he went and drop out on a Cadillac to ride in as a everyday car. Flex like the CTS cause it was low key but it spoke money at the same time. Bri-Bri also like the CTS and wondered what it would take for him to put her behind the wheel of a matching one.

Flex wasn't the only person thinking bout a new whip as T.Z rode shotgun in Derrick's BMW as they arrived at Hector's dealership. Hector had called T.Z early this morning telling him the car had arrived and bring $75,000 dollars with him he promised. T.Z he wouldn't be disappointed in the least. Both of them got out the car and Hector came out the building "Hello guys" Hector greeted them as he shook their hands. "Whats up?" They both responded "I know you have been patiently waiting but the wait is over. Follow me" Hector told them leading the way to a garage where car repairs were being done. "It just got here when I called you this morning I haven't even had a chance to drive it." Hector said excitedly "If you haven't even drove it how do you know I'm gone like it?" T.Z asked "This is how I know!" Hector said stopping at a car with a car cover over it then snatching it off revealing its Candy Fire Red paint and

unique design. "Damn!" Is all T.Z could say as he did a 360 view of the sports car "This is a Venom GT specially design by Hennessy out of Houston only 29 made, has 1,200 in horses zero to 200 in 15.9 sec. Top speed 260 mph a Bugatti Veyron can't even beat this." Hector explain T.Z open the door to the driver side and sat down on the bucket leather seat "I also had the rims specially design for this car by Hennessy not to take away any speed or torque from the car. Offset 20's on the front 22's on the back Vizzo M. Forgioto's." Hector said "Like I said but for 75 thousand you can leave with it right now. I'll set you up on a payment plan with me until the car paid off then I'll sign it over to you as a gift or should I say a donation from my company until then the car remain in the company's name with full covered insurance." Hector explain "How much a month?" T.Z asked" $25,000 a month until amount is paid in full!" Hector said "I can do that!" T.Z said. "Here's the contract between us for you to agree upon." Hector said with only his hand extended. T.Z looked at Hector realizing he wasn't speaking of a written contract but a verbal one "Word is bond!" T.Z said shaking Hector hand

143

upon agreement "A man's loyalty to his word is the most important thing for him to have." Hector said handing T.Z the car keys with his other hand. Hector walked around getting in the passenger seat "I'll meet you at your car." T.Z said to Derrick a he closed the driver door starting the car, the electronic dash lit up sky blue. T.Z use the gear shift located on the steering wheel to put the car in 1st gear to take off. T.Z eased out the garage slowly feeling the horse power through the pedals as he crept the car around to the front of the building were Derrick car was parked. T.Z left the engine growly as he got out and retrieved the black bag containing the $75,000 dollars out of the backseat of Derrick BMW. Handing it to Hector as he approached. "Thank You!" T.Z said "Anytime. Derrick let me know when you are ready to shop around" Hector said "Let me know when you get something else that can top this." Derrick said pointing at the GT Venom "You'll be the first I contact." Hector promised "Aight!" Derrick said "See you on the 1st of the month" T.Z said getting back inside the GT Venom. T.Z pulled out the lot

slowly getting a feel of the car coming directly to a red light. Derrick pulled next to T.Z on his driver side, letting down the window "I guess you the shit now?" Derrick shouted out the window "I been the shit nigga I thought you knew" T.Z shouted back out his window. They both shared a laugh Derrick nodded his head towards a middle-aged white man pulling next to T.Z passenger side in a black and red Bugatti Veyron that he just purchased from Hector dealership as well. The white man looked at T.Z with a smirk on his face then hung his arm out the window to display his Bugatti watch that comes with the new car. Derrick seen the cockiness the white man displayed thinking he was driving the fastest car on the road Derrick mouth the words "Smoke him!" T.Z as they looked at each other. T.Z revved the engine making the rpm shoot up as they waited on the light to turn green. The man caught the signal cause he started revving the Bugatti motor as well. The light changed to green both cars tires screeched as they smash the gas pedal. T.Z went from 0-60 mph in bout 2.7 seconds in second gear. The white man was right there along side as T.Z switched to third gear on a residential street going 100mph the two raced the expensive cars onto the ramp getting on 75 south. T.Z made it to the ramp first as they white man tailed him getting onto the highway. T.Z was so caught up in the race he didn't realize he was going 175mph in 5th gear but still T.Z couldn't pull away. T.Z watched the white man hit his last gear as the Bugatti jumped in front of him by an inch. T. Z switched to 6 gear sending the GT Venom rocketed to 200mph passing the white man up as he watched T.Z speed past him giving more speed T.Z held the steering wheel with two hands as he looked in the rear-view mirror of the Bugatti showing down defeated. T.Z felt the rush of driving a vehicle 200 plus mph it was a feeling that only having a lot of money can buy. T.Z touched the in-dash screen turning on the satellite radio picking up on Lil Waynes featuring Bruno Mars song "Mirror on the wall" T.Z smiled to himself thinking about how less than a year ago he was sleeping in a cell using a community shower and looking at Butt in men magazines jacking off. Now he had a loft downtown,

a bad bitch with a career and cars people dreamed of driving with a million in cash saved up. T.Z bobbed his head to Wayne as he rapped understanding the pleasure plus agony that came along with being a young nigga getting money. Only thing bout T.Z the agony he faced only motivated him to get more money. "These niggas to scared to even leave earth how they gone get to Mars! Wayne? "T.Z said to himself talking out loud about the song that played through the speakers as he drove. T.Z decided to go surprise Yvonne so he exited University Drive heading to her Condominium to show off his new car to her but T.Z got a surprise of his own as he turned on her street. T.Z pulled the car over at the top of the street. T.Z pulled the car over at the top of the street knowing she wouldn't know it was him in it. T.Z heart sunk in as he watched Yvonne stand next to a yellow Lexus IS talking to a tall slim nigga with his hair cut in a mohawk. T.Z watched as she hugged the nigga then he got his long leg ass in the little car driving off. Something about the situation just didn't seem right to T.Z as he drove off not even bothering to ask Yvonne bout what he just seen. T.Z always kept the thought in the back of his mind telling him people say all men lie T.Z believe most women lived a lie. As soon as T.Z felt Yvonne might be one of the few she shattered his dreams and lost his loyalty as respect for her and he would make sure she felt the repercussions of it. Yvonne must had telepathy and read T.Z mind cause when he got back on the highway his phone vibrated and it was her calling ("Nah you want to call a nigga!") he thought. T.Z forward the call to his voicemail. As he pictured Yvonne hugging the funny looking nigga in his mind making his blood boil but he regained his composure remembering what he told himself while in prison. ("He would never lose any sleep over a woman again!") T.Z replayed them words over again in his head. T.Z knew just the place to go to clear his head at a time like this. T.Z sent Derrick a text message telling Derrick to meet him their cause knowing his childhood friend he never refused to go where T.Z had in mind.

Flex stood up with sweat covering his body as Bri-Bri laid on her stomach with cum all over her ass and lower back. Flex had finally got to hit that ass and he made it worth it. Flex had took two Stamina RX pills on the low about 30 minutes before so when he did finally slide in he went long and strong. Bri-Bri has had her share of dicks but she had to admit she probably hadn't got fuck that good since before T.Z went to prison cause with most niggas when she got to throwing that phat ass on them they usually instantly started cumming but Flex as going pound for pound with her. Bri-Bri had so many orgasms she lost count she couldn't believe her vagina could still ache like it was. Bri-Bri could barely get up and go to the restroom to wash the cum off of her. Flex grin as he watches Bri-Bri struggle to the restroom from being sore. After almost 2 hours of straight sex she better be sore. Flex felt he had to make her suffer for waiting. When he heard the shower turn on he had to get boost for round 2 as he dug in his pants pocket that laid on the floor. He got his powder pack out and his key sitting on the edge of the bed with his back turn snorting a few hits. Bri-Bri was about to come out the restroom cause she forgot her towel but stop when she seen Flex hunch over snorting coke off the key she quietly close the door back not wanting Flex to know she seen him. Flex wasn't the first nigga she been with that use coke but that wasn't Bri-Bri choice of drug even though she smoked weed and might pop a ecstasy pill on the occasion she was against using coke, crack or heroine. She had seen the drugs ruin to many lives around here so she vowed to never try them. Bri-Bri got inside the hot shower as the hot shower eased her muscle her mind went to T.Z she wondered was he using as well since Flex and him was good friends and most homeboys damn near do the same shit. She heads the bathroom door open it as Flex entered. He pulled the shower curtain back as he stared at Bri-Bri body covered in suds as he stroked his manhood. Bri-Bri just continued to shower as Flex pleased himself. It was a weird feeling but it turned Bri-Bri on just standing there watching him masturbate to her. Bri-Bri decided to give him a little entertainment as he watched the show. She bent

over letting the shower water splash her butt then inserting two of her fingers inside of her then taking them tasting her own juices. Bri-Bri propped one leg up on the side of the tub then began to play with her clit and squeeze her nipple. Bri-Bri closed her eyes and bit on her bottom lip as she please herself. She opened her eyes as she felt Flex grab her hand making her jack him off now. Flex put his hand on the top of her head guiding her mouth down to his rock hard manhood. She squatted inside the shower as he stood on the outside receiving a head job and a head job was Bri-Bri specialty. Help from T.Z made her a beast cause every morning they woke up together before T.Z got out of bed he would make Bri-Bri give him head it became so much of a routine if she woke up before him she would just start giving him head in his sleep to get it out the way and unless she wanted to be sucking until she had lockjaw she had to get good at it to make him cum quick as possible. She was a professional slurp and swallower if you could put her head job in a bottle and put it on a shelve to sell it would sell millions. Flex hump her face as he bobbed her head faster forward and backwards side to side while cupping his balls spit was dripping from his piece and the side of her mouth. Flex had two hands on her head stroking as if her mouth was the pussy her throat matched every thrust until he pulled out as warm cum shot all over her face. She opened her mouth sticking out her tongue with her eyes close making sure all the cum was out. Bri-Bri close her mouth on the tip sucking on it double checking as she looked up at him smiling with cum on her face.

T.Z and Derrick paid and enter the gentlemen's club it was a light crowd enjoying the happy hour special. They took a seat at the table close by the stage watching the Hispanic woman on stage perform on the pole. "Can I help you guys?" the waitress wearing a referee shirt asked. T.Z eyed the light brown skin woman up and down admiring her hour glass figure "Yeah let me get some Ciroc and Nuevo mixed on ice with a six-piece wings." T.Z ordered. "Crown black and coke with some cheese sticks" Derrick ordered.

"I'll be back in a minute" she said smiling back at T.Z looking him up and down as he rocked his 8732 fit with some white low top air force ones with his jewelry shinning from the club color lights. "Damn nigga what made you want to hit the strip joint at 5 in the afternoon this usually something I do not you" Derrick said. "A nigga can't come just to chill and watch some ass and titties!" T.Z told him. "Yeah if you say so nigga!" Derrick said knowing that couldn't have been the only reason. The waitress returns with their drinks "25dollars all together" she said. "What's yo name?" T.Z asked "LaLa!" Everybody calls me. T.Z he said introducing himself extended his hand as he watched her eyes stare at his platinum bracelet covered in VVS Diamond "Nice to meet you!" she said shaking his hand. "Let me get 75dollars in singles the rest is for the bill." T.Z said giving her a hundred-dollar bill. Even though T.Z wasn't big on tricking his money he decided he might as well waste a few dollars while he was here. "Let me get some singles" Derrick said handing her two hundred dollars. As she left to go get change." I see you bout to have a good time" T.Z joked talking to Derrick "I'm already here why not!" Derrick always felt it was better to come to the strip club around this time of day cause all the stunters were still out making their money they would blow making it rain at night. Yeah Derrick and T.Z had the money to match them niggas but it didn't make any sense to waste stacks making it rain when the would get the same result at the end by only throwing a few dollars early in the day enjoying themselves. LaLa returned sitting the crisp dollar bills on the table Derrick one's still had a seal to break. "I can't have yo number before you leave" T.Z said. "I don't leave until 7:30" she said sarcastically knowing he didn't mean it that way" I guess we will be leaving together then" he told her "Maybe so!" she said walking off smiling. The strippers must have smelled the money being brought out to them cause soon LaLa walked off two dancers appeared asking them do they want a lap dance. The decline the lap dances but the women dance in front of them at their table. T.Z tossed a few dollars at the two not to impressed. "You niggas bet not be throwing away all y'all lunch money?" the

deep voice said from behind them. "Edge!" Whats good nigga?" Derrick asked dapping him up "Whats good? T.Z asked "Blessed and highly favored." Edge said pulling up a chair. "I can dig that. You must be in here collecting from yo hoes." Derrick said "Never that I don't do the strip club pimping only the track but I am on the hot pursuant for a brand-new prostitute. "Edge said T.Z shook his head listening to Edge spit his pimp talk. Edge was certified with his pimping. T.Z couldn't deny that Edge keep at least 10 hoes in his stable and if that wasn't enough proof five platinum chains hanging from his neck and 4 rings on each hand covered in diamonds with a six-row bracelet and a Audemars Piguet Watch. Edge was in his mid 30's and had been having cash since the 90's when T.Z was still playing sandlot football. T. Z had respect for the man and his hustle but the pimping thing never impressed T.Z. He always thought them type niggas were just to scary to get in the trenches of the street themselves but Derrick on the hand he loved hearing the fly talk and pimp story "I haven't seen you in a minute Edge where you been at?" Derrick asked "You know traveling the globe like a true pimp suppose to. I had a one year tour from Florida up to Jersey across to Vegas and Cali. I just came to visit my peeps then I'm back off probably to D.C or Memphis just depends." Edge said. "How is Rome doing. I seen him at my sister funeral but I didn't get to speak to him." T.Z said "Same shit still wasting time with the dope game. I'm sorry to hear bout yo fam to "Edge said "Shid nigga's like us ain't wasting no time in the dope game money is plentiful out here in these streets." Derrick said "I can't knock yo hustle if you eating then eat greedy then youngin" Edge told him. The three sat and talked as LaLa brung their food and more drinks as different dancers came over and performed for them. Edge was serious about his pimping so he refused to throw any money at the strippers his words was "Why waste any money on paying one bitch when I got 13 paying me tricking is against my religion" That still didn't stop T.Z or Derrick though. T.Z looked at his cellphone checking the time "7:15pm" T.Z was ready to go plus the night shift was bout to come in. "You ready to go?" T.Z asked Derrick "Hell yeah!" he said

seeing he was out of ones "I got to get ready for tonight anyway" Edge said as he stood up. T.Z felt the alcohol soon as he stood up getting light headed. Derrick as well they headed towards the exit. The sun was setting when they step outside they didn't have to walk far cause all three cars were valeted in the front. "This you in the Rolls Royce Drop head White on White?" T.Z asked "Yeah you already know a pimp got to ride clean" Edge bragged "What y'all in?" Edge asked "I'm in the 760Li!" Derrick stated "I got a 750Li money green on 22in Ashanti" Edge told him. T.Z hit the auto-crank for his GT Venom making it growl as it idle Edge smiled at T.Z "GT Venom" I see you niggas doing y'all thug thistle I like to see that. Let me know that y'all entire generations ain't all fucked up!" Edge said A few dancers came out the club dressed "Time for me to work youngins" Edge said leaving them as he walked over to the women. T.Z was on a mission of his own waiting on LaLa to come out. When he seen her walk out the exit doors he approached her. " I see its 7:40 now!" T.Z said looking at his Rolex "You must have had to many drinks thinking Im leaving with you." she said "Our not enough!" he said She grabbed his cellphone off his holder on his waist and put her number in his phone. "Call me and we can discuss it" she said handing him his phone back then walking to her car. The phone began vibrating as he held the phone he seen it was Yvonne calling again but he forwarded the call to voicemail again. He still wasn't in the mood to speak with her yet. Him and Derrick got back in their cars to leave the club. T.Z was already spinning from the alcohol so he went home as Derrick went to one of his lady's crib.

CHAPTER 14

Derrick had it all set up the would be the second time Ken Ken come and re-up from him even though Ken Ken was the type of nigga that would spend plenty money and made sure it kept coming to you. He had to be dealt with the decision had already been made amongst the three of them. Flex was apart of the crew and if a nigga threatens one nigga life then it's just like he threatened all three so the nigga had to be handled regardless of how much money he would spend. Derrick drove his 760Li to the meeting spot in Oak Cliff along with 5 kilos and 10pounds of weed in the trunk of his car as T.Z trailed him not to far behind in a stolen Gray Honda minivan with Flex in the van with him. A homicide was about to transpire because of some cooked-up story Flex made up cause he was too afraid to admit the truth. Flex figured soon as as this shit was over this could be another one of his skeletons he hung in the closet and wouldn't have to worry about it coming back to haunt him later. The sun was starting to set as Derrick pulled into the shopping center parking lot. Ken Ken was parked at the back of the parking lot in a Nissan Altima that Derrick already knew he was in. This time Ken Ken had somebody else in the car with him that Derrick didn't know. Derrick parked behind the Altima leaving his

BMW engine on as he went to the trunk taking the two duffel bags out the trunk. Ken also got out the car with a bag in his hand. "Is this all the cash!" Derrick asked

as he sat his bag on the hood of his car looking inside Ken bag observing the stack of money "You already know. This is all my shit!" Ken Ken asked looking inside the other two bags. "You see it don't you!" Derrick told him. Ken Ken did a mental count making sure it was all there before he zipped the bag back up. "Get at me!" Derrick said tossing the bag full of money in the back seat of him BMW then getting inside. Ken Ken also got inside his car to leave. He trailed behind Derrick coming to a four way intersection stop sign not paying attention to the minivan coming across the front of him until he seen the sliding side door open "Tat, tat , tat, tat, tat, tat, tat, tat" the .223 bullets flipped out the barrel of the AR-15 that had a hundred round drum attach to the bottom of it. Ken Ken and his passenger ducked down in the seat as the masked man fired repeatedly into the front windshield. Flex counted squeezing the trigger on the weapon as Ken smashed the gas pedal swerving right into a fire hydrant sending water gushing into the air. Flex jumped out the van with a adrenaline rush. Firing into the driving side window until there were only pieces of the window left. Water from the hydrant rain down n Flex as he opened the driver door. Ken Ken laid slump over with blood soaking into his clothes. Flex looked at the passenger with his head laid on the deployed airbag also bleeding. Flex seen the man back raise taking breath His lat breath as Flex fired a fatal head shot in him and one to Ken Ken just in case. "Tat, tat" Flex fired two shots at a approaching car quickly making them reverse. He opened the back door grabbing one bag tossing the straps around his shoulder then carrying the other running back to the van wet from the hydrant water. T.Z made the tires screech as he took off with the sliding door open as Flex jumped in

Lil D was wondering what was taking Ken and nephew so long to get there it had been over two hours since they left and every-time Lil D tried to call him they phone would go straight to voicemail. He knows they only went up the street to meet Derrick so what could be taking so long. Lil D got worried thinking they

might have got rolled by the laws and got locked up that could be the only explanation to the situation. Lil D got in his BMW and drove up there just to check. His stomach drop when he seen all the DPD cars and the street blocked off. Lil D assume the laws had jammed Ken Ken and Lil Loc up. Even through the flashing lights in the night every time scene didn't set right with Lil D. From years of experience in the streets he could tell something bigger went on then a few bricks being found the biggest give away was the local media tryna get a story. Lil D hit his hazard light parking on the side of the road getting out. A she got closer realization came to him when he seen Ken Ken Altima covered in bullets and detectives huddle up talking as the A&E cameras captured them investigating what happen for the television show First 47. Lil D didn't need to question to know what happen it was obvious were just murdered at a stop sign why it happen didn't matter to Lil D cause regardless he was gone make sure the nigga responsible reaped the same fate. ("Derrick!") Lil D thought as he ducked out the crowd going back to his car. Lil D would call his sister to break the bad news and she could come speak with the detectives cause he had too much illegal shit going on to be talking to the police about anything.

Flex was laid back with his hands folded behind his head and his 9mm next to him on Bri-Bri bed looking at the ceiling fan rotate, thinking about how he just got away with murking Ken not really caring ow he then put Derrick in the cross if Lil D had a clue Ken was going to meet Derrick for a transaction. Flex figured long as his problem was out the way shit was good and if things got that bad for Derrick all they had to do was murk Lil D as well. The value of like wasn't worth more then a Mexican food stamp to Flex now knowing he possessed money and power. "Here you go baby" Bri-Bri said passing the lit blunt to him as she sat down next to him. Flex took a long pull inhaling the hydro smoke slowly releasing the smoke into the air. Bri-Bri kissed him on his exposed chest "The streets are your baby so don't stress!" Bri-Bri said between kisses and

stroking his ego. "You right the streets are mine!" Flex said "So am I!" Bri-Bri said Yeah you my bitch! Flex said "That's right baby I'm Flex bitch!" she said working her way down his stomach as he unbuckled his pants guiding her head down as he continues smoking the blunt.

"I know we solved one problem but we might create another one." Derrick told T.Z "You think the nigga Lil D had a clue Ken was coming to meet up with you." "I can't really say for sure I just knew that would be the only way to get Ken Ken without missing." I can dig it!" T.Z and Flex decided to let Derrick keep all the profit from the murder since Lil D owed Flex Four more bricks he fronted him which Derrick already concluded he would have to charge to the game after Ken Ken got knocked off it would be too risky tryna judge rather or not Lil D know

Derrick played a role in the murder so Derrick would just take it as if Lil D know just to be safe. Derrick could tell Flex was a little upset about not being able to get a cut but after T.Z broke down the situation and if it wasn't for him the shit wouldn't have transpired" So take the nigga Ken Ken head as our cut!" T.Z told him closing the discussion. Derrick was they homeboy so why should they trip about him getting a few extra stacks if that the case Derrick should have charge Flex for setting the nigga Ken Ken up. "Yo boy Flex act like he was heated when you told me to keep the cash and the drugs" Derrick said. "I ain't sweating Flex ma'fucking ass he just tryna be greedy, we fam so shouldn't no greedy shit be in the mix of us he now that if he don't like it then oh well sue me!" T. Z said "You hell nigga!" Derrick said laughing "Anyway whats the business on this Lil D nigga anyway where he be at in the Cliff?" Just in case the nigga do become a problem." T.Z said "The nigga from fifty second street he still be over there and he be over there off Sunnyvale and shit." Derrick said "Bight nigga long hair mini Slim Thug looking nigga!" T.Z said "Yeah thats him!" Derrick said "I was locked up with a few of his young niggas they had pictures of the nigga Crip Nigga!" Hell, yeah thats him!" Derrick agreed "Yeah I heard the nigga get full

of that juice and act a fool nigga say he bout that pistol play real street nigga" T.Z said "Yeah he a cool nigga thats why I'm hate to have to murk him cause he gone play by the rules of the jungle!" Derrick explain "Eat or get ate!" T.Z said knowing what Derrick meant "Stay on point until the shit is handle!" T.Z added "Believe that!" Derrick said

It was true everything Lil D had seen was just verified with the phone call he just received back from his sister his nephew and cousin had just been murdered. Real tear drops ran on top of the three he had tattoo under his left eye. His nephew was only 17 years old even though he played the game of a grown man and suffered cause it he was still a lil boy in Lil D eyes. Lil D scrolled in his phone until he got to Derricks name pressing talk on the touch screen Galaxy phone he put the phone on speaker as it rung. Derrick answer and play dumb founded are not even answer at all giving his self away cause Lil D still owed him for the bricks so why wouldn't he answer. "Hello?" Derrick answered. "What's up?" Lil D asked listen for any signs of guilt. "You tell me nigga" Derrick said "I got that lil change I owe you want to meet me and get it." Lil D asked hoping he took the bait. "You a O.G and I'm a Y.B in this shit gone be a O.B so enough with the bullshit we both know the business that means we both know the consequences in this shit. I'm ready to face mine!" Derrick spat "I hope so cause you will nigga!"

Lil D said "To let you know it wasn't nothing personally against you Derrick said. The kid was 17 everything personal now! Lil D said between clench teeth "It is what it is nigga!" Derrick said ended the call. Lil D had to respect Derrick for not playing pussy but would give him a closed casket for being too tough as well.

Derrick ended the call looking over at T.Z since the phone was on speaker T.Z heard the conversation. When Derrick heard Lil D tell him to come pick up the cash he owed he knew right then Lil D already figured the shit out and Derrick felt he was

too much of a real nigga to play the I don't know what you talking about games. Derrick would put a bullet in his own head before he caught that pussy scared of any nigga. Nigga like Lil D whenever they sense fear they would prey on it. Derrick laid all his cards on the table letting it be known ain't no fear on his end. "Fuck the nigga he gone have to get the business to T.Z said "He is gone get the business" Derrick said with Venom coming from his words "Tonight!" Derrick added T. Z dialed Flex number to see where he went. "Hello?" Flex answered "Where you at?" Flex lied "Come to the apartment like yesterday we got business to go take care of" T.Z told him "I'll be there!" Flex said ended the call. "We gone need a car" T.Z told Derrick "We can crank one on the way." Derrick said "Yeah that would be better instead of driving out there in a stolen car with straps. T.Z said "Yeah I know where his trap at on Fifty second, more then likely that where he at or on his way too!" Derrick said. "We can stop by one of my spots and pick up a chopper since its closer" T.Z said T.Z hated to do reckless shit in the heat of the moment cause little mistake could be costly but his dog was ready to ride out and if the situation was vice versa Derrick wouldn't hesitate to ride out with T.Z so if something did go wrong then they was prepared to suffer the repercussion.

Flex buckled up his pants as he stood up. Bri-Bri wipe the spit from her mouth as she just finished giving him some head. Flex put his tank top on tucking the 9mm inside his waistline. Flex understood what that call meant shit was about to get ugly. Yeah Flex was still a little hot about not getting a piece of the cash but he was the cause behind all the bullshit so he couldn't back out now plus Flex enjoyed the power of having somebody else life in his hand regardless of why. Flex was mentally fucked up something about busting a nigga head just excited him. Flex got inside his CTS started the car as Jezzy "Thug Motivation 103' CD Played. Flex took out his powder pack to hit a line needing the high to take him to the next level. Flex snorted 3 lines still not satisfied but he had to go meet up with T.Z and Derrick. Flex sprinkle a little coke

inside a blunt before he rolled it experimenting Flex fired up the lovely as he drove off.

Lil D was on full alert as he rode shot gun in the 88 LTD Crown Victoria. His homeboy Clue was behind the wheel as Clack and Ced rode in the backseat armed with SK's. Lil D gripped the handle of his .45 Desert Eagle hoping they ran across Derrick as they crept through the streets of the grove. Clue drove in and out of every set apartment complex they seen hoping they spotted Derrick BMW. They were even asking niggas do they know Derrick just to find out where he be at. Lil D hit the sherman cigarette laced in juice blowing the smoke out towards the cracked window. "Pull up on them right there" Lil D said pointed at two chicks who couldn't be older than 18. "Y'all know a nigga name Derrick drive a white 760Li? Lil D asked speaking slowly, the girls looked like a zombie "Naw" they answered in unison. Lil D let the window back up as Clue drove away. Lil D regretted himself for being so lazy every time him and Derrick had to meet up instead of Lil D coming to him, He would always just meet Derrick somewhere instead. Lil D couldn't have known one day they would be nemesis instead of business associates so he never had a reason to wonder where Derrick stayed at.

On the opposite side of the city in Oak Cliff, Derrick, T.Z and Flex was also on the hunt for blood as they sat behind the tint of a stolen Delta 98 also armed with choppers and pistols watching the blue and white house with burglar bars on it. Derrick had only been to the house once before watching the traffic pulling up to the house and leaving in less then 60 seconds verified to him that his was the same trap house belonging to Lil D but Lil D kept somebody working the spot 24/7 365 to make sure his money stayed flowing in constantly. "I say we just air the house out I'm sure that will make the nigga come out if her in there." Flex said. "We don't need no extra attention we gone murk this nigga and mash out the neighborhood already on fire from that shit early with Ken Ken." Derrick said "This nigga need to bring his bitch ass on." Flex

said impatiently "Nigga stop crying!" T.Z told him. Flex couldn't sit still in the backseat skitzing from the lovely smoke before he met up with them. "Nigga you acting like you paranoid or sitting on ants back there nigga" Derrick said to Flex cause he kept on moving in the backseat. "Naw nigga I just got to piss thats all!" Flex lied saying "Ah! This nigga nervous now he got to go pee pee now. Need me to bring some huggies next time? "Derrick said joking "Fuck you nigga!" I'll be right back" Flex said getting out the car walking by the trunk to pee Flex needed the breeze from the night air cause he had started perspiring and for some reason he couldn't be still. Flex was geeking for real. Flex began urinating behind the car in the street. Flex pushed harder tryna hurry up and finish as he seen a set of headlights turn onto the street headed to him. The unidentified vehicle stopped about 50 feet away making Flex cautious as he reached for the 9mm tucked in the back part of his waistline. The spotlight that sat on the front of the car instantly turned on surprising him. "Pow! Pow! Pow!" Flex reaction made him fire at the car immediately the Cherry's and Berry's light flashed on top of the car identifying itself. "What the fuck!" T.Z shouted as him and Derrick ducked down looking backwards hearing the gunshots. Flex had just fucked up he shot at the laws it was too late for him to turn back now.

Pow, Pow, Pow! Flex fired 3 more shots at the car as heard the car crank up Pow, Pow! he fired two more times jumping inside the car "GO NIGGA GO!" Flex shouted. Derrick smash the gas pedal on the old school Delta 98 burning off "What the fuck you doing nigga?" T.Z shouted looking back tryna see was the police car in pursuit of them. Flex didn't respond as he turned around wondering the same thing. Derrick sped down the residential streets turning on backstreets tryna get back to T. Z Benz that wasn't parked too far away on Fordham. "Turn, Turn nigga right here" T.Z shouted as Derrick made a right turn swerving the big Delta 98. Flex continue to look back wondering if he hit the officer cause they weren't being chase. Derrick parked behind T.Z Benz as all three of them jump out "Leave the straps!" T.Z said "What?" Flex said carrying the chopper "nigga leave the fucking

guns" T.Z demanded. Flex and Derrick wiped the finger prints off with their shirts then tossed them back inside the Delta. "Hurry the fuck up" T.Z growled hearing the helicopter in the distance. Derrick got in the passenger seat. T.Z drove off tryna get away from the stolen car. "What the fuck you shot at the laws for?" Derrick asked "I didn't know it was the fucking laws until after I already shot!" They could hear sirens coming from every direction as they fussed. "Chill, Chill!" T.Z shouted as a police car zoomed headed towards them. T.Z looked in his rearview mirror as the police car passed him then suddenly the brake light lit up. "Fuck!" They U-turning!" T.Z said "Dip off on them!" Flex said "Hell naw, that's to suspicious just relax nigga.!" T.Z said as the police car was right behind them more then likely running the tags. T.Z had license and insurance and the car was clean so all he had to do was remain calm and don't panic. "Fuck!" Flex shouted as the police turn the Cherry's and

Berry's on signal T.Z to pull over "Just chill nigga don't panic, we on our way to the loft coming from hoes house Derrick know. T.Z coached them getting prepared for the police officer questions. T.Z came to a stop rolling down his window as two officers approached with their hands on their weapons. The black officer went to the driver side as the white dude took the passenger side both shining flash lights through the tint tryna see inside "Where you gentlemen headed this late?" the black officer asked. "Home!" T.Z answered squinting his eyes from the flashlight "License and insurance" the black officer said "Slow!" The black officer shouted as T.Z reached into the center console getting his license and insurance handing it to the office. "Step out Mr. Zonders" the black officer said. T. Z could see the helicopter circling the neighborhood with the spotlight on. Flex sat in the backseat praying and hoping they got away. "Step back here for me." the black officer motion toward the police car. T.Z remain calm as he went along with the familiar routine. "Is there a problem?" T.Z asked "I'll just like to ask you a few questions that all" the black officer stated. "What's that?" T.Z asked "Are they any drugs are weapons on you are inside the vehicle?" the officer asked "No Sir!" T.Z said "Is it okay if I search

the car then?" the officer asked "I'm sort of in a rush to get home my girl be on that bullshit I ain't tryna hear her mouth tonight. I know you understand being married and all." T.Z commented looking at the officer wedding band. T.Z heard the walkie talkie "We have located the suspect vehicle on Fordham drive." "Copy that!" the black officer responded back. T.Z glanced in the air at the helicopter hovering over a certain position with the spot light on it. "Yeah I understand make sure you go straight home to her." the officer said handing T.Z back his information then waving to his partner to leave. T.Z walked back and got in his car as the two officers did the same "What they say?" Flex asked "To stay away from stupid mutherfuckers who like to shoot at them" T.Z spat as he pulled off. That was a close call for sure all their shit could have been jeopardized behind a simple mistake T.Z didn't have a clue what the fuck was going on in Flex head but whatever it was couldn't be tolerated at all. "My bad T dog!" Flex tried apologizing now that he had sober up out of fear. "Whatever my nigga!" T.Z said brushing him off. Derrick shook his head thinking about the fuck up Flex just made. They all have had their share of doing some crazy dumb shit but Flex took the cake with this one. ("This nigga tryna get us for sure lethal injection!") T.Z thought looking in the rearview at Flex! ("Damn I tripped the fuck out I honestly didn't know who the fuck that was creeping up on us, better to shoot first ask questions later") Flex thought as he stared out the window. This had ended as a hell of a day to much of hell if you asked him.

Lil D ended the call, he had just received a call from X-man one of the young niggas he had running the trap house. X-man just informed him on they had to close up shop for the night. He wasn't exactly for sure what happen but somebody got shot on the same block and police was everywhere on a man hunt knocking on people doors they even had the ghetto bird in the air. X-man told him all he could see was a old school Caprice or Delta burning off after hearing the shots fired. Lil D wonder what was going on that street was one of the worse streets in the hood but Lil D practically owned that block he made sure his neighbors were all taking care of that's why he never had to worry about no nosey neighbors calling the police. If any gunshots popped off on that block they were coming from Lil D or his people. And if anybody else was to pop some shit off they best had informed Lil D cause when the laws come that means his money stop. Stopping his money was something niggas shouldn't do. Now he had another problem he had to go handle but how X-man explained the scene it would have to wait until tomorrow morning before he could get the scope on what happen and who did it.

CHAPTER 15

"Bang, Bang, Bang" T.Z jumped up out his sleep wondering who could be at his door banging on it at 8:25 in the morning. "Bang, Bang, Bang!" the banging continued as T.Z got the .40cal out he top drawer then approaching the door slowly. "Bang, Bang, Bang" T.Z peeped through the peephole "What the fuck?" T.Z said looking at the angry Yvonne. He unlocked the door then slightly open it "Move!" Yvonne said pushing the door all the way open bumping into T.Z ignoring the pistol he held and heading straight for the bedroom. He heard Yvonne checking the closet and bathroom even going into the other bedroom and the upstairs living room. "Where the fuck is she Tyrone?" She barked looking at him standing in only a silk pair of polo boxers and socks with the pistol in his hand." How did you get upstairs?" He asked her calmly, that doesn't matter where the fuck is the bitch that got you on some bullshit!" She spat "It doesn't matter cause you just got somebody fired from their job and second ain't no bitches in here so you can leave if you satisfied now." T.Z said as he waved his hand towards the door. "Oh yeah!" Thats how you playing the game now." Yvonne yelled twisting her face up. "You started the games so live with it" he said "Nigga I ain't start shit!"

166

Yvonne barked stepping in his face. "I ain't got no time for this it's too damn early in the morning" T.Z said tryna walk past her "I knew you were just like the rest of these no good ass niggas. Yvonne said pushing T.Z out the way

as she stormed out the door leaving it wide open. T.Z closed and locked the door behind her returning back to his bedroom sitting the pistol on top of the dresser then flopping down on his king size bed "FUCK!" T.Z said out loud to himself hoping today wouldn't end up being another fucked up day. He stared at the lights in the ceiling fan thinking if he made the right decision by letting Yvonne leave without questioning her about what he saw. T.Z was to frustrated to go back to sleep so he decided to take a hot shower and get dress then hit the D-town streets early morning.

Detective Simmons sat in his unmarked Impala drinking coffee and eating doughnut holes. He wondered why the sexy lawyer woman was upset as she mumbled cuss words to herself leaving out the building. Simmons had his binocular aimed closely on her reading her lips only words Simmons could make out were "Bitch ass nigga!" Simmons laughed thinking T.Z must have just got caught with another woman that could be the only reason she was furious leaving his building. It had been a few days since Simmons watched T.Z especially since after almost blowing his cover last time so he had to back off not to draw any suspicion to himself. Simmons had been outside T.Z building since 7 in the morning. Simmons had contacted a friend of his that work vice and narcotics to see if any of the three men was on the DPD radar but they weren't Simmons figured they have must have been low-key in the drug market cause by the expensive cars and lofts they stayed in he was for sure they were making plenty of money to catch the narcotics division attention. Simmons swallowed the doughnut hole quickly as the star of the show pulled out the garage in his Camaro. Simmons hurried and started his car to trail T.Z as he pulled into the downtown traffic headed to highway 35

Yvonne couldn't believe the way T.Z had just started acted. Yeah Yvonne expected niggas to be on bullshit at time for no apparent reason but T.Z wasn't the typical nigga not what she thought anyway but she proved to be wrong. Yvonne as even ashamed of herself for going over his crib and causing a scene the way she did

that wasn't her style at all. Maybe her feelings is deeper then she thought for T.Z but Yvonne refused to beg any nigga to be with her cause it was a half billion niggas out there who would love to have a chance with he so Yvonne wasn't gone sit around and cry over one nigga. Bet not never have before and never will. Yvonne paid to park in the lot of the Frank Crowley Courthouse as she got out her BMW carrying her Louis Vuitton briefcase the attorney worked as a paralegal for had an important hearing this morning. A client that she represented name Kenneth McDonald had been charged with 3 counts of aggravated assault with a deadly weapon causing serious bodily injury had a grand jury indictment hearing proceeding. Kenneth was out on bail fighting the charges that he claims he didn't commit. Yvonne walked into criminal district court #6 as the attorney sat next to Kenneth whispering to him before the proceeding began "Hi you guys doing?" Yvonne greeted them as she took a seat in the open chair next to Kenneth. "Hi you doing Yvonne?" the attorney greeted back "What's good?" Kenneth asked looking at Yvonne with lust in his eyes. ("Damn why all the bad guys got to look so damn good!" Yvonne thought looking at Kenneth as she unlocked her briefcase to get ready for the hearing proceeding.

"I'm telling you my nigga she came banging on my door at 7 o'clock she swore I had a bitch in there with me. "Ha, Ha nigga I told you nigga ya'll was in love cause only a female in love gone do some shit like that!" Derrick explain "I can't stunt I got strong feelings for her but that the shit I seen the other day kind of knocked her out the box with me I might still fuck but that's about it." T.Z said. "Nigga you ain't never even asked her with the deal was on the shit anyway. "Derrick said "Cause I ain't tryna hear no fairy tales." T.Z said. "Nigga don't you fuck other hoes?" Derrick asked "Hell yeah!" Okay so why you tripping then?" Derrick told him "Nigga she can't do what I do ya dig!" T.Z said. "My nigga its 2012 bitches doing just as much as any nigga if not more." Derrick said "Well not more then this nigga!" T.Z protested. "At least call her and get all the details. Peep I was planning on taking Pauline on a trip you

know get away for about 2 weeks what's up with Yvonne she might want to come with you" Derrick said "Nigga did you just not hear me if I go anywhere I'm going solo-dolo and nigga let me find out you running from Lil D!" T.Z joked saying "nigga you got me fucked up!" Derrick spat "I'm just bullshitting but where you planning on going?" T.Z asked "Hawaii!" Derrick said. "Damn I can dig that one!" T.Z said "I mean what the use of having or getting money if you can't enjoy some of it" Derrick said "I feel you. I still ain't fo so about Yvonne going but I'll think about it. You talked to Flex about it. T.Z said "After last night hell naw!" Derrick said as T.Z laughed "I'll think about it though!" T.Z said "Aight let me know the business cause I want to leave by the first of the month!" Derrick sad. "Aight!" T.Z said ended the call. T.Z parked in front of the trap house that he took over after Roxy died that he still had the two ex-hoes working in. T.Z walked towards the front door with a backpack hanging off his right shoulder the front door and burglar bars were opening as he got closer "What's good baby girl?" T.Z spoke to the bright skin woman with a lace front wig and a hour glass figure nickname Asia cause her eyes were always low like a Asian. "I'm Gucci T!" How you doing?" she said giving him a hug "Tryna get at this cash!" he said as she closed the door behind "I heard that!" she said "Where Kasha at?" he asked taking a seat on the leather sofa "Her ass in the room still sleep" Asia said. T.Z stood up and went to the bedroom where Kasha was knock out sleep in the queen size bed her T-Shirt was pulled up above her waist exposing her phat red ass cheeks in the G-String. T.Z eased up on her as she snored lightly "Smack!" T.Z slapped Kasha ass cheeks bruising it "Damn Asia wh-" Kasha caught herself realizing Asia wasn't the culprit behind the ass smack "I told you I was gone whoop that ass" T.Z said smiling "You know I like that freaky shit!" Kasha admitted biting her bottom lip seductively looking at T.Z half awake. Before Kasha actually ever laid eyes on T.Z she had been infatuated with the guy Roxy spoke so highly about then when she finally met him she really couldn't resist him. T.Z would tease Kasha but nothing more even though Kasha was pretty with

a ass like that Pinky the pornstar. T.Z kept his hormones in check with it came to her. Being a ex-hoe Kasha was use to niggas wanting to dick her down on sight and by any means necessary but not T.Z he passed the self-control the normal nigga didn't have and she believe that was what made her want him even more. "Wake yo ass up you ain't bout to sleep all day!" T.Z said as she put her face back in the pillow "Smack!" "Umm..." Kasha moaned into the pillow as he slaps her exposed butt cheek again "Get up!" Kasha was beautiful. He have thought about taking her up on her offer for a sexual escapade but Kasha and Asia were certified trap stars so T.Z refuse to let his personal feelings end up effecting his business cause they did numbers trapping out the house. He didn't want Kasha or Asia to think since he was sticking dick in one of them they could start coming up short or start slacking on their grind. T.Z was serious when he vowed money over bitches during his prison sentence "Come to the living room I got something for y'all!" T.Z told them excited the room. T. Z lit up a freshly rolled blunt on the sofa. Kasha walked out the room in the oversize T-shirt and panties with a stack of cash in her hand "Here's your money daddy!" Kasha said handing him the cash pretending as if she was paying her pimp. "Keep playing!" T.Z mumbled with the blunt hanging from his lap as he counted the money with two hands "Let me help you out!" Kasha said taking the blunt out his mouth and flopping down next to him "Yeah thanks nigga!" Y'all something else!" T you need to gone head a punish that hoe with the dick so she can calm down." Asia said not minding if T.Z punished her with the dick as well either before or after he hit Kasha it didn't matter to her she had shared dick with Kasha before and they never had a problem. "Naw she ain't ready maybe when lil one get older." T.Z said making excuses T.Z was sure if he chose to he could have a threesome right now if he wanted to cause even Asia ass isn't as phat as Kasha she was still a dime. A stranger could be fooled and they think they wore simple girls and wife them just off they beauty alone. T.Z just flipped through the bills not counting all of it trusting the girls to give him 15 racks as always. T.Z removed a zip lock bag with 4 1/2

ounces of hard and 4 1/2 of soft and 5 pounds in separate bags "I need 12thousand off this!" T.Z said sitting the drugs on the table knowing they would make a little extra but he did that to all his workers just on GP when people had something to profit off they seem to work harder. "We'll be finished with this in about 3 or 4 days tops" Kasha said blowing the smoke in the air "Hell yeah!" Asia agreed "Good the quicker the better!" T.Z said grabbing his blunt back out Kasha mouth before she smoked before all of it. "T when you go stop bullshitting a sell me the Camaro I'm tired of driving that bitch ass Ford focus!" Asia complained "Girl you already know that's my everyday car I ain't tryna get rid of it but I might can help you get one." T.Z told her Oh for real come on T you already know I love them Camaros" Asia said excitedly motion like had had her hand on the wheel driving. "Yeah give me a couple of days and I'll let you know the business. How much you got saved up? He asked curious "Bout 34 stacks" Asia said "Damn girl you been stacking" T.Z admitted "Hell yeah best to believe it "Asia said How much you got? He asked Kasha "Bout 28 thousand" she said smiling T.Z knew they wasn't lying cause all they did was trap 24/7 hardly ever went out did each hair. The rent and utility bills were paid off the dope money the house made so where else would they money be going? "I'm proud of y'all real nigga shit!" T.Z told them "For real!" they said amazed cause their pimp use to always tell them they were to fucking dumb to manage money that's why they needed him. So, to hear a compliment gave them self confidence "Yeah for real. Now y'all start bagging that shit up its cash to be made T.Z instructed. T.Z watched Asia break down the crack ounces into fifty's, quarters, twenties and dime rocks as he worked the razor blade skillfully. While Kasha made up ponder pack weighting 0.4 grams that would sell for ten dollars a piece the girls had got so good at the shirt only time they needed a scale was for 8 balls and up their eye ball game was accurate T.Z noticed as he dropped a powder pack on the digital scale then a couple rocks. T.Z help sack up the weed as they continued doing that. "Somebody coming!" T.Z said looking at the monitor that displayed four

different angles of the outside of the house. Asia grabbed the Smith Western 9mm off the table heading to the front door to meet the customer. "What's up?" Asia asked the young-looking white dude "Let me get a zone of that corn!" he said sticking the money through the hole in the gate. Asia made sure all $120 dollars was there counting the money "Hold up!" she said closing the door back. T.Z had heard the young dude so he was already weighting out the 28 grams of weed. Most niggas in the trap would be a little cautious bout serving the young white boy but out here in North Dallas these was they little type of ma'fuckers that stayed coming through on a regular. T.Z handed her the zone of weed in a sandwich bag then she went to back to the door to serve him. T.Z watched the monitor as the white boy left could have sworn he was tripping again as the familiar car pass by on the screen. T.Z sat with the lady's sacking up the weed for about another 45minutes as the morning traffic came to get their morning dose of whatever it was they got high on. When T.Z seen that same car parked at the end of the street on the monitor it really caught his attention this time from a different angle.

Asia where yo car at?" T.Z inquired "In the garage!" she said Let me see yo keys!" he said as she gave them to him. T.Z wanted to make sure of something as he got inside Asia Blue 01 Ford Focus pulling out the garage in the alley. He drove around to the front of the house driving right past the unmarked Impala undetected because of the tint on the focus "Bitch Ass Dick!" T.Z said as he drove right past the front of the house back around to the garage. T.Z was right that was the same Impala that he seen at the furniture store but this time he seen who it was Detective Simmons. T.Z assume he had to follow him to know where he was unless the nigga had a tracker on his car can't underestimate these krackers. At least T.Z knew it wasn't the DEA or FBI only local. T.Z had to leave the spot cause to much traffic would come and with Dick outside watching he would for sure have enough say-so to get swat a warrant to hit the place for drug distribution T.Z hated to have him follow him but he had no choice. T.Z told the girls he would catch up later with them to pick up the

money they just gave him. He kept the information to himself not wanting to alert them. T.Z was right cause soon as he got into traffic he spotted the Impala trailing him from a distance. T.Z was at a standstill he couldn't just pull next to the detective and say hey stop following me!" and he couldn't just set the nigga up to run straight into a trap or could he. (I'm on some Flex shit now!") T.Z thought to himself now wondering how long had the detective been trailing him and what all have he seen. T.Z made the RPM on the dash board shoot up as he smashed the gas pedal down getting on I-635 headed south. He dipped in and out of between cars hoping to gain enough distance on Simmons. T.Z watched his mirrors as he gain distance doing 115mph taking a risk knowing police sit on the side of the highway this time of morning shooting their radar guns looking for people speeding. He was blessed this morning cause there were no police posted. He made a quick exit on Lake June Road.

Detective Simmons did his best to keep up without getting to close and being notice. Simmons didn't know if the youngster just drove crazy cause he was in a rush or realized he was being followed. Whichever one it didn't matter cause when T.Z made the last-minute exit crossing over three lanes it was to late for Simmons to exit without causing a massive collision pile up behind him. Simmons had to take the exit which was Elam Rd hoping he could cut into him. Simmons use his training remembering most people are creatures of habit and routine so Simmons headed over to the apartment complex he followed T.Z to that one day he meet up with his accomplices.

T.Z hadn't seen the Impala in the last two and half miles so he figured he exited at the last-minute trick worked. T.Z phone vibrated on his hip as he drove still checking his rearview being cautious "Hello?" he answered "What's good nigga?" the deep voice asked "In traffic what's happening Slick?" T.Z asked seeing the caller ID "A couple of my lil niggas came up on some heat last night they tryna get rid of for the low low. I know niggas like us

there's never been a such thing of having too much heat so you were the first person I call." Slick said. "Where you at?" T.Z "At my spot in the East" Slick said "I'm on my way" T.Z said. "Bet!" Slick said ended the call. That was exactly what T.Z needed to hear cause the way shit been going lately he would need all the ammunition he could come across instead of going to the apartment T.Z headed over to Slick spot.

T.Z parked in the driveway behind Slick Red 04 Cadillac DTS on Chrome 24in Dub Floaters with a Red lip around the rims. T.Z walked to the front door as a brown skin nigga let him in. His name K.P., K.P was one of the niggas Slick had working for him. Slick sat around a fold out table along with three other young niggas who T.Z never seen before "What's good T.Z?" Slick asked dapping him up. "Slow motion!" T.Z said as he eyed all the different variety of weapons that were laid out on the table next to each other. "These my three lil nigga's Slick introduced them with no name including. "Y'all tryna get rid of these?" T.Z asked and these!" Slick said opening a duffel bag packed with guns ("DAMN") T.Z thought. The lil niggas had to hit a lick on a gun store or pawn shop to have all them weapons and they looked brand new. T.Z did an estimate of how many guns it was total it had to be probably around 25 guns from .380, .38, 9mm, .40, .45, 5.7, AR-15, MAC-90 and one desert eagle 50cal and .357 snug nose and T.Z favorite .44 Bulldog. "Fuck the 380 if I only get six shots I need all six to be lethal shot ya dig" T.Z explain picking up the .44 bulldog examining it remembering the replica he use on RedMack. "Give us $3500 you can take everything even the .380 one of the youngsters said I got 2000 and a zip of hard." T.Z said "Like I said you can keep the four .380" T.Z added saying. The three lil niggas looked at each other "Aight!" the same one said who had to be the spokesperson for the trio. T.Z counted out two thousand dollars as the trio put the weapons inside three black trash bag "Look out Slick give the lil niggas two zips for me I'll reimburse you." T.Z told him giving the lil niggas a extra ounce just on the strength "Appreciate!" the lil nigga said "It's all good just next time y'all come across some more shit y'all make sure y'all get at Slick first he'll contact me ya dig." T.Z said "Aight bet!" the trio agreed Them type of young niggas came in handy they stayed hitting licks breaking into shit them lil niggas probably would take everything that wasn't nail down to the floor. "Y'all help me carry this shit to the car" T.Z said grabbing one of the trash bags T.Z had to purchase all the high powered weapons from the young niggas cause bargains such as that amount didn't come every day the youngsters could have made triple the amount selling the guns separately but T.Z figured they just wanted fast cash anyway for the shit.

Yvonne mind was still on T.Z as she exited the courthouse getting into her BMW the hearing didn't last all day as expected when the victims got on the stand and suddenly had amnesia about what happen that night after the club the district attorney decided not to fight the motion for dismissal the defense filed on the spot. It was only 12:45 and she was finish for the day. Yvonne decide to go treat herself to make her feel a little better. She went to North Park Mall to do a little shopping compliments of the Black American Express card her daddy had given her. Yvonne went inside the Bulgari Store and swap the credit card spending 5,500 on a purse then swiped the card to purchase a set of bangles by Charles Krypell for a thousand dollars. Yvonne walked through the mall buying items as if she had never heard of the term rescession before even though she have the term never applied to her one bit. Yvonne went into Nordstrom's she seen T.Z homeboy Flex over at a register paying for some items. Yvonne was about to go speak until she recognized the woman face that stood next to him with shopping bags in her hands from the Gucci store. Yeah Yvonne was green when it came to the street life but one thing she understood for sure that most homeboys didn't fuck with each other's exes. Maybe that was how they got down cause by the way she was all up on Flex it couldn't have been just a friendly outing. Yvonne assumption of Bri-Bri was exactly as she figured a trashy ass hoe cause what type of female goes and fuck

with her exes' man homeboy but long as T.Z wasn't fucking with her she didn't care. Yvonne kept on walking finishing her shopping.

Detective Simmons had got a call letting him know that Ms. Richmond had been moved into a normal room and she would recover just fine only problems she might still suffer from is post-traumatic stress. After waiting for bout a hour in the apartment complex for T.Z to show and he didn't. Simmons decided to head up to the hospital to talk to Ms. Richmond now that she was a little better and see would she revealed some reliable information on T.Z as well. Simmons knocked lightly as he entered the hospital room. Ms. Richmond was in her bed watching General Hospital "How are you doing today?" Simmons asked "Still in pain but not as bad as before." Ms. Richmond admitted "Like I told you before I pray you have a full recovery. Thank you! She said "I hate to take you back to that awful night but I'll like to ask you some follow up questions" Simmons told her. "Okay!" Ms. Richmond said after taking a deep breath. Simmons took out his pocket tablet and a pen to jot down some notes. "Is there anything different you might able to remember about your attacker that you couldn't remember at first? Simmons asked Ms. Richmond thought about t then answered saying No! "Okay" the guy was asking about your God Son Tyrone Zonders would you might have a clue why, does Tyrone owe somebody any money or in a gang are involved in the drug trade" Simmons question Ms. Richmond pondered over the question yeah her attacker was only there mainly because of Tyrone but Ms. Richmond had a built bond and love for Tyrone as if he was her flesh and blood so Ms. Richmond didn't want to say too much and entrap Tyrone but she also wanted her attacker caught as well. "Detective Tyrone is a grown man so if he owed any money out I wouldn't know of it and like most young boys he was involved in a clique or whatever they call it and honestly I never wanted to know if he sold drugs." Ms. Richmond explain "What was the last job you know of him working at? Simmons asked "I'll say at a detail shop a few years back before he went to prison I believe." "I

looked Tyrone up and I see he's been out for at least 9months and still unemployed how does he maintain without being involved in some type of illegal activity." Simmons said. "Look detective I don't know what he's into when I'm not around yeah I love him like a son but the questions you are asking me I cannot answer cause I don't have the answer you might need to go speak with Tyrone." Ms. Richmond said tryna to remain calm. "Listen Ms. Richmond I'm not tryna upset you by any means you are the victim here I just know the more information I have on Tyrone the closer I'll be to catching the culprit behind this crime." Simmons explain tryna relax Ms. Richmond realizing she was getting upset "I understand that detective I also want the bastard behind this caught. I just don't want to give you know assumptions as answers to your questions as well" Ms. Richmond told him. Detective Simmons had a genuine reason to be asking all the questions he asked bout Tyrone but her gut feeling told her it was some interior motive involved somehow. Ms. Richmond wasn't as green the street life as people suspected her to be. Roxy father was a D-boy but when Roxy was 15months he father was killed in a drug deal for 16kilos of cocaine but right before that Roxy father Raymond had just found out that he was under investigation by the FEDS they were constantly being followed phones taps but when Raymond got killed the FEDS backed off but Raymond had prepared Ms. Richmond for the questions and turn on your own family routine the laws played but the wisdom Raymond install in her at a young age stuck like glue to her so she vowed never to rat on a love one cause at the end these krackers don't give a damn about none of us. They just help us out to boast their own careers. Simmons spoke with Ms. Richmond until the nursed came in to give her the pain medication which would make her drowsy so Simmons decided to leave still with no concrete information.

T.Z had a fresh arsenal of weapons right on time for the two wars he was fighting on two different fronts he had just drop the weapons off at the apartment it was only 3 o'clock in the evening.

T.Z was still observing as if he was being followed by Simmons but hadn't seen the Impala since he lost him on the highway this morning. Derrick offer on a vacation was seeming like a good idea now but T.Z didn't want to go alone either but after catching Yvonne with that nigga he felt he would be a sucka just accepting her back and he refuse to just take any random hoe on a trip. T.Z thought about it and figured he would at least give her a chance that night when Bri-Bri tripped the fuck out. T.Z dialed her number waiting on her to answer but the automatic voicemail picked up. He hung up cause leaving messages he didn't do.

T.Z phone vibrated signal he had a text message "What do you want?" the text read from Yvonne. "We need to talk!" he responded texting "Now you want to talk. You full of shit nigga!" she text "Probably is but we still need to talk." he responded "I'm on my way home, I suggest you beat me there not meet me if you want to talk." she text T.Z laughed when he read the text "Whatever!" I'll meet you there!" He texted back then attaching the phone back to his hip. Yvonne was already at home when T.Z parked in front of the condo. T.Z walked to the front door ringing the door bell "who is it?" Yvonne shouted like she didn't know who it was already from looking out the upstairs blinds. "Open the door girl" T.Z said as the door half open with her body standing in the door way. They stood looking at each other in the eyes. "So I can't come in!" he protested "I thought I told you to beat me not meet me" she said with a fake attitude "People tell me to do a lot of shit I ain't never been good at taking and following orders." he said "Well I'm not anybody so we can talk out here!" she said stepping outside closing her door. T.Z wasn't in the mood for games so he got straight to the point "Who was that nigga I seen you out here with that drive the yellow Lexus?" Yvonne started laughing when she heard that "You spying on me Tyrone." What type of nigga you take me for? I was coming to surprise you and show you my new whip on the real" he said "I guess you the one that got surprise huh! She said T.Z gave her a death look and turned to leave Yvonne watched him leave but reconsider what she did" Tyrone, Tyrone! She shouted then ran after him stopping

him as he got in his car? "What?" "Got yo ma'fucking hands off me!" he Spat! Tyrone I'm just playing I just said that to make you mad you hurt my feeling this morning. That was my friend Kim I told you about

181

when we first meet." She explains "Kim! I thought you was talking about a female" T.Z said now understanding why the nigga looked odd "So Kim is really a him not a her" T.Z said "Let me show you!" Yvonne took her cellphone out her bra and dialed Kim number "Hello?" the voice said tryna sound feminine "Kim what's up girl?" Hey Von Von!" I'm tryna tell somebody who say they know you what kind of car you drive and color" Yvonne said "Who?" Kim asked "This fine ass nigga!" Yvonne said as T.Z mumbled the words stop playing "Tell him I drive a canary yellow Lexus IS!" Kim said 042. as Yvonne turn her lips up at T.Z "Okay girl I'll call you back!" Yvonne said ended the call. T.Z instantly felt bad for the way he had been acting with Yvonne. "Damn my bad baby I fucked up" he apologized grabbing her hands. "Next time you assume some bullshit about me just ask me first about it". She said "I will I promise how you want me to make it up to you" he said "That's for you to figure out" she said "How bout a trip to Hawaii and some of this dick right now!" he told her then kissed her. "That's a start!" She said smiling leading him back toward her door.

CHAPTER 16

"Your ticket please sir" T.Z handed the flight attendant his boarding pass as Yvonne, Derrick and Pauline did the same thing. The four were escorted to their seats in first class. T.Z couldn't believe how fast the month has went by. Yvonne had passed her American Bar Exam and now was a certified attorney her and T.Z were on great terms with each other. T.Z had gone and visit Ms. Richmond after she was released from the hospital she let him know that she didn't blame him for what happen to her she just wanted him to be careful cause she can't handle having to attend another funeral if something happens to him. She also informed him on how Detective Simmons was questioning her bout him which wasn't a surprise to T.Z since every chance possible he was tryna trail him. Ms. Richmond advised T.Z that taking a two-week vacation would be a smart idea just to get the heat off his back from Simmons. T.Z tried to convince Flex to come along with Peaches but said he couldn't get nobody to watch the kids for two weeks which was a lie Flex made up just because he didn't want to leave Bri-Bri for that long alone and since their relationship was still unknown by T.Z he damn sure couldn't bring her with him. T.Z and Derrick had supplied all their traps and people with enough work to last them until they return if they happen to need more T.Z could just call Flex and he would supply them until T.Z returned. T.Z took his seat anxious and a little nervous this would

be the first time ever flying somewhere. Derrick and Pauline had flown before and Yvonne and had flown plenty of times. "First class is nice but still nothing out dues a private flight! "Yvonne said "Everybody doesn't have a G4 jet!" T.Z said to her "Shame ain't it!" Yvonne said sarcastically. Damn! Yvonne yo Pops got a private jet?" Derrick asked "It's actually a G5 to be exact and yes he does plus a yacht!" she said as T.Z inhale deeply not really tryna hear about her father. "You should have asked him to borrow that Ma'fucker and a nigga could have saved $3500 dollars on these tickets!" Derrick stated "I was somebody told me not to" she said looking at T.Z "Aww!" Dawg you passed a offer up that good" Derrick complained "Nigga if you wanted to fly in a private jet you should have rented one or brought one" T.Z told him "Game keep treating me this good best believe I'm gone buy one nigga." Derrick stated "Well until then stop complaining nigga!" T.Z said. The pilot came over the loud speaker as the "Buckle seatbelt and turn cellphone devices off" symbols lit up. "It's okay baby we haven't even took off yet!" Yvonne told T.Z as he quickly tried to buckle his seat belt and put his phone on airplane mode. "I'm Good!" he assured her. To make sure on the way to the airport T.Z popped two prescription Zanex pills and down it with four ounces of codeine and promethazine couch syrup mix with 20oz sprite to make sure he stayed calm by sleeping the 13-hour flight. T.Z could feel the prescription drugs kicking in cause he watched the safety video the flight attendant on the video sounded as if she was talking chopped and screwed and T.Z could hardly hold his eyes open.

Will had been keeping a low profile the last past month ever since he shot the Hispanic man in the head and tried killing his accomplice in the parking lot of the county morgue. Will had to be on the safe side just in case police had link him to the murder. Aaron Will friend who worked at the morgue did say the police came in questioning him about if he knew what happen of course Aaron denied any knowledge of the crime. The police even ask to see the surveillance camera luckily Will was just out of view of the

lot cameras. Will had three different passports and ID's so going to prison wasn't in Will's head but since he was around Jax on a daily basis and Jax rubbed elbows with prominent people he didn't need his face plastered on every local media news cast looking for him and it led back to Jax. After this long and his picture haven't shown up Will assume it was either the police didn't know shit or didn't have shit mostly it was both. Will hated taken a leave of absence when on a mission for souls and not to save souls either more like the grim reaper. Will had been waiting across the street from the parking garage entrance for almost 30 minutes in a black Audi A8. He still had T.Z address and had unfinished business with the youngster. Will was bringing the shirt to T.Z front door. Just when his patience was running thin a H3 hummer was pulling up to the gate to enter the garage. Will quickly drove out getting behind the Hummer trailing the vehicle since he was also a expensive car he figure trailing the H3 wouldn't draw suspicion to his which was right cause the white woman in the Hummer glance in her rearview mirror but seeing the $80,000 dollar car she wasn't worried as if the driver belonged in the building. Will drove through the parking garage until he got to T.Z assign parking spaces. The parking spaces were occupied by

T.Z Benz and Camaro SS. Will assumed that meant T.Z was home. He went and found an empty parking spot not worried if the resident showed up cause it was the middle of the day so the average person should be at work and Will wouldn't take long he would just run upstairs murk T.Z and back out. Will twisted the silencers on a barrel inside the strap holster he wore under is Sean Jean suit jacket. He made sure the Kevlar bullet proof vest was covering his mid-section properly under his shirt. Will watched the same white lady step on the elevator disappearing that was his cue to get out. Will jumped out walking towards the elevator pushing the up button. Will took out the Dallas Mavericks fitted cap already aware that most garage elevators had cameras. As the elevator door open Will kept his head down and back turn as he stepped on the elevator. The camera was place in the top corner right above the floor buttons. He pressed the correct floor without

exposing his face even when the door open reaching the floor he stepped out backwards. Will reached T.Z door gently pressing his ear against the door to see if any sound was coming from inside. It was silent Will removed his lock and pick it from his pocket to get inside. Will had a surprise for him. Will quietly unlock the door then pulled out one of the 9mm easing inside the door. He didn't shut the door behind. He left it cracked just in case. Will crept through the living room quietly heading straight towards the backroom with the door open. Will didn't hear any sound coming from the room so he thought T.Z might be sleep. Will pulled out his second gun then rushed into the room in attack mode with both guns pointed and ready to fire but all he found was a made-up bed. Will went and check the other room and the upstairs den still nothing. T.Z was nowhere to be found. He went back inside the master bedroom and started searching through the drawers then a picture on T.Z night stand instantly caught Will attention. Will couldn't believe his eyes at what he was looking at. It was a picture of T.Z and Yvonne. Will didn't understand how the hell did the enemy get on the picture with Jax's daughter. Will was confused, did Jax know that his daughter was dating T.Z? Is that the reason why he didn't want to give the green light on murking the youngster but if that was the case why didn't Jax just tell Will? Will continue to search the room entering the walk-in closet. He rambled through the clothes sitting in the back of the closet was a safe. True, Will didn't come for any money only thing valuable he wanted was T.Z life since he would be unable to get that. Will hope taking the safe would set T.Z back. Will pick the safe up and took it into the room. He snatched the comforter off the king size bed to cover the safe up as he took it downstairs to the car.

T.Z and Yvonne enter the hotel suite at the Hilton Hotel with a beach front view of the Pacific Ocean. The suite had a bedroom with a separate living room dining room area full kitchen with appliances and a 42in flat screen in the living room and bedroom. T.Z left the Gucci luggage in the living room as he went straight to

the balcony to his right he could see the beach and his left the city of Waikiki the view was amazing from the 16th floor. He went back inside and into the bedroom where it was a king size bed and the bathroom had a jacuzzi tub with jets and a stand-up shower that sprayed water from 3 different angles. "This gone be the first thing we do" Yvonne said sneaking up behind him wrapping her arms around him from behind." Naw you gone be the first thing I do!" T.Z stated as he turns around kissing her it must be the air cause since T.Z exited the plane his hormones been raging. "Let me freshen up first!" Yvonne said breaking the lip lock T.Z had on her "Aight!" T.Z said after one more kiss. He left out the bathroom taking a seat on the end of the bed. Picking up the remote control turning on the T.V. It was only 4 o'clock in the evening the flight took 13 hours total they boarded the flight at 7 that morning but the 4 1/2 hour time zone difference made the day seem longer. Yvonne came out the bathroom in only her natural smooth brown skin making blood start straight to his manhood. Yvonne signal with her finger for T.Z to come here as she turned around giving him a view of the pretty brown round as she headed into the awaiting shower with him on her heels like a trained dog.

"How much?" Derrick asked "1200!" The young dude said. "Aight!" Here's for yo trouble" Derrick said giving him $1,300dollars. "Thanks, let me know if you need more!" the young dude said.

"Believe I will in bout 3 days so get at me!" Derrick told him as he let the guy out his suite. "Damn this some good!" Derrick said to himself picking up a bud out of the sandwich bags that was completely the color gold. As Pauline and Yvonne checked into the room. There was a young Samoan dude who couldn't be over 19 working as a bellhop for the hotel. Since the airport TSA was so tight now days Derrick and T.Z wasn't gone take a risk by tryna bring some weed on the plane so that meant now they would need something to smoke on. T.Z spotted the dude and told Derrick "I bet he knows where the dro at" "Hell naw he a square!" Derrick said "Bet!" "Call it" Derrick said "If so you got to pay for it" T.Z said as they agreed upon the bet. When T.Z approached the dude, you can tell he wasn't for sure but looking at the two men with their county talk and platinum grills and chains the dude knew they were only tourist and agreed upon the request. Derrick suite was exactly the same as T.Z Pauline sat flipping through a brochure of the many fun and romantic events the island had to offer. Derrick called T.Z on the suite phone "Yeah!" T.Z answered "Look out nigga you busy?" Derrick asked "Lil bit what's up?" T.Z asked "I got that for you and its some good some shit a nigga only see in high times magazines." Derrick said. "Give me bout 20minutes!" T.Z said "Aight!" Derrick said hanging up. Even though the hotel had no smoking policy, Derrick didn't give a damn worse you could do was kick him out and keep the $150 deposit so he put a wet towel under the door and made sure the security latch was on then twisted up a Dutch cigarillo. Derrick fired up the Alcopoco Gold inhaling the high quality weed smoke then blowing it in the air. Pauline wasn't a smoker but she would hit a blunt from time to time and since she was on vacation these was one of them times. She grabbed the blunt out of Derricks mouth taking a pull. "Cough, cough, cough!" Pauline instantly started chocking with her eyes watering "Take it easy baby!" Derrick said laughing "Shut up!" she said wiping the spit from her chin. Derrick already could tell this was gone be the best two weeks he then had.

Will sat across from Jax inside Jax chill room where they came to watch sporting events on the 82in flat screen and relax the room had a mini refrigerator and a poker table. Will sipped on a glass of Glendfiddich with ice. Jax ended his conversation with the unknown caller turning his attention back to the Monday night football game. Since Jax was a gambler he had $50,000 on the cowboys but the eagles were already up 21-0 second quarter. "Jax I haven't seen Yvonne lately where she been at?" "She then started fucking with some knucklehead since she passed her bar exam she said the dude wanting to treat her to a trip to Hawaii as a gift." Jax said never taking his eyes off the T.V "Who is the knucklehead?" Will asked

wondering if Jax would expose if he knew. "Some lil nigga name Tyrone!" Jax said. "You never met the nigga?" Will asked "Naw I didn't get to but Linda did. Why you ask that?" Jax asked looking at Will curiously "I know you just don't let your daughter go out of town some some random nigga." Will stated "You right I don't but Linda been pressing the issue telling me I need to ease up she's grown plus she said the guy seems like a genuine dude he reminds her of me 25 years ago." Jax said "Is that right!" Will said 'Yeah!" Jax said Will couldn't believe that Jax had no clue his daughter was sleeping with the enemy. Will decided not to drop the bombshell news on Jax not just yet cause Will wanted T.Z head as a trophy of his own. Jax if he heard that news he would be on his private jet heading to Hawaii as they speak. Will wondered if T.Z was aware that he was dating Jax daughter. How could he not Yvonne had to speak of her parents to him. Jax was right the youngster was playing Chess not Checkers cause having Yvonne in arms reach was smart but Will didn't sweat it cause to him it would be checkmate soon as they got back. He figured Jax would thank him later. Will finished watching the game still astonish about the information he found.

CHAPTER 17

F lex cruise down South Boulevard in his CTS making sure he was going the speed limit cause the laws patrolled the area frequently cause of the high crime rate in that section. He was still in South Dallas but wasn't on his side. Flex still receive love from the niggas and the ladies on the side. He didn't too much like driving through the hot ass area especially with 10kilos of cocaine in the backseat but he knew the risk of being out here chasing cash. He pulled into the Angel Tree Apartment Complex that were mostly vacant the dope fiends used as shooting galleries and smoke rooms to get high. You could see a extension cord running from a unit with utility working all the way to a apartment window into another vacant. "They straight thuggin" Flex said laughing at the site. A black and Red challenger SRTS on some 22in Diablos pulled next to Flex. A nigga got out the driver seat resembled Rubin Studdard size and looks. He grabbed a black duffel bag out the back seat then got in the passenger seat of Flex car "What's good big homie?" Flex asked him. Big homie was the name he gave Flex when they happen to just meet each other by chance one day. Big homie bad been buying 2 or 3 bricks at a time form Flex the past 8months. He scored bricks from Flex at least twice a week now that Big Homie wanted a whole ten piece. Flex was cool with making the $250,000 dollars "I'm good. What about yourself?" Big Homie asked. "Tryna get it as always!" Flex stated "Let me not hold you up

then!" Big Homie gave Flex the duffel bag. Flex looked inside "This the hole 250 right" Flex said trusting Big Homie since he always came correct" Have I ever been short!" Big Homie told him. "Get the bag off the floor in the backseat." Flex instructed. Big Homie checked the bag counting the bricks of coke making sure it was ten. "After I get rid of these I'm need probably bout 25 or so can you handle that?' Big Homie asked "I can handle any order you need ain't no such things as droughts on my end long as you got the bread I got the dope!" Flex said estimating the cash he would make off 25 keys. "Aight give me about a week tops then fly these birds" Big Homie said as they dapped each other up. Big Homie got out then got into his Challenger to leave. Flex pulled out the parking spot soon as he got ready to leave out the apartment complex Three unmarked police cars cut him off with Cherry's and Berry's flashing in the grill and visors When he tried to reverse two more unmarked Dodge Durangos also with matching lights had him pinned in. Officers wearing DEA and FBI swat gear surrounded the CTS and MP5 and AR15 pointed ready to fire.

T.Z and Derrick whipped the 2011 Ducati Diavel 11 Motorcycles around the mountains on Highway 2 with Yvonne and Pauline holding on tight to them. They ears began to pop cause of the altitude of the mountains. T.Z dropped his head switching to fourth gear going upwards. Derrick did the same thing as his eyes began to water from the wind hitting his face. T.Z pulled up to one of the many rest spots that accompany the Highway that was on the side of the mountains looking out on the ocean. They parked the motorcycles side by side as the ladies took off the helmets. The four walked out to the safety railing that kept a person from falling to their death looking out at the view. "Ya'll stand still let me take y'all picture" Pauline said pulling out her digital camera they all took several different pictures with the beautiful Hawaii sky as the backdrop. "You never see no shit like this at home!" Derrick said "For real nigga can get use to this!" T.Z agreed thinking about how it would feel just to make an early retirement and move out there.

Yeah cost of living was expensive as hell but with the million he had stashed away he figure that he could start something legit to live comfortable from. "That would be nice huh!" Derrick commented looking at T.Z reading his mind cause he had the same thoughts. "What?" T.Z asked "Wayne said gangstas don't die they get chubby and move to Miami. I say thugs don't die they get rich and move to Hawaii!" Derrick said "I can dig that Fam!" T.Z agreed smiling Yvonne love to see her man happy she could see the difference in the stress that he streets gave him being at home. Had to always be on alert couldn't go to the grocery store without a gun on him phone stayed ringing it was always something but the last couple days he been relaxing. She had no idea T.Z snored when he slept cause in the city he was always so paranoid if he got into a sleep to deep he might not be able to hear the things around him which might determine if he lived or died in his sleep. She told him he was just sill institutionalized that's all. He didn't care what she called it T.Z refused to get caught slipping sleep or awake cause the element of surprise is a great strategy to conquer the enemy. But out there, T.Z felt comfortable enough to go into a deep sleep not on guard.

They got back on the motorcycles to finish their journey around the island. They went by different neighborhoods the more expensive homes that were on the hills were gated off these were three or four million-dollar homes and only could enter the neighborhood if you live there or was invited. Other neighborhoods they would have to leave their ID's with the gate attendant until they left black out but the island was magnificent to them. Yvonne had been out there before but the experience was just as excited as her first time being with T.Z made it even better.

Flex had been in a cold room for almost 2 hours, he realized looking at his Frank Muller watch. He couldn't see the camera watching him but he was positive they were watching him. Flex had been in a interrogation room before so he was already up on their scare tactics. Yeah he got jammed up with $250 thousand cash and a eight ball of coke he was snorting out of but something

was telling Flex it had to be bigger then just that cause that baby shit compared to what the FEDS dealt with. Flex was about to find out as a fake ass Starsky and Hutch walked into the room with the white guy carrying a brown folder. They both sat down at the table across from Flex "I'm special agent Moss. This is special agent Rice" the black officers introduce him and his partner. Flex didn't budge or even speak back he just looked at them. Mr. Xavier Johnson, I see you was recently released from prison now your back in trouble I see you also just finish your parole as well. My partner and I would like to discuss a few things with you if that's fine with you." Agent Moss informed him. "I want my lawyer!" Flex stated not breaking the eye contact. "I told you why you

194

even waste your damn time even tryna consult with this scumbag just lock his ass in a cage in Florence, Colorado until they strap him down to the death table." Rice blurted out "Just hold up a second Rice I think this young man deserves a chance." Agent Moss said. Flex was already prepared for the good cop bad cop routine. "Whatever!" I'm not risking my career on this joker." Rice said standing up exited the room slamming the door behind him. "Look Mr. Johnson or do you prefer Flex?" Moss asked Flex just shrugged his shoulder "Here's the deal I'm give you the opportunity of a lifetime here and now only once. I'm save you from the State of Texas sticking a needle in you veins for killing and robbing Nathan Hooks or as the Streets call him Nate! Not to mention the large amount of cocaine you been selling to an undercover Drug enforcement Agent and the marked $250,000 dollars you were arrested with to prove it all along with these. "Moss pulled out several pictures of Flex making transactions with Big Homie including the one form today. Flex dropped his head knowing he was fucked with no Vaseline. "Not to add salt to you already open wounds but if I make one phone call you will also have other charges as in shooting at a police office and another capital murder for killing Kendrick Smalls and 17yr old Stacie Smith cause I know that was you behind the ski mask jumping out the van," Moss explain knowing he had Flex by the balls "What you want?" Flex asked "Them and everything that comes with them!" Moss stated laying out a picture of Derrick, T.Z, Felex, and some other Hispanic man who Flex didn't know. Moss was right Flex had a choice of a lifetime either stay stuff and tell agent Moss to suck a dick and take his chances hoping he at least receive a life sentence or go against everything he stands for and become a snitch to save his ass. "What about my girl and kids?" Flex asked They can all join you in the witness protection program. When all this is over." Moss said "Damn!" Flex said out loud taking a deep breath looking at the pictures again notices Felex and the unknown Hispanic man resemble each other. "I'm in!" Flex said in a low tone voice "You made a wise decision for you and your family" Agent Moss told him. It might have been wise on Moss behalf but Flex knew if anybody found out he would be found hanging from a light pole or in the Trinity River Floating.

T.Z, Yvonne, Derrick and Pauline continued enjoying their vacation having as much fun as possible. The group strolled own Kalaka street hitting up all the expensive stores the street had to offer. Louis Vuitton, Bulgari, Prada, Coach, Burberry, Gucci, Fendi even went inside the three-story Nike store for T.Z and Derrick could get a couple of exclusive Jordan's and Air Force ones between all four of them it had to be at least $65,000 dollar's worth of merchandise. Derrick all most past out when he heard Yvonne tell T.Z to put his knot up and she pulled out the American Express Black Card. Derrick then been with a few women that had careers and a little money of their own but not like Yvonne so for him to see that was shocking. It shocked Pauline too. T.Z had on some light brown Gucci linen shorts with a button-down matching Gucci linen shirt with no undershirt on showing off his chest and abs with the shirt unbutton with some Gucci sandals. Yvonne had on pink and white Fendi sundress with some Fendi flip flops showing off her fresh manicure toes. They were headed downstairs to the beach for the weekly Friday Lua the hotel presented. T.Z had his arm around Yvonne waist as they walked through the sand to the luau. Since T.Z didn't eat the swine he couldn't taste the juicy pig the islanders had roasted on the ground over the fire. T.Z had to admit the aroma was pleasing but T.Z discipline made him remember everything that look good or smell good ain't food. "BOOM! , BOOM! , BOOM!" Firecracker erupted in the sky as soon as roasted sun settled in the ocean from a distance signal the start of the Island traditional cookouts. Drums began sounded as a group of women ran out forming a like shaking their hops to the beat. A woman came and pt a flower necklace around T.Z and Yvonne neck as two of the dancers came and grabbed T.Z hand. T.Z tried to refuse but even Yvonne push him from behind to join the woman shaking their butts on the man it was harmless to her. T.Z was kind of cautious thinking Yvonne might trip but he seen her clapping her hands with the drum beat encourage him on just like the rest of the crowd. One of the Hawaiian dancers put her nice shape soft booty on T.Z and grinned on him. She felt his manhood get rock solid cause she made sure she didn't back off of it she just grinned harder turning her head around smiling. When the drums stopped the dancing stop. "I see you had yo'self a good time!" Yvonne said looking down at T.Z shorts. His print was visible through the linen shorts. "Don't worry this dick belongs to you." he said wrapping his arms around her "Trust I know why you think I let you have your fun" Yvonne said smiling at him "Find out you the type who like to watch their spouse fuck other people y'all sophisticated folks be into that type of shit." T.Z said "Maybe in your dreams" Yvonne said "How you know!" T.Z said They continue to party since T.Z didn't eat none of the pigs, Yvonne decided not to as well just for the sake of him, so they ate plenty of the different fruit that was available and had all type of mix drinks by 12 o'clock they were wasted walking down the beach. Yvonne couldn't walk straight or

197

stop giggling. Yvonne just stopped and took a seat in the sand. T.Z sat down next to her pulling the blunt out his pocket that broke in half when the woman was dancing on him. T.Z lit up half the blunt exhaling the smoke into the night. T.Z looked into the sky at the full moon as the stars lit up the sky. Yvonne took the half of blunt from T.Z taking a light hit not to choke "I guess you thuggin now!" T.Z told her as she hit the blunt passing it back to him. All she could do was giggle leaning her head on his shoulders. "Look baby!" Yvonne said pointing at a shooting star "Make a Wish!" she added saying T.Z dropped the blunt in the sand and began kissing her while easing on top. The only light on the beach was the moon and stars so he wasn't worried about nobody seeing them. Yvonne was already soaking wet as T.Z rubbed his fingers on her clit causing her to moan. He pulled his swollen manhood out them moved Yvonne thong to the side. "ummmm!" She moaned as he entered her. He guided himself deeper inside her watching her vagina muscles contract as he went in and out with long deep stroke. "Ummm Baby!" I Love You. I Love you! Yvonne moaned as he sped up. He flipped her right leg over making her lay on her side as he continued the pounding. She raised up to her knees for he could hit it doggy style never letting him slide out. "AHH!" she screamed as he smacked her ass. "Tell me who pussy this is." T.Z said as he felt her climaxing "It's your baby! Yours!" she pleaded having back to back orgasms gripping a hand full of sand. T.Z couldn't hold back any longer as her erupted all inside Yvonne.

Flex sat in the living room of his home with 63 grams of his cuban finest white girl thinking about the deal he made with the devil just cause he was scared to take his on heat. All the fucked-up shit Flex then done in his 21 years he never would imagine that he would become a rat and get his whole crew pinch. He leaned over sticking the end of the rolled fifty-dollar bill in his nose snorting the thickness line he ever hit before. "Uummm!" He grunted as the coke ate away at the gristle in his nose. He chased the drain with a swig from the Ciroc bottle. At the moment he didn't want to face reality cause the life of Flex the real street nigga was over he was a certified bitch nigga now. Flex snorted another huge line and swallowed the Ciroc. His mind drifted back to when he was in prison and T.Z and him would be up riding after night time rack off. They would be discussing how one nigga testified on his co-defendant to get less time now the nigga running around like he real or how some other

nigga be in yo face smiling then go turning on his homebody. He had even heard the term is not call "snitching" it's called "getting down first" that still was some bullshit. Flex and T.Z felt snitching was snitching no matter what you call it. Flex was so high and drunk when Peaches came in the house he was just sitting in a daze. She took the kids in the room not wanting them to see their father high as a kite. "Flex!" she called his name nudging him "What?" he responded slowly looking up at her with his eyes blood shot red with cocaine residue in his nose and on his face. Peaches just stared at him in disappointment. And disgusted at what he had become since he started using. He had lost his muscular frame. If it wasn't for the jewelry and expensive clothes he wore you would think Flex was smoking crack. "Look at you Flex, get up!" she said but all he did was lean forward reaching for almost empty Ciroc bottle. Peaches yanked the bottle away "Damn bitch why you did that for?" Flex slurred as he spoke. 'You look a hot as mess come to the room" she said pulling on his arm tryna stand him up "Get off me I don't need yo help!" he spat. Flex leaned forward to snort another line of cocaine "I'm not gone stand here and let you put that shit up your nose!" Peaches stated "Bye!" he said before continuing. Peaches tried to grab him for he would stop thinking she could over power him since he was drunk and high but she was wrong. Flex jumped up grabbing her by the neck and in the same motion slammed her into the glass table. "AHHH!" Peaches screamed as she broke through the glass table only suffering a scratch from the fall but the heartache was tremendous. Flex stood over top of her as she cried "Oh, now you want to cry!" Flex shouted "Momma what happen?" little Khadijah asked scared with tears in her eyes "Go to your room, yo momma okay" Peaches lied tryna make her daughter feel like she was okay. Khadijah walked back to her room with her head down not understanding why her mother was laying through a broke table. Flex you scaring the kids please stop!" Peaches pleaded. Flex was zone out and did feel like taking his problems out on Peaches but he thought about his princess Khadijah and Kia in the next room. "You lucky! Now clean this shit up!" Flex instructed Peaches

leaving her on the floor to cry. Peaches couldn't understand how her relationship went from great to terrible in a matter of months. Yeah Flex did provide for her and the kids but since they stop having money problems they began having relationship problems. Peaches was fed up and tired of the constant ass whooping for no reason then on top of that she knew Flex was cheating cause he would be gone all night then she went through his phone finding several text messages from Bri-Bri. Peaches had never in her life been the type to tolerate bullshit so why was she now?

CHAPTER 18

It was unbelievable how fast the two weeks went by. T.Z mind came back to reality as he looked out the window riding in the back of Pauline Ford Expedition paid for by Derrick. Fantasy land was gone as the downtown sky scrapers appeared in full view they were back home and it was time to get back serious cause it was a lot of business that needed to be handled good and bad. They talked about all the fun they had as Pauline pulled into the garage. They had to buy extra suit cases just to pack all the clothes the purchased while in Hawaii. It would take two separate trips just to bring all the luggage upstairs. Derrick and Pauline got off on the 8th floor to go to Derricks crib as T.Z and Yvonne got off on the 10th floor. I had so much fun baby!" Yvonne told T.Z as they approached his door "Me too baby" we go ho- T.Z paused as he was about to insert his key into the lock "What's wrong baby?" Yvonne asked getting worried cause the frown on T.Z face T.Z quickly dialed Derrick number "Hello?" Derrick answered "You good?" T.Z asked in a low tone of voice "Yeah!" why you whispering nigga?" Derrick asked "Come up here now bring a strap!" T.Z said ended the call "What's wrong baby?" Yvonne asked now worried "Somebody in there or been in there!" he whispered Yvonne thought T.Z was just losing his mind to just assume something like that. "Why you say that?" she whispered back. Look at the lock I never turn the key hole all the way back I always leave it slightly at an angle for only

I can tell to know if somebody been in my shit." T.Z explain to her his secret that only two people know about which was Derrick and Flex. Derrick got off the elevator jogging towards them "Yvonne go to Derricks apartment with Pauline I'll call you and tell you what's up!" T.Z said "Okay!" she said understanding the seriousness of the situation now going to the elevator. Derrick removed the two .45 smith & western from his waistline handing one to T.Z., T.Z made sure one was in the chamber before he slowly unlocked the door. T.Z looked at Derrick as he nodded his head confirming he was ready. They rush through the door like they were trained for that type of action. They checked upstairs and the second bedroom and bathroom and hallway closet leaving the master bedroom last. The door was open to the bedroom he could already see where the culprit was rambling through his drawers. They entered the room checking the bathroom and closet. T.Z knew immediately as he checked the closet what was missing "Damn they got me D!" "What they get?" Derrick asked "My safe!" T.Z said angrily already tryna figure out who did the shit. T.Z pace the room unable to control his anger. "What all you have in there?" Derrick asked "All my jewelry I didn't bring 3 straps and all my bread over a mill" T.Z said "Damn!" Derrick said feeling his homeboy pain "Who you think done this shit?" Derrick said It only a few people who knew T.Z even lived downtown besides Derrick was Flex and Dot! Derrick protege but only Flex know what floor and door. "Have you ever told Dot what apartment was mine?" T.Z asked "Hell naw!" Derrick said All fingers

202

pointed towards Flex cause he also knew about the trip knowing T.Z said "I know nigga was mad about not getting a cut of that money from Ken Ken shit but I can't see the nigga hitting you maybe my crib but not yours!" Derrick explain T.Z was tryna find a reason not to blame Flex as well then Detective Simmons came to his head. He had been following T.Z so he knows where T.Z lived and Dallas laws did all type of dirty stuff. T.Z called Yvonne and let her know it was okay to come up to the apartment. T.Z ran the following events down to Derrick about how Simmons had been following him up until they went out of town. And how he

thinks Simmons might be behind the break-in or had something to do with it but still wouldn't ex Flex out the equation. "You okay baby?" Yvonne asked walking inside the apartment "Yeah I'm good!" "What they take?" she asked noticing all the electronics still here "Just my safe!" he stated "I'm sorry baby!" I'm start cleaning this mess up Yvonne said looking around at the drawers on the floor and clothes everywhere. "Fuck this shit!" Go get me a room at the W hotel I'm gonna stay there until I find another place." T.Z said "You can stay with me if you want to" Yvonne said "That's straight. Get me a few things to wear and I'll meet you at your place!" T.Z said giving her the keys to the Benz. "Let's head to the hood!" T.Z told Derrick as he dialed Flex number.

"I'll meet you there in minute!" Flex said hanging up the phone. Flex was a little nervous about meeting T.Z. He could tell something was wrong by the tone in T.Z voice plus he needed to see him right now. Flex wondered if T.Z had found out about him snitching already. The agents told Flex that his cell phone would be tapped and try and get them to incriminate themselves much as possible plus they would be trailing him at any give time they needed much evidence as possible on everybody. The agents even instructed Flex how to download a Federal phone app that would be undetected by the user it allowed the FEDS to listen to whoever as around the phone without using it just as long as the phone was powered on the agents could activate the app. That wouldn't be easy to get done without drawing suspicion to himself. Most of all he wasn't supposed to blow his cover by no means if so the deal was off and he would be tried and convicted with the rest of them. Flex has a helluva task on his hand and could feel the pressure and eyes ain't on him. Flex had went and purchased a metro phone cause he was sure the Federal phone app had been put on his iPhone as well. T.Z Camaro was already parked outside the building when Flex pulled up at the apartment. As Flex walked to the door he peeped the unmarked Dodge Charger driving by making Flex remember that shit was real and not a game. "Knock" T.Z open the door soon as he heard the knock letting Flex inside. "What's good Fam?" Flex asked walking inside seeing the cold look on T.Z face. Derrick sat on the couch smoking a blunt "What's good?" Derrick asked "Slow motion!" What's so important y'all needed to talk about ASAP? Flex asked acting concern "I ain't about to play Sherlock Homes with you I'm ask you straight up and don't fucking lie my nigga." T.Z came off saying. Flex prepared himself for the question about to be exposed. "What's that?" Flex asked "Did you break into my crib and get my safe?" T.Z asked actually surprising Flex but making him mad for being asked some shit like that. "Nigga hell naw how the fuck you go ask me some bullshit like that." Flex responded "Cause I did nigga" T.Z spat. "Nigga What the fuck I look like to you I ain't got to steal yo shit!" Flex spat standing up walking toward T.Z "Nigga my shit missing so everybody who know where I live suspect." T.Z said "I advise you to talk to them don't come to me sideways niggas" Flex said "Nigga I'm grown don't tell me how to do a ma'fucking thing" T.Z said "Y'all chill, chill!" Derrick said tryna defuse a bomb waiting to explode. "Chill yo boy out he the one on the bullshit!" Flex shouted upset "Ain't no bullshit when my paper missing nigga!" T.Z shouted back "I ain't tryna hear this hoe ass shit nigga I'm gone!" Flex said as he left out the door headed to his car. The unmarked Dodge Charger was parked by the last building he seen as he drove off. Flex wasn't prepared to hear no shit like that. Even though he was in motion of doing some hoe shit but he still felt a nigga didn't have the rights to accuse him of doing no hoe shit regardless. Flex now felt the things he was doing could be justified believing it wasn't no loyalty in the first place to make T.Z think something like that about him. Flex would get the things the FEDS needed and then get out of dodge. "First rule in life is self-preservation!" Flex psyched himself out saying "You don't really believe he did it do you?" Derrick asked T.Z "Naw but now a days you never know until it's too late" T.Z said "True Dat!" Derrick agreed "Even if it wasn't Flex that mean whoever did it probably know about this apartment as well and I damn sure can't afford to take a lost on the dope too! T.Z mention. "What you want to do then?" asked Derrick "We got to move the drugs to another spot just to be safe." T.Z advise "Yeah that would be smart." said Derrick "I got to make a few runs to!" Derrick added saying "Yeah I do to. Go ahead and take care of your business and I'll get at you later" T.Z told him. "You sure!" stated Derrick "Yeah go head!" T.Z said. Derrick left out the apartment getting in his BMW unaware of the eyes watching him through the binocular as Derrick pulled out so did the unmarked Dodge Charger. T.Z was still inside the apartment trying to figure out where he could stash the drugs on short notice. He refused to put Yvonne in harm's way so he wouldn't dare take it to her place and didn't trust to many other people to leave them with all he had left to get back on his feet. He still had about $100,000 dollars floating around the streets to pick up from the work he fronted out before he went out of town and at this time he would need every penny. He was still cashing out on delivery with Felex so he didn't have to worry about him because he didn't owe him any money, that's the main reason T.Z never got fronted nothing because in the game things could happen at any given moment and never wanted to be in the hole with somebody. T.Z had a stack of bricks and pounds he had to dispense just to get his re up money so he had to grind hard.

Flex didn't give a damn no more about hiding his coke habit he sat in the living room of Bri-Bri apartment snorting line. The day he slammed Peaches through the glass coffee table he went to Bri-Bri house he was so wasted to the point he didn't care what she thought he felt since he paid all her bills and supported her expensive lifestyle she bet not say shit or suffer the same fate as Peaches. Unlike Peaches, Bri-Bri didn't give a damn about his well-being long as he keep on coming out his pockets. It was so good for her she quit her job and just depended on Flex. Bri-Bri had some money saved up but it wasn't no reason for her to spend any of her savings. She had finally convinced flex to pay the down payment on her a new car but instead of a Challenger she pushed her luck and got a E-Class Benz. Flex was paying the car notes for her as well. She refused to mess her shit up just because he like getting high long as he left her some cash he could OD for all she cared her mind was only on the Benjamins. As she walked into the kitchen watching Flex she figured this would be a good time to hit his pockets up. She closed the refrigerator after grabbing a soda out she walked over by Flex standing in front of him in some boi panties and shirt that stop at her belly button. Flex admire her voluptuous body as he caressed her thigh. "I miss you daddy!" Bri-Bri lied! "Daddy missed you to!" Flex said grabbing his crotch not taking his eyes off her camel toe print. Bri-Bri staddle his lap as Flex cupped her cheeks. She began kissing on his neck. "uuummm..." She moaned as he rubbed her clit and she rotated her hips "I Love You Daddy!" she said as the juices came out her on his fingers "Love you too!" she said as she pulled his limp manhood out. Bri-Bri pulled her panties down to her thighs as she squatted on him she rubbed the head of his manhood on her wetness hoping that would make it rise for the occasion but still it didn't the coke he snorted had him out of service. Bri-Bri started getting frustrated cause money and dick was the only things she liked about him. "What's wrong?" she complained knowing the only way she would get the 10stacks she wanted was to give him a good nut. Bri-Bri got up then drop to her knees she put the limp dick in her mouth swallowing it making it dripping wet. She began rotated her head on the tip while stroking it with one hand and rubbing her clit with the other. He grabbed the back of her head when he felt the blood started to flow causing a erection" Finally!" Bri-Bri thought as she stood up to straddle him backwards.

Derrick pulled up in front of Head Swag barber shop to collect his paper from his homie DeDe. DeDe was a barber there but also Derrick fronted him pounds of weed that he would flip. "Ha! Seven dice!" DeDe said as he rolled the dice as a group of niggas huddle on the sidewalk playing craps. Derrick walked up next to DeDe not speaking not wanting to break DeDe concentration as he rolled the dice tryna hit eight. "44!" DeDe said as he rolled. Derrick looked at the twenty's, tens and fifties on the concrete hoping DeDe hit his point. "AWWW!" the group shouted as the dice fell on six deuce. DeDe picked up around the board. He looked up and seen Derrick "What's good nigga?" DeDe asked "Shit!" What's good with you?" Derrick replied "Taking these niggas money!" DeDe said straighten out the money he just won "I pass my roll!" DeDe said to signal to Derrick to walk to the car with him "You running nigga!" a dude shouted to DeDe "I wouldn't think about leaving long as you got money in your pockets" DeDe said to the dude. Derrick got in the passenger seat of DeDe Black 645i BMW on Black 22in BBS "How was the trip nigga?" "Good a nigga needed to get away" I need to take me a vacation but ain't never find the time." DeDe said as he pulled a Bank of America money pouch out the glove compartment handing it to Derrick. Derrick unzipped the pouch flipping through the hundred-dollar bills. "I know what you mean but do what I did just set a date and get things in order" Derrick said putting the money in his pocket giving the pouch back to DeDe. " The shit sounds easy but you already know it ain't" DeDe said. "Yeah I know" Derrick said.

Lil D was headed to one of his various women's house. Hoes and money were bout the only reason he would be on this side of town cause this wasn't his jurisdiction. Lil D had to take a double look as he rode by noticing the white on white 760Li. "Naw can't be!" he thought as he got ready to make a U-turn in his Silver S550 Benz he just recently purchased. Lil D could recognize Derrick BMW from anybody else cause Derrick had the symbol "Limited Edition" put on the opposite side of the 760Li symbol. This had to be a lucky day for Lil D and a curse for Derrick cause ever since Lil Loc and Ken Ken got killed he hadn't seen Derrick especially when he was hunting for him. Lil D parked in the parking lot not too far off but for he could see the entrance to the barber shop and Derrick car. He didn't see Derrick gather amongst the group of niggas gambling but Lil D knew he wasn't too far away.

"You go come get in this dice game?" DeDe asked "I might let me see what you niggas got to lose first." Derrick said "Come on then!" DeDe said as he opened the door as they got out the car to join the other men "Nigga I got fifty to say you don't hit" DeDe shouted to the same dude who said something to him at first "I bet I bar!" the dude said "Naw nigga straight four" DeDe shouted "10 or 4" "Bet!" DeDe said dropping his money "Lil Jae!" Emmit Smith!" the dude said rolling the dice tryna hit the point four.

Derrick seen the dude eyes get big right before he jumped to his feet. Derrick turned around unsuspected to see Lil D running toward him with a pistol pointed. "Boc, Boc, Boc" Lil D start firing at Derrick not caring who the stray bullet hit. Derrick tried running almost tripping over a dude who was also trying to get out the way. Derrick was reaching under his shirt tryna get his gun as he dodged the flying bullets. Right when Derrick got his gun out. "Boc Boc Boc Boc" one bullet his Derrick in the shoulder almost making him fall but the second bullet to his thigh did the trick making him fall and throwing the pistol out his hand and out of reach. Derrick laid on the pavement unable to get up. He never looked back to see Lil D but he felt the man presence coming up behind him. All the rumors were true Lil D he was a damn fool with that pistol and Derick would find out first hand. "Forgive me of my sins father!" Derrick said a silent prayer getting ready to meet his maker "Boom! Boom!" Derrick tighten his eyes hearing the shots right next to him erupt "Derrick hold on bro!" DeDe yelled as he turned Derrick over cradling him. Derrick eyes went to the .357 revolver in DeDe hand then to Lil D body lying face down bout 1foot away right before Derrick blacked out from the pain.

CHAPTER 19

T.Z sat in the waiting room with Derrick grandmother, little brothers and Pauline. The doctors had rushed Derrick right into surgery soon as the EMT's arrive at the hospital. When T.Z got the call from Derrick cellphone some nigga name DeDe was explaining to him what happen. T.Z couldn't believe what he was hearing the only reason DeDe knew to call T.Z was cause Derrick informed DeDe when they were talking in the car that his homeboy T.Z went out of town with him. DeDe was unable to identify the nigga or the man but described him and T.Z had a good idea who it was. Hearing that Lil D was dead didn't bring any sadness to T.Z heart he was only concern about Derrick. Flex walked into the waiting room high as a kite. T.Z had called him and delivered the news. Flex was still mad about the situation early but had to let that rest for now. "How is he?" Flex asked "He still in surgery. Only thing we know he got shot twice" T.Z said "Who did it?" Flex asked in a low voice. "Lil D!" T.Z whispered back. All this beef began of the lick Flex did on Ken Ken so Flex would have to kill Lil D getting his mind ready to lay the murder game down once again unknowing Lil D was already dead. Do the laws know who did it?" Flex asked "Yeah!" T.Z answered "How?" "Lil D got murked at the scene" T.Z told him That was a relief for Flex to hear that Lil D was already dead cause with the FEDS watching

his almost every move ain't no way he was gone be able to be the trigger man but in a situation like this T.Z would want to be the man ending Lil D life for sure. "Excuse me are you the family of Derrick Shaw?" the Arabian man asked dressed in scrubs. "Yes! How is he?" Derrick grandmother jumped up speaking. "I'm doctor Malik Abu. Mr. Shaw was shot twice and the bullet enter through the right shoulder and exited out the front not causing any long-term damage. The second gun shot wound was in his left thigh the bullet also penetrated from the back severing several tissue and muscles in his leg. I was able to remove the bullet fragment from his thigh but after some rest and off his feet for a couple of days he will make a full recovery. I will keep him here for at least 72hours to make sure his wounds are healing properly." Doctor Abu explain. T.Z was thankful to hear that Derrick would be okay cause another death of a love one would be beyond devastated for him. "Can we see him?" T.Z asked "He is sleepy from the surgery but only three at a time." the doctor informed them. "We'll wait out here!" T.Z said to Derrick grandmother. She followed the doctor to the room while T.Z and Flex stood in the waiting area. "Look dawg my bad if you felt like I came at you sideway, a nigga was just hot bout my shit coming up missing ya dig!" T.Z apologizing. Flex looked at T.Z for a moment before he spoke back "I ain't tripping dawg I already know you didn't mean the shit!" Flex accepted the apology "We good huh?" T.Z asked sticking his hand out Flex dapped him up "We good!" Let me see your phone I forgot my shit on the car charger. Peaches told me to call her and let her know how Derrick was doing." Flex said T.Z went in his

212

pocket pulling out the iPhone 4 handing it to Flex. Flex walked off acting as if the phone couldn't get signal. He quickly logged on to the Internet site then downloaded the app. To the phone not knowing that was Derrick phone instead of T.Z. The EMT's gave the phone to him along with Derrick keys and wallet when T.Z got to the hospital not far behind them. Flex dialed Peaches number then quickly pressed the end as he put the phone to his ear. T.Z watched Flex from where he was not suspecting him to be doing no foul shit. T.Z was just a little curious about the way

Flex was looking. He still dressed expensively but his health was deteriorated. T.Z wonder was Flex sick cause in the last two months he had to lost about 40 pounds. Then he been hiding Peaches out lately she much be sick to cause if he got it she damn sure do. T.Z hope that wasn't the case. Maybe it was just stress from the street life. Flex walked back over to T.Z handing him the phone T.Z put the phone in his pocket. "You been aight since we been gone?" T.Z asked "Yeah! Why you ask that?" Flex asked suspiciously Nigga you done lost a lot of weight" T.Z said. "Bro smoking, stress and a lot of fucking" Flex said. "A lot of good fucking can be the result of losing weight if you know what I mean" T.Z said "Naw I refuse to get caught slipping like that" Flex said "I'm just checking nigga" T.Z said laughing.

Will chauffeur Jax in the Double R Ghost they were just leaving the gambling spot that Jax used to let RedMack run. Jax had just collected his money that the gambling spot produced. They were headed to Jax daughter house to surprise her upon her return from her trip. Will wonder if he should reveal the information that he had found out. Will seen the gas tank was low something told him to fill up when they left Jax house but thought they were only going to the gambling spot and back. "Need some gas Jax!" Will stated as he turns into the Exxon Mobile. Jax just nodded his head as his attention was focus on his iPad 2 checking his states. Will parked at the gas pump turning the engine off to pump the gas. Will exited the vehicle placing the nozzle inside the hole then swiping the debit card. Will pressed the 93 buttons then began filling the Double R up with supreme gasoline. Will back was turn as the Mercedes Benz Coach van pulled into the Exxon. When Will turn to look hearing a door open it was already too late four masked men were jumping out pointing MP5. Will reached for his conceal weapon under his blazer but one of the mask men fired a taser gun hitting Will in the chest stunning him making him collapse. Jax quickly locked the car pulling out his 9mm. The car had bullet proof windows and side panels Jax had custom done. Jax watched from behind the limo tint has two of the men stood pointing their weapons at the car. Jax figured they were coming for him as he prepared himself but two of the men dragged Will to the van putting him inside. The men had specific orders not to touch Jax's in any way only get Will so soon as Will was in the van the last two men retreated to the van as it sped away.

Derrick was still a little dizzy and could feel the pain from being shot but he was just thankful that was alive. His grandmother little brother and Flex had left about a hour ago. Only T.Z and Pauline was there."You okay baby!" Pauline said joyful "I'm good!" Derrick said in a groggy voice. "Damn nigga you tryna get ghost on me" T.Z said "Fuck you!" Derrick spat smiling. "Aight nigga thats why yo motherfucking ass where you at now cause you always talking shit." T.Z said joking tryna add some humor to the situation. "Long as I'm here and not the morgue then I'm keep talking" Derrick said boasting his escape death. "I'm go get the nurse" Pauline said leaving the room. "Nigga what the fuck happen? I get a call from a nigga name DeDe saying you been shot" T.Z explain sending Derrick mind back to the frightened event. "I remember talking to DeDe then watching them niggas shoot dice in front of the barber shop I just happen to look back and see Lil D coming at me busting. I tried running but I remember the burning feeling in my shoulder then my leg and I couldn't move. I heard a couple more shots then Lil D was lying right behind me with blood leaking out his head on the pavement and now this." Derrick explain to him Doctor Malik Abu and a nurse came into the room with Pauline checking his vitals and making sure he was okay. They ran the usual test making sure he could see, hear, feel and remember, then told him to press the button on the bed if he needed any type of assistance then they left out the room leaving the three of them alone. "You might want to call DeDe the nigga saved your life" T.Z said handing Derrick his phone and car keys back. Derrick went to DeDe name in his contacts calling him. He hopes DeDe answer the phone even though it was one in the morning. "Hello?"

DeDe answered "I never thought yo ugly ass would be my guardian angel" Derrick said. "Damn nigga you had me spook the fuck out I thought you was out of there when I seen you on that ground" DeDe said "I probably would have if you weren't there. Thank you, my nigga, for real I owe you one" Derrick said. "Come on dawg much as you bless my game. Oh yeah I got yo money out yo pockets to cause all that cash would have alerted suspicion at the hospital." DeDe told him "I ain't tripping that's all you take it as a thank you gift." Derrick said.

"Appreciate!" "You good just get at me on that issue when you ready" Derrick said "You already know" DeDe assured him "Aight then" Derrick said ended the call. "I'm glad that nigga Dee was there if not a nigga would be dead" Derrick thought as he took a deep breath thankful he had a second chance at life cause most niggas wasn't that fortunate especially when he was the one holding the gun. It was already late so T.Z told Derrick he was about to leave. Pauline promise to take care of him. T.Z left the hospital driving to Yvonne place. Yvonne was probably sleep T.Z had call and told her about Derrick soon as he got to the hospital. She offered to come up there and wait with him but he told her that wasn't necessary he would be there later on. T.Z parked behind his Benz and headed to her door about to call her on the phone but before he could open her front door and she was standing there in a pair of his silk boxers and tank top shirt looking as if she been waiting on him for hours to come. "You still up?" he asked as she hugged him extra tight" How could I sleep, Is Derrick okay?" she asked letting go of the embrace. "Yeah he good!" T.Z said "Who shot him?" she asked "One of his many haters!" he said closing the door behind him "Was he trying to rob Derrick or something?" Yvonne asked "Naw baby it was just some beef shit that had been building." T.Z explain seeing the concern on her face. He knew Yvonne was worried about if something like that would happen to him. T.Z wasn't invincible so it could also happen to him at any given moment if he got caught slipping "I'm gone be okay baby!" T.Z added as he kissed her forehead then lips understanding her concern for his safety. "Let's get some sleep"

CHAPTER 20

"**R**ing, Ring, Ring" T.Z phone rung from the unprogrammed number that was calling him at 7:30 in the morning. He started not to answer but figure it could be Derrick calling him form the hospital room. "Yeah!" T.Z answered in as sleepy deep voice "Hola amigo!" the man voice spoke in Spanish T.Z instantly recognize the voice "What's up?" T.Z asked still half sleep "I have a gift for you and we need to talk" Felex told him "When?" T.Z asked "Now!" Felex stated "Right now!" T.Z repeated "Yes right now!" Felex instructed "Aight I'm on my way" T.Z said as he ended the call. T.Z had just fell asleep only two hours ago and here he was right back up. "Baby who was that?" Yvonne asked still half sleep "I got to go handle some business!" T.Z said "Can't it wait till later" she whined putting her arm on him tryna keep him in bed. "I wish it could!" T.Z admitted. If that call had been from anybody else T.Z would have refused to get up this early but with dudes like Felex that's a sign of disloyalty they expect when they ask for your presence you were suppose to come when they call for you. After taking the lost from his safe T.Z couldn't afford falling off with his connect because he was tired. T.Z got dressed putting on a Jordan jogging suit and Red and Black #11 and a

Chicago Bulls Derrick Rose jersey. Yvonne had picked for him. Yvonne had brought the hook up for him when they were in the Nike store in Hawaii. She said Derrick Rose was her favorite basketball player and if she ever met him she would probably cheat on T.Z then T.Z didn't like that part to much. T.Z tucked his .45 in his waist. "I'll be back!" T.Z said kissing her goodbye. Yvonne open her eyes smiling as he seen T.Z wearing the clothes she brought him. "Are you smiling cause of me or are you thinking about D. Rose again" T.Z said joking. "You know us sophisticated women can't resist a thug ass nigga!" Yvonne said "I know cause our millions be in cash!" T.Z kissed her one more time before he left the house hopping in his Benz. T.Z wondered what Felex needed to speak with him about that was so urgent it couldn't wait till later. T.Z figured it had to be drug related cause wasn't too much else for them to discuss. T.Z arrived at Felex furniture store. He parked next to the Escalade truck that had two of Felex same bodyguard that always stood by him in the front seat. The back door to the Escalade was open. T.Z looked at the customize interior in the truck as Felex reclined in a leather seat. T.Z got inside the Escalade and took a seat in the empty seat next to Felex. The back of the Escalade had been transformed into a lounge area it had a mini refrigerator, touch screen panels in the arm rest with a 42in flat screen built into the areas that would allow you to see the driver and passenger. Felex had the movie Scarface showing on the screen. T.Z had never been inside any vehicle like this before. Felex handed T.Z a cuban cigar. The tint was so dark even from the inside it was hard to see out. The T.V screen roll down as Felex pressed a button like a limo driver do when needed to speak to the driver. "Vamos!" Felex said to the guard driving before rolling the T.V screen back up to see the movie.

Tyrone you have been a trust worthy business partner that's why I ask you to meet with me I would like to discuss this matter before I give you your gift as promised." Felex said as he touched the screen on the armrest that was install in between them. A newspaper article popped up with a picture of four men two were Lil D and Derrick "Witness say suspect Donald Banks open fire yesterday in front of a barber shop on a group of men hitting Derrick Shaw and Tate Wilson before getting shot and killed himself by DeAndre Madison. The shootout was supposed to be over a on going drug war." T.Z read the brief article "Okay and?" T.Z asked wondering where the conversation was going. "I understand unfortunate event happen beyond your own control but the business we are in it's not good to have your picture on the front of the newspaper." Felex explain "That wasn't by his choice" T.Z said defended Derrick "I'm sure it wasn't I never suspected it to be his idea but unfortunate events such as this also brings heat by the police and that's is what we don't need you see!" Felex said T.Z nodded his head in agreement "That's from now on I'm only dealing through you only. I understand them are your amigos which is fine I have no hard feelings against them but this is business you understand." Felex told him "I understand!" T.Z said puffing on the cigar.

Jax had all his top Lieutenants assemble early this morning none of them had a clue why Jax call the meeting but by the look on his face they knew it had to be serious. Ten men sat around the table as Jax took his seat at the head of the table. "Brothers I know you are wondering what was so urgent I needed you all her at 8 in the morning. The reason as you can see is the 12th member of our family isn't present." Everybody eyes focus on the empty seat that Will would always occupy. Jax continue speaking "The reason for his absence is not by choice or because of betrayal. Our loyal brother was kidnapped yesterday!" Jax explain shocking everybody. "Who is behind this act is still unknown that is why you are all here now. I know each man in here has control in a different area inside the DFW metroplex, Cole-Oak Cliff, Jerry-North Dallas, Eric -Pleasant Grove, Rick -West Dallas, Sammy-East Dallas, Allen- South Dallas, Psych- Agg Town, Zeus-Grand Prairie, Justin and Pete y'all split Fort Worth. If anybody can find out information I know you ten can. Put the word out to your soldiers and find out who is behind this to whichever man find out, I have a million dollars for the reward." Jax stated. "Your money is no good Will is family.!" Jerry spoke out "he's right, for one of us Will wouldn't hesitate to go to work so Jerry's right the money is no good "Cole said as the other men nodded their heads in agreement. Jax love seeing the loyalty between his soldiers "Very well let's get to them streets!" Jax instructed unleashing a spree of violent murders and other crimes into the metroplex. The men stood to leave knowing they had the okay to unleash chaos upon the city to find Will. It was seldom that Jax called a unit meeting as such either it involved a lot of drugs or a lot of murders either way 911 would be receiving a lot of calls until Jax said other wise to cease fire. All ten men already on their phones calling a meeting with their top soldiers as they left Jax presents. Jax sat alone at the table tryna piece the puzzle together. At first Jax thought the kidnapping was ransom but after not receiving any calls asking about ransom money he ex that out his mind. He replayed yesterday events in his head. The four men were professional and how the scene played out Jax realized they were only after Will. The men showed no sign of even attempted to get Jax. Jax could tell the men were

220

most likely hispanic decent but that still didn't narrow to much down. Jax contemplated on making the decision should he contact Pedro.

The Escalade truck pulled into the open gate of a warehouse compound as the gates electronically closed back with the push of a button from Felex on the touch screen panel. The Escalade parked inside one of the warehouses. The bodyguards come and open the doors for T.Z and Felex. T.Z frowned up as the unpleasant smell from anywhere the stench of blood and death was a unforgettable smell. T.Z looked around at all the machinery "Welcome to my slaughter house!" Felex said standing next to T.Z puffing on the cuban cigar. Felex signal for T.Z to follow him as the guards trailed them. As T.Z walked past the machinery he could tell it was used for slaughtering animals of all kind. Felex stopped at a door that looked to be a freezer. Felex pulled the handle opening the door. There was was a massive freezer but the temperature wasn't freezing cold just around 50 degrees. T.Z seen something big hanging from a chain in the darkness but didn't know exactly what it was but he was sure it wasn't no cow meat. Felex turn the light switch on revealing it was a person hanging from a chain tied around him with a hood over their face. They proceeding towards the body T.Z was wondering who the person was maybe a dis loyal member of Felex crew who Felex was about to make an example out of to show T.Z he didn't tolerate disloyalty. "When we first met remember all I asked was loyalty and respect!" Felex said. "Yeah!" T.Z said "Well thats all you have showed me and that is very hard to find now a days but here is a gift of my appreciation!" Felex explain then pulling the hood off the hanging man head. T.Z had a evil grin on his face as he stared into the eyes of Will. Will had knots and bruises on his face but he was still conscious and return the stare right back at T.Z "Fuck you!" Will spat "Hush Puppy!" Felex said as Will tried spitting a glob of blood onto Felex but he got out the way in time just to miss. One of the bodyguards come a duck tape his mouth. "Uuummm!" Will tried to yell as Felex put his cigar out on Will eyelid. "Don't worry there's not way to get yourself out of this one you are destined to receive what you have gave to so many other people, Death!" Felex stated. T.Z had been waiting for this day since the day Roxy was murdered. T.Z wasn't for sure if he wanted to torture Will first or hurry up and just end his life. Felex picked up a machete that stood had animal blood on the blade handing it to T.Z letting him know it was okay to take his time in killing Will. T.Z planned on inflicting so much pain upon Will he would still be suffering in the other life. First thing T.Z did was explain to his ass. Will that's what people from the Caribbean call it when you smack a person with a machete. T.Z hit him several more times slicing Wills face. "You been looking for me huh ma'fuckers!" T.Z growled hitting him even harder several more times making Will do a 360 as he hung from the chains. "You like to stick yo dick where it don't belong I hear. Let me show you what happen to ma'fuckers who do that." T.Z barked as he yanked Will slacks down to his ankles exposing his shriveled-up dick and butt. Will eyes got big "Ummm!" Will began to move in the chain tryna avoid what was coming next as T.Z line the machete up raising it above his head with two hands "UUMMMM!" Will screamed in pain as the sharp blade cut right through his flesh chopping his prize possession off. "Ummm! Ummm!" Will muffled cries fell on deaf ears as blood skitted and oozed out from the little piece of flesh he had left. "You lucky I ain't making you suck yo own dick bitch!" T.Z spat kicking what use to be Will dick across the floor. They watched Will go unconscious from the pain. "Let this bitch bleed to death he ain't worth wasting my bullets" T.Z said to Felex "I got a better plan!" Felex said enjoying the show. Felex said something in Spanish to his bodyguards. One walked out the freezer to a massive machine pressing a button the machine roared as it came to life. The other guard went to the levers the control the chains movement. "Follow me!" Felex said as they exited the freezer. They walked over by the machine as it roared. Wills body came out a hole in the top of the wall on a conveyor belt headed right into a drop off into the opening of the machine. "This is how we dispose of no good animals" Felex stated as they watched the body get closer to the drop. "AWWWW!" The sharp blades sounded as Will body fell into the pit of the machine being chopped to pieces. That was cruel being chopped up in a machine while still alive. T.Z felt Will had got exactly what he deserved only thing else he needed that eternal hell-fire. The machine began to quiet down as the guard turned it off. Felex and T.Z walked back to the Escalade truck getting back inside the customize truck. "Good looking out Felex I owe you a big one I been looking all around town for him and Jax but them niggas are like ghost only appear unsuspected." T.Z said "Which I know is true thats one reason he lasted so long in these streets. Will has been killing niggas since late 80's early 90's but today he received punishment!" Felex said. The bodyguards got back into the truck then left the warehouse.

At first T.Z was gone keep the information about losing his safe to himself but decided he would tell Felex. As they rode through the city burning gas T.Z explain the situation he was in not asking for any help but since he took Felex to be a friend he thought he should let him know.

Felex admire the determination in T.Z and told him not to worry loses was apart of the game just make sure

loses don't happen often and promise T.Z he would get him back on his feet over night. Felex revealed a lot of information to T.Z about how his brother Mario ran the Cuban Cartel out in Miami and central Florida and how Felex migrated to Texas to expand their empire. A lot of which T.Z already knew because of Felex Uncle Leto. They also talked about him and how he would be up for parole, T.Z felt the bond with Felex understanding it was loyalty between the two men and know for sure it would be plenty more millions he ran across while in these streets. Felex would have T.Z as the new Rayful Edmond of the south.

CHAPTER 21

Flex rode in the backseat of the tinted unmarked F-250 truck it had been over a month since Flex cop a deal with the FEDS and now the pressure was on him and with his increasing drug habit, Flex felt was beginning to look like shit. He was still wearing expensive clothes and jewelry but his health was diminishing day by day. The FEDS still didn't have any hardcore evidence on T.Z and none on Felex since only T.Z dealt with him first hand. It was at the point where the FEDS install a hidden camera inside the I-45 emblem on Flex chain to try and help incriminate T.Z, agent Moss and Rick were steady threatening Flex with prison time if they found out he wasn't holding up his end of the bargain. Flex was tryna hold up his end and still get money and not have his cover blown at the same time. The streets had actually become a 24hr job. The agents wanted Felex to introduce Big Homie the same undercover agent who got Flex jammed up to T.Z. Flex still had animosity on his chest towards Big Homie but would have to put it aside for now.

Flex knew T.Z was far from being stupid and would be extra cautious about any new niggas coming around it had to get to a level where if T.Z hadn't been dealing with you he wouldn't at all first hand. You would have to by one of his spots and get served even if a nigga wanted a few bricks or a couple pounds he only

kept a hand full of niggas who could cop work personally from him now. The F-250 pulled up next to Big Homie car. "What's up?" Big Homie asked Flex didn't bother to even respond. "Look here young punk I don't give a fuck about your damn attitude we got a job to do so make sure it get done and if you even think about blowing our cover, I'ma blow yo head to the fucking stars my damn self you understand!" Big Homie barked. Flex stared at him with malice in his eyes knowing he would have murked a nigga for even speaking to him out of line like that but now that he was Uncle Sam bitch he had to deal with it. "Nigga yo ass bet not get me knocked" Flex said

T.Z was at the car wash on M.L.K getting his GT Venom shinned up. He had a dope fiend washing his car as he sat in a lawn chair smoking a blunt with young Kobe standing next to him. Lately he had been keeping Kobe around him closely he really like the youngster "One time on the block!" a local well-known dope fiend name 6'4 shouted alerting everybody the laws were coming "Two time on the block!" he shouted letting everybody know they were pulling up in the carwash. T.Z put the blunt out of sight as the police cruise crept by checking out the scene and looking at all the D-boy cars getting shine up. Everybody relaxed as the cruiser left the carwash driving off. Who didn't know the carwash was an area use for drug selling so the police would always ride by but that still didn't stop the lock block hustlers from doing their thang up there. If a person actually just tried to get some order up there the carwash could be a million-dollar spot but every time a nigga tried to get order it only lasted about 2days before somebody got shot or stabbed. A black and red challenger on 22parked next to T.Z GT Venom since T.Z car was parked away from everybody else's he was curious of who it was. Until he seen Flex getting out the passenger seat with some big ass nigga driving looking as if he supposed to be playing D. End for the Cowboys. Flex had been wanting T.Z to meet this nigga. T.Z had been avoiding the shit he wasn't busy he agreed to. Flex bragged how the nigga supposed to have a mean connect on that "ICE" T.Z wasn't into the meth game but figure he might as well listen might be worth is while. "What's good dawg?" What up lil nigga? Flex spoke to T.Z and Kobe "What's good?" They both responded back "This my nigga Big Homie!" Flex introduced them. "What's up?" Big Homie asked. "Slow Motion" T.Z said "I been telling T.Z how you got the plug on that ICE!" Flex jumped straight to business "Yeah I do but I hear you the man round here" Big Homie said "Naw I ain't shit just another nigga tryna survive" T.Z said. "I ain't tryna be no middle man in this shit you know we do everything as partners just how with Felex!" Flex said "I don't know Felex!" But where you from Big Homie?" T.Z said switching subject cause of Flex loose lips. "I'm really from Houston but I been living in Dallas for bout 7 years." Big Homie said "What part of the D you stay in?" T.Z asked. "I got a crib out in Desoto but I be everywhere hustling." he answered T.Z talked to Big Homie about general things where was his family how many kids he had but nothing drug related. Something about the big nigga swag didn't sit right like the nigga was tryin too hard to be hood. T.Z took it has maybe Big Homie was raised on the good side or Houston and just choose the street life that's probably the way he got a connect on the meth cause don't to many niggas fuck with that shit better yet have a connect on it especially in the D. T.Z promised to get in contact with Big Homie as him and Flex headed to the car "A Flex come here right quick" T.Z said as Big Homie keep walking."Yeah!" Flex said "How much you know about this nigga?" T.Z asked "Enough! Why?" "The nigga seemed like a square or a wolf in sheep clothes" T.Z said "Naw he good people fuck with him and you'll see" Flex said "I'll see whats up?" T.Z said as him and Flex dapped each other up before Flex left. "Something seemed wrong about that nigga big bro!" Kobe said "You ain't never lied!" T.Z said watching the Challenger leave. "L....L....Look out B...B.B Boss man!" 6'4 the dope fiend call T.Z stuttering "Whats up?" B.B.B. Careful I think that...that nigga working for them people." 6'4 said really catching T.Z attention "I knew something was up with that big ass nigga!" T.Z stated N.N not him the ... the other one." 6'4 said surprising T.Z "Who Flex?" "Yep" "Hell naw! Why you say that?" T.Z asked "I ...I was on the boulevard about a month ago in the smoke house. I ...I seen a lot of laws had him jammed up and these laws wasn't DPD. Now he back on the street explain that" 6'4 said "What kind of car was he in?" T.Z asked "Cadillac!" T.Z was puzzled when he heard that the whole time he suspicious of Big Homie when his homeboy might be the snake. T.Z handed 6'4 a fifty-dollar bill one thing about dope fiends they might steal and do fucked up shit but they don't miss shit in the hood. T.Z just hope 6'4 had Flex mixed up with the wrong person. If the information turned out to be true. T.Z know what he would have to do cause snitches get stitches. T.Z was glad he didn't tell Flex about Felex fronting him the 100bricks of cocaine and thousand pounds of weed but he did tell him about Will.

Yvonne had been having morning sickness for the past few days then on top of that she hadn't had her period since before they went to Hawaii so she wasn't surprise when the doctor told her she was 8 weeks pregnant. As she drove her Porsche she wondered what T.Z would say is he gonna be happy or not. Then she thought about her parents she knew her mother would be excited and happy but her father was a different story. Yvonne decided it was time T.Z and her father met anyway so she would deliver the good news to both of the men at the same time so far right now she would keep the pregnancy as her secret. Since T.Z had moved into another loft also in downtown Yvonne tried her best to spend much free time as possible with him she even had a key to his apartment. Now that she was a certified lawyer she also stayed a little bit more busy than before.

Flex sat in the passenger seat of Big Homie car as Big Homie relayed the report back to Agent Moss on the phone letting Moss know Flex as doing his job. Flex was so tired of all the James Bond shit he had to do but remember it was either this or the death table. After Big Homie wrapped his phone conversation up. Flex was allowed to leave but already seen the FEDS kept a close eye on him. Flex got inside his Benz SLS and waited for Big Homie to drive off before he removed the eight ball of coke from the glove compartment spreading it out on a CD case then twisting up a twenty dollar bill snorting a line. This was how Flex took the pressure off himself tryna stay high as possible all day not wanting to face the facts of reality much as he could. After snorting bout a gram of coke Flex put the paraphernalia up then lit up a blunt laced with coke and headed to his crib.

T.Z and Kobe were inside the trap waiting on Derrick to come through. Derrick had just bout made a full recovery from getting shot that day. T.Z had explained to Derrick about what Felex said Derrick was upset about it when T.Z first told him but understood as well, but long as T.Z still had the connect Derrick wasn't tripping. T.Z was still charging him and Flex the same price. Even though he was the only one access tot he drugs the still looked at them as a team so out of love and respect he wouldn't never change the price on them. T.Z felt his phone vibrating on his hop and seen it was Yvonne calling "Hello?" he answered "Hey Baby?" she said "Chillin on it what you got going on?" he asked "Coming to see you" She responded "Damn! I'm out here in the hood but you can go head and go over there" T.Z said. "If you not there what the point." She complained "I got to handle some shit with Derrick first" he explained "Okay! How is he and Pauline?" she asked "He good and I'm sure she is since he haven't been complaining about her" T.Z answered "What about your other friend you don't talk about that much anymore" she said. "Who Flex?" he asked "Yeah the one who mess with the bitch I had a fight with!" Yvonne told him "What?" T.Z asked confused "You remember the hoe I had the fight with at the club that lied and said y'all fucked around" she explain "Yeah Bri-Bri but Flex don't fuck with her"T.Z said "Well I seen them at the mall together with shopping bags all in they hands" Yvonne said "When was this and why you never told me?" he asked "Honestly I forgot cause it was doing that period when you call yo self being mad at me "Yvonne said "You sure that was her?" T.Z asked "I'm positive cause I almost decided to give her ass beating number two but didn't feel like going to jail. "Yvonne said. "Baby Derrick just got here so I'll see you at the house." T.Z said.

"Okay Love You!" "Love you too!" he said ended the call. "What's wrong dawg?" Derrick asked as he sat down next to T.Z on the couch. "You ain't go believe that shit I then heard today" T.Z said shaking his head. "What?" First, I hear from a smoker that Flex got jammed up a few weeks ago by the FEDS. Then Yvonne tell me she seen him and Bri-Bri in the mall together before we went out of town" T.Z told Derrick as he also looked confused. "I don't know dawg can't be believing no crackhead" Derrick said "I know Yvonne ain't lying" T.Z said "True that" Just all Bri-Bri and ask her" Derrick said T.Z dialed the last number her known Bri-Bri to have but that was when he first got locked up over 3years ago. The automatic recording picked up saying the number was out of service. "Her number don't work!" T.Z said pressing the end button on the screen. "Let's go by her crib then." Derrick said "Yeah I'm sure that broke bitch still live off John West! T.Z said "I'll drive!" Derrick said as they got up to leave Kobe had to stay and work the trap. T.Z had no feelings towards Bri-Bri it was just the point of Flex fucking with her and not letting T.Z know. They all yell M.O.B so why would Flex let a bitch come between them then all in the mall with the bitch on some girlfriend/boyfriend shit. T.Z felt if he couldn't trust the nigga behind some shit that got to do with a nothing ass bitch ain't no telling with other shit the nigga might be doing. They got inside the expedition Derrick brought for Pauline heading over to Bri-Bri apartment to question her. Derrick mashed the big body down Buckner reaching the apartment complex. "So you actually haven't fucked with Bri-Bri since you been out?" Derrick asked "Hell naw I almost decided to but after that bullshit she pulled that night at the club I squash that idea!" T.Z explained. They drove through the apartments

231

when they got close to Bri-Bri building. Flex SLS stuck out like a sore thumb and so did the E Class Benz parked next to it. T.Z couldn't believe he had this hoe over here living ghetto fabulous but even that the disloyalty he felt was ten times worse. "Park over there!" T.Z pointed to an open parking spot past her building but still making her building visible "We should go murk his bitch ass" Derrick spat "Naw thats giving him the easy way out and especially not over no bitch" T.Z spoke calmly but his blood was on fire. "Nigga want to be greedy so you just starve him to death thats all!" T.Z said. T.Z had seen enough he was ready to go he would make sure Flex pockets felt his pain. "Let's Go!" T.Z said right when Derrick was about to pull out a CTS came speeding through the apartments stopping in the middle of the street.

Flex was on the bed getting some head from Bri-Bri as usual he had tried going home but ended up arguing with Peaches and beating her up the beatings had become a every other day routine for them "Bang Bang Bang" both Flex and Bri-Bri jumped up slipping on his pant walking to the door shirt less. "Damn"! he said as he looked through the peep hole "I know you in there open the ma'fucking door!" Peaches screamed "You need to control yo bitch" Bri-Bri said coming in the living room "Shut yo ass up I got this!" Flex barked at her before he opened the door to a raging Peaches. "What the fuck you doing over here?" he asked "Nigga what the fuck you doing over here is the question!" she screamed pushing past him about to charge at Bri-Bri. Bri-Bri prepared herself for the battle but as she looked at Peaches she could tell somebody had already been beating her ass by the black eyes and swollen lip. Flex caught Bri-Bri by her ponytail yanking her back almost falling. "You gone save this bitch? You put yo hands on me instead of her?" Peaches scream with tears in her eyes "Cause you tripping now go home!" he ordered her pushing her towards the door. Peaches reached inside her jacket pulling out one of Flex's 9mm he kept at home. "Don't neither one of y'all fucking move!" Peaches shouted as tears ran down her face.

T.Z and Derrick was shocked when they seen Peaches jump out the car with the pistol in her hand. Peaches was a pretty woman but with all the bruises on her face you could hardly tell from a distance. They decided to wait and see how the situation played out but when they heard several gun shots ring out they knew what happen. They watched Peaches run to the CTS crying then burning off fleeing the scene they didn't really think Peaches would use the pistol mostly just scare them but they both knew somebody got shot that's what happen when disloyalty happens. T.Z did feel bad for Peaches cause if the police found out she did it she was for sure headed to prison and would leave two beautiful little girls out here without parents and would probably end up being a product of their environment.

CHAPTER 22

Agent Moss and Rice walked into Detective Simmons office while doing surveillance they had spotted Detective Simmons also watching their mark. At first, they wondered was Simmons involved in the Drug ring but after investigating they found out he was only a local officer looking for his name to appear in a headline of a newspaper. The agents weren't about to mess off months of hard investigating because some local cop wanted to be a hero and try and save the community." Detective Gary Simmons! I'm agent Moss this is Rice we need to speak with you" Simmons had already seen this coming while doing his investigation he spotted a few cars that he was concern about and called the plates in finding out they were government issued vehicles" I'm listening! Simmons said. "Doing a ongoing investigation we have noticed you, I guess doing your own investigation as well we appreciate your dedication but we ask you to stop for your own safety and let us handle this from now on!" Moss said "I'm in the middle of a home invasion rape assault as well." Simmons said "Listen here we tried this shit the nice way but I'm telling you to stay the hell out the way from now on cause if you fuck up this you gone need a lawyer for your damn self" Rice informed him "Is that a threat?" Simmons said standing to his feet in defense. "I don't make threats Simmons I only carry out promises!" Rice said "Detective Simmons!" Simmons corrected him "Well Detective Simmons we prefer to do things the civilized way and not have to go that route that's the reason we are here now, so I'm asking you to stand down on this one." Moss explain tryna calm the situation. "So what am I supposed to do about my investigation!" Simmons asked "Fax the details over to our office and if we find something out during our investigation we will contact you!" Moss said "Alright!" Simmons agreed just for the agents to leave. Rice gave Simmons a hard look before they both turn to leave. Simmons didn't care what the agents tried to threaten him with, he was determined not to let this one go.

The crime rate had sky rocketed in the last month and local officials couldn't understand why the crime against person division all across the metroplex had more cases coming in more then ever. Jax closed the newspaper after reading the article in the paper knowing why the crime rate on violence was at a all-time high. Because of him and the way Jax was thinking and feeling shit was only gone get worse until he found out who was behind taking Will. It had been over a month since Will got kidnapped and not a word had been heard from the captors so Jax had already concluded Wills fate. Jax was sure that Will body probably would show up any day now. Since Will had no close relatives Jax was his only family he wanted to make sure Will had a proper burial for a soldier that served a life term in the streets. First Jax had an appointment with his guardian angel, whenever she wanted to meet it had to be serious. As Jax sat in the booth drinking coffee and finishing his french toast, bacon and eggs. A slim white lady with blonde hair sat in the booth directly behind him for their backs were to each other. The woman picked up a menu to block her mouth. "The DEA and FBI are about to come down on a Derrick Shaw and possible Tyrone Zonders "the woman spoke low" I don't even know who they are so what does that mean to me?" Jax whispered back "I thought you knew that Tyrone was Yvonne boyfriend" she told him. The name Tyrone instantly click in Jax head remembering Yvonne boyfriend name. "Is Yvonne in any trouble?" Jax asked "Not that I know of but the two guys are best friends and under heavy surveillance." the woman said. "Thank you my little angel." Jax said

"Anytime!" she said. Jax dropped a fifty-dollar bill on the table and left out the Denny's restaurant. Jax got in the driver seat of his 2011 Range Rover. He dialed Yvonne number as he drove off. "Hello?" Yvonne answered the phone "Hey baby girl?" "Hey Daddy?" "What are you doing?" he asked "Working hard" she said "After all them tuition fees I'm glad I'm finally seeing my money go to use." he said joking "Daddy that's not funny!" She said "Babygirl, I actually call you to ask you about your little boyfriend of yours really" Jax said. "What now?" Yvonne asked knowing how her father felt about her boyfriends. "Why you sound like that?" he asked "Cause I know how you are" She stated "Is something wrong with me wanting the best for you?" he said "No there's not but I Love him daddy" Yvonne said "Girl you don't know what no love is" Jax said "Yes I do. How bout this, you and mama come over this Friday for dinner and you can sit down and talk to him. How's that?" Yvonne asked. "It's a date!" Jax agreed "Okay see you Friday! " she said excited before hanging up Yvonne had always been his weakness he would do anything for his babygirl. He could tell Yvonne had strong feeling for this dude and watching him going to prison would really hurt her so Jax had to warn the boy before destruction hit. Linda had already told Jax the boy reminded her of him 25 years ago now he understood why she said that.

T.Z had just hung up the phone talking to Yvonne she was over excited about a dinner she was planning on Friday with her parents and the two of them. She said it was bout time her father and him met each other plus she said she had a surprise for T.Z as well. ("Damn the laws been hot lately!") T.Z thought as he drove his Benz through the Grove. Seem like every corner he turned there was a police car. Kobe had call and told him early that the police was doing random road blocks on various streets. He looked in the air through his windshield at the ghetto bird circling the sky. T.Z was wondering what happen that the laws were patrolling so hard today. T.Z had to hurry up and get out the hood cause it was to on fire for him to be driving around.

Derrick also was noticing the increasing pressure of DPD. He was on his way to pick up some money from one of his spots in Oak Cliff and almost drove straight into a police road block on Keist and Polk he just happened to turn off on a backstreet because traffic was backed up. He was riding dirty with ten pounds and a whole brick of coke in the trunk of his BMW. "Ring, Ring, Ring" "Hello?" He answered "A big bro?" "What's good Dot?" "Don't come by the spot no time soon! "Dot informed him "Why not?" Derrick asked "Laws posted on both ends!" Dot said "What they doing?" Derrick asked "Just sitting there!" Dot said "Damn them hoes everywhere" Derrick said. "Keep a eye out just in case you got to get rid of the issue. "Derrick told him "Aight!" Dot said as they ended the call. Derrick changed direction cause he was about to head on the end of the Cliff when he missed the road block but now it was also hot on the Wood Town side as well. He let Dot run the trap on that side on a street called Goldwood. Every street on that side ended with wood so everybody called it wood town. He made phone calls checking on his other two spots he had wasn't any laws posted but they are was hot today both of his other two lil soldiers name Big Boy and Pacman told him. Derrick couldn't risk getting rolled with the drugs in the car. Looking for a safe spot so he jumped on I-35 headed North to get out of the way.

Agent Moss and Rice hovered over the top of Derrick in the helicopter listening to his phone calls and watching his every move. Agent Rice couldn't get the local squad cars moved off the street on Goldwood in time enough when they noticed him going in that direction the Derrick received the phone call warning him not to come just in case he was coming. Since the increase in violent crimes then went up in the last month the mayor forced the chief of police to put more men on the street to crack down on crime. Agent Moss and Rice know that would send alert signals to their suspects and possible scare them to slow down or stop their illegal activities trying not to risk getting caught by local police with is crack down on crime going on, Agents decided they had to move in fast before somebody caught wind of them watching. They continue to follow Derrick making sure no local police didn't decide to make a routine traffic stop and stumble upon the petty drugs Derrick was concealing in the truck and arresting him cause the agent knew that was nothing to the amount of drugs Derrick dealt with and could be caught with.

Jax enjoyed the sight of all of DPD finest working their asses off because of the terror he released in society. It was bout time DPD actually did some work for their paychecks and unless Jax got some answers real soon. Police headquarters would end up having a help wanted sign posted in front of it thanks to Jax.

CHAPTER 23

Two days later and hadn't to much changed, the laws were still patrolling extra hard but Yvonne had informed T.Z on the plan the mayor and chief of police had come up with to crack down on violence. And until the violence calm down the constant reminder of squad cars would stay present. T.Z had found out Peaches got locked up for the shooting. He paid the head lawyer in Yvonne law firm 50 grand to represent her since she was being held on a 2-million-dollar cash only bond for some odd reason. T.Z had just left the county jail from visiting her. She admitted to T.Z she had about $150,000 dollars of Fed money that was all she had saved up in the safe at home. T.Z told her to just make sure the money stayed in a safe place for whenever she got out. T.Z assume Flex had to have some more money stashed away somewhere else cause that 150 thousand wasn't shit compared to the money he should have saved up. T.Z would go by Flex two traps to pick up whatever money he had their as well to give to Peaches and the kids. Cause he felt awful for Peaches knowing she would be locked up because Flex powder head ass couldn't stop beating on her. T.Z thought it had to be something going on with Flex all the weight he lost and the attitude change. T.Z parked his Benz in front of Flex old trap on Pine street in

South Dallas. Right before he got out his car he noticed a Dodge Charger at the top of the street only reason he peeped it cause wasn't no other cars in the path of their view. T.Z started the Benz back up and drove off noticing the unmarked car as he passed by. T.Z understood the local police were hot but that was a FED car what made it so bad they wasn't even tryna hide they were letting it be known they watching.

Agent Moss stood in front of the marker board talking to a room full of DEA, ATF, and FBI agents giving play by play instructions on a drawn diagram on the board of several different houses. Next to it was a group of about 20 photos in columns. "We must hit them fast and hard these men are extremely dangerous" Moss coached the group. Rice stood up. "Team one you take down these spots. Team Two you got these spots. Team three you got these spots. Team four you have these two." Agent Moss and myself well go with Team five to take down these two." Rice instructed pointing at the diagrams. "Let's be careful guys!" Moss said as the room of agents raised for action on operation "Greedy Intentions" take down.

Jax looked himself over in the mirror as he wore the 3-piece Brown Gucci Suit with matching Gucci shoes. Linda had on her silver Prada dress and Prada heels with a 10 ½ karat Platinum necklace to match her 10 karat Platinum wedding ring. They were both dressed to impress as they got ready to leave their house in Forney to go to Yvonne dinner party she had planned. Jax was ready to meet this Tyrone fellow that his daughter loved and spoke so highly about. Jax could tell his daughter did have strong feelings for him cause she never talked about any other guy so much before and Linda like him so Jax figured he might as well give the kid a chance but wonder how would he react when Jax revealed the FEDS were coming for him if he didn't get his shit in order. Jax and Linda got inside the White 2011 Bentley Flying Spur to head over to Yvonne house.

Derrick rode in the passenger seat of Dot Black 2009 Ford Mustang on 22in Barra Forgiatos. Since the hood was still swarming with laws Derrick decided him and Dot should just go out and kick it, he called T.Z but Yvonne had some special dinner going on that he couldn't miss. Dot pushed the mustang on the highway headed to Club Onyx one of the hottest strip joints in Dallas. Dot was to busy bobbing his head to the song by Dorrough while hitting the blunt of kush he didn't peep the Dodge Durango following him since he left the spot to pick up Derrick. Derrick had the seat reclined sipping on a cup of lean so he was unaware as well.

T.Z had went by Flex spot and also seen a unmarked car parked not to far from it and one by his spot as well. The shit had him a little paranoid he stayed looking in his rearview all the way as he drove to Yvonne place but he wasn't being followed. He hated to miss the cash but he called his workers and told them to close up shop for the night don't serve or even answer the door for nobody until he called and let them know to do so. He helped Yvonne set the table cause her parents had already called and said they wasn't to far away. "Are you nervous baby?" Yvonne asked cause she was "For what?" ain't yo pops human like us?" T.Z said "Yes but I thought you might just be nervous!" she said T.Z wrapped his arms around her waist "Look baby you the only person who determine if you love me or accept me. Do you love or accept me?" he asked staring in her big brown bedroom eyes. "Yes I do!" she said "that's what's important!" He said they kissing her. That's why Yvonne loved him so much cause he gave her the security and confidence a woman needed in a man.

Jax pulled up behind the Benz "I want you to be nice!" Linda told Jax "I'm always nice!" Jax said as they exited the Bentley. Jax could tell the youngster was on top of his paper pushing the new AMG 6.3 Benz. Jax rung the door bell.

The butterflies instantly came back as Yvonne heard the doorbell. It was time to reveal her big secret about being pregnant. "Relax!" T.Z told her as they both headed to the door to greet her parents. Yvonne took a deep breath then opened the door.

Agent Moss strapped on his Teflon vest as Rice double checked the 30-round clip in his MP5 again. The armor truck came to a stop in front of the duplex house. Agent Moss, Rice and bout 8 other officers dressed in swat gear jumped out the back of the truck rushing the house. Five agents ran to the back of the house as the other five hit the front yanking the burglar bars off the windows and front doors. "Boom!" Moss threw a flash bang grenade through the window before the front door was knocked in. Right when the agents thought they had access inside the house they ran into a cage blocking access to inside the house. "Get the cable's there's another set of bars! "Moss yelled into the ear piece. "Bloc, Bloc, Bloc, Bloc, Bloc" somebody started shooting at the agents. "Tat, tat, tat, Tat" all the agents returned fire. "AH!" a agent screamed being shot in the neck hooking the cables up to the other set of bars. Rice dragged the wounded agent out the line of fire. "It's clear!" Moss shouted for the bars to be pulled off. The agents rushed the house with rapid fire.

"Hey mom, Daddy!" Yvonne said hugging her mother soon she opened the door. It took bout 10 seconds for each other faces to register in their heads but it did. "You!" both said simultaneously T.Z had his pistol upstairs in Yvonne bedroom he figured it wasn't no reason to have it on him but when he seen Jax hand bout to reach inside his suit jacket. He made a lifesaving move reaching grabbing Jax hand knocking the chrome pistol on the ground. Both ladies jump back in shock not understanding why this was happening. T.Z punched Jax with a left hook but Jax countered punched with a gut shot with a right hook. Jax was almost 60 but he was in excellent shape. Jax threw a straight jab but T.Z ducked it throwing a right upper cut. Jax grabbed him tryna use his size as advantage slamming T.Z against the wall. "Daddy stop!" Yvonne screamed "Jax was tryna choke T.Z but he kneed Jax in the balls making him let go. Then punched Jax square in the nose stunning him. T.Z eyes searched the floor for the gun but it wasn't there. Then he realized why Linda had the gun pointed at him. T. Z froze knowing he was fucked now. "I don't know what is going on but I suggest you leave now!" Linda warned Yvonne stood in shock with tears in her eyes looking at the catastrophe happen in front of her. T.Z look Yvonne out of breath then sprinted out the front door to his car.

Derrick and Dot were sitting at the table with five thousand ones in front of them making it rain. Then all of a sudden it seemed as if time just froze. People in normal clothes drew their weapons "Freeze!" then several more people with black jackets DEA, ATF and FBI letters on the back emerged out the crowds. The music stop playing. Dot was shocked the look on his face. Derrick already knew what it was, he took one last swig of the Rozay out the bottle then put his hands in the air. "Derrick Shaw you are under arrest!" Agent Moss said coming out the crowd with Rice by his side arrest Dot as well. They escorted them outside where at team of other agents were waiting as well. The agents put Derrick and Dot in the backseat of two separate unmarked cars but before they got in Derrick nodded his head at Dot letting him know to stay strong it was plenty of days Derrick warn him that this could happen. Now it was time to man up and handle it.

T.Z tried calling Derrick but his phone was going straight to Voicemail. T.Z couldn't believe what the hell just happen out of all the fathers in the world Jax had to be Yvonne's. T.Z was tripping as he paced in his living room smoking a blunt. He wanted to murder Jax so bad but he also wanted to be with Yvonne so bad as well. His emotion was flying in two opposite directions. "Knock, Knock" T.Z paused at the sound of the door. He picked up the Desert Eagle 50cal wondering if Yvonne told her father where he lived. "I'm alone!" she shouted. From the other side of the door. T.Z was cautious as he opens the door pointing the gun. "I'm alone I promise! "She said. Yvonne eyes were red from the crying and arguing with her father he demanded she stay away from him but she didn't care what Jax said she love her baby daddy and wouldn't allow anything to come between them. T.Z let her in closing and locking the door behind him. Yvonne was hurt and didn't have a clue what was going on between him and her father "What's going on?" She asked tryna hold back her tears. T.Z just hugged her as she broke down crying in his arms. He had a major dilemma on his hand. Either hurt Yvonne or make Jax feel his pain or let her make it. T.Z mind went to Roxy and the horrible death she suffered. He tightened his eyes close taking a deep breath. "I made a promise to Roxy after your father had her killed!" T.Z said in Yvonne ear shocking her hearing the devastated information. T.Z pushed Yvonne off of him pointing the gun at her Yvonne froze in fear knowing this was the end." BOOM!"

THE END

GREEDY INTENTIONS II
(THUGGIN HARD)

COMING SOON

Made in the USA
Columbia, SC
18 June 2022

61867215R00137